CANADIAN JEWISH SHORT STORIES

CANADIAN JEWISH SHORT STORIES

Edited by
MIRIAM WADDINGTON

Toronto
OXFORD UNIVERSITY PRESS
1990

Oxford University Press, 70 Wynford Drive, Don Mills, Ontario, M3C 1J9

Toronto   Oxford   New York
Delhi   Bombay   Calcutta   Madras   Karachi   Petaling Jaya
Singapore   Hong Kong   Tokyo   Nairobi   Dar es Salaam
Cape Town   Melbourne   Auckland

and associated companies in
Berlin   Ibadan

Canadian Cataloguing in Publication Data

Main entry under title:

Canadian Jewish short stories

ISBN 0-19-540813-6

1. Short stories, Canadian (English) – Jewish
authors.* 2. Canadian fiction (English) – Jewish
authors.* I. Waddington, Miriam, 1917–

PS8321.C35 1990   C813'.01088924   C90-095070-6
PR9197.33.J49C35 1990

1 2 3 4 5 – 94 93 92 91 90

Printed in Canada by Webcom Limited

For Marcus, Gail, Jonathan, and Paula.

CONTENTS

viii *Contents*

ACKNOWLEDGEMENTS

TED ALLAN 'Lies My Father Told Me' used by permission of the author.

MONIQUE BOSCO 'The Old Woman's Lamentations on *Yom Kippur*' original French from *Boomerang* (HMH, L'Arbre, 1987) © Monique Bosco. English translation © Patricia Sillers. Used by permission.

MATT COHEN 'The Watchmaker' from *Columbus and the Fat Lady* (House of Anansi Press). Used by permission of the author.

SHARON DRACHE 'The Scribe' from *The Mikveh Man and Other Stories* (Aya Press). Used by permission of the author.

SHIRLEY FAESSLER 'A Basket of Apples' from *A Basket of Apples*. Used by permission of the author.

NAOMI GUTTMAN 'Practising' from *Celebrating Canadian Women* edited by Greta Hofmann Nemiroff. Reprinted by permission of Fitzhenry & Whiteside Limited.

NAIM KATTAN 'The Pact' originally published in French as 'Le Pacte' from *La reprise*, Naim Kattan, Editions Hurtubise HMH, Montreal (Quebec) 1985. Reprinted by permission. English translation © Sally Livingston, 1990.

A.M. KLEIN 'Prophet in Our Midst: A Story for Passover' from *A.M. Klein Short Stories*, edited by M.W. Steinberg © University of Toronto Press, 1983. Reprinted by permission of University of Toronto Press.

ROCHL KORN 'Earth', from *Erd* (1935). Used by permission of I. Kupferszmidt, M.D. English translation © Miriam Waddington 1990.

HENRY KREISEL 'The Almost Meeting' from *The Almost Meeting and other stories* by Henry Kreisel, reprinted with permission of NeWest Publishers Ltd.

NORMAN LEVINE 'By a Frozen River' from *Champagne Barn* (Penguin Books Canada). Used by permission of the author.

JACK LUDWIG 'A Woman of Her Age' © 1958 Jack Ludwig, from *The First Five Years: A Selection from The Tamarack Review* (Oxford University Press). Reprinted by permission of the author.

MORDECAI RICHLER 'Playing Ball on Hampstead Heath' reprinted by permission of the author.

CHAVA ROSENFARB 'The Greenhorn' from *Kanadish* (1974, edited by S. Rojanski). Used by permission of the author. English translation © Miriam Waddington 1990.

J.J. STEINFELD 'The Chess Master' from *The Apostate's Tattoo* (Ragweed Press) by J.J. Steinfeld, copyright © 1983 by J.J. Steinfeld. Used by permission of the author.

MIRIAM WADDINGTON 'Breaking Bread in Jerusalem' from *Summer at Lonely Beach* (Mosaic Press). Used by permission of the author.

HELEN WEINZWEIG 'My Mother's Luck' from *A View from the Roof* (Goose Lane Editions). Used by permission of the author.

ADELE WISEMAN 'On Wings of Tongue' from *More Stories by Canadian Women* (Oxford University Press). Used by permission of the author.

INTRODUCTION

What is Canadian about a Canadian story? What is Jewish about a Jewish story? And how do Canadian Jewish stories reflect both? Since I still believe that we can learn from history, in spite of the prejudice against it in the last few decades, I wanted this anthology to portray, in literary terms, the development of the modern Jewish Canadian imaginative experience. The latter is an experience that takes for granted that 'somewhere in the vicinity Spinoza is [still] breeding his spiders in a jar'.* Along with its modernity, the development of the Jewish imaginative experience can best be shown by a selection of stories grouped chronologically, according to the author's year of birth. Beginning with stories that depict the Yiddish East European roots of the Jewish immigrants who came to Canada before and after the two world wars, this anthology goes on to portray the variety of situations they encountered after settling here. Finally, stories by younger writers show how the children and grandchildren of those immigrants have perceived and interpreted both their Jewish and their Canadian cultures.

In making my choices I have excluded stories containing the Jewish stereotypes based on what John Stuart Mill, writing in the nineteenth century, called received opinion, and that today consist of second-hand ideas and images derived from the conventions of cinema, television, and stand-up comedians. Although accents and gestures, yarmulkes, candle blessings, cantorial chantings, chicken soup and the like are all authentic aspects of Jewish life, they have been so debased by commercial use that serious writers have usually avoided them. Since space was limited, I chose only stories that had been previously published in books—either individual collections or anthologies. This decision meant that I could not include every writer I might have, and there are many young and not-so-young Jewish writers who

---

*Osip Mandelstam, *The Noise of Time,* translated by Clarence Brown (London: Quartet Books, 1988). This is another way of saying that the modern Jewish literary tradition is like all other Western traditions in that it had its roots in the European enlightenment.

still await discovery by some future editor.

I have argued elsewhere* that there is no single tradition in Canadian literature. There are many. The reasons are to be found in our history: in the influence of a particular climate and a varied geography; in the effects of a lingering colonialism that lasted up to the Second World War; and in the fact of two official languages, English and French. The presence or absence of one language, be it either English or French, does not remove the shadowy syntax, the special sound, or the spicy flavour of the second one, no matter which it happens to be. There is also the issue of multiculturalism—the Canadian attempt to integrate immigrants into their new country while at the same time allowing them to preserve the language and traditions of their mother countries. This has resulted in an important national characteristic: the awareness of otherness, of difference, whether or not that difference is accepted or even recognized. Awareness of difference is not only politically sanctioned in Canada, but operates socially in a thousand ways, and can be expressed both positively and negatively. The awareness of difference and the tensions and barriers it creates, the necessary hesitations, even at such a basic level as language, have been mistakenly seen as symptoms of a national inferiority complex—a simplistic interpretation that overlooks the intellectual effort and emotional cost of living out the awareness of otherness.

The stories in this book are Jewish not only because they are written by Jews, but because they reflect definite Jewish values even when these are expressed indirectly. Chief among the values portrayed here is the continuity of a Jewish tradition containing religion, ethics, and a culture that includes two languages besides English and French—namely Yiddish and Hebrew. Linked to continuity is the individual's sense of belonging to a marginal group and being part of that collective. Being born into and part of the Jewish people also includes, these days, the knowledge that always, in some other place on this earth, distant or near, Jews are being oppressed and persecuted. In art the issue of oppression usually generates themes of exile and problems of uncertain or divided identity—what Klein called the twinship of his thought.

Pervasive and important as these aspects are in Jewish writing,

---

* 'Canadian Tradition and Canadian Literature', in *Apartment Seven: Essays Selected and New* (Toronto: Oxford University Press, 1989).

I believe there are still two even more important characteristics. Though it is not the only writing that is moral, Jewish writing always has a moral dimension, and nearly always reflects the age-old quest for knowledge—a quest that has resulted in the description of Jews as 'People of the Book'. Yet book knowledge and learning are only one part of knowledge. The other way of gaining knowledge is personal and emotional. While reading for this anthology I found, over and over again, that the drive to learn—the need to know and the urge to possess knowledge in oneself—was one of the main concerns in most stories. Sometimes it consisted only of the longing for something as apparently simple and ordinary as the 'reminders of a Canadian winter' that send Norman Levine's narrator to a small northern town where he finds much more than he bargained for. Other times it is the search for the knowledge of authenticity in love, a search that propels Naomi Guttman's young narrator into the activity she calls 'practising'.

How do Canadian Jewish stories unite and integrate both Canadian and Jewish themes? How do they deal with the problem of assimilating Canadian culture while still holding to a Jewish culture or, if you like, an ethnic identity? An examination of the stories will show how different writers have dealt with these matters—even though it is never a question of integrating just one issue, but several overlapping ones. Among them are locale and the sense of place, families in an immigrant context, generational clashes, exile, identity, suffering, and the effects of the Holocaust. And most of the stories touch on not one but several of those very issues.

It should not surprise us that the Holocaust and its effects are dealt with in as many as five of these eighteen stories. In Chava Rosenfarb's 'Greenhorn' (translated from the Yiddish), the hero is an involuntary immigrant from a Displaced Persons' camp. Monique Bosco's 'Old Woman's Lamentations on Yom Kippur' (translated from the French), gives us a survivor who mourns losses that have robbed her of everything but her loneliness. Naim Kattan's hero in 'The Pact'—also translated from French—is the son of a 1920s immigrant who is not especially interested in his Jewishness but who is nonetheless compelled to visit Dachau, where he feels a new and unfamiliar connection to other Jews. 'Here we were in the past, in history.' Matt Cohen's surrealistic story about a watchmaker, a survivor who lives a life within a life, reveals a past and present that combine in a jigsaw of questions with menacing undertones. And finally there is J.J. Steinfeld's story about the suffering of the child of survivors who plays chess (and more than chess) in a Toronto street café with a former Nazi. 'The past,' Steinfeld writes, 'can be transmitted from generation to generation.'

In a class by itself is the single satire in this collection. Mordecai Richler's 'Playing Ball on Hampstead Heath' depicts 'showbiz expatriates . . . come together on a Sunday morning for a fun game of softball on Hampstead Heath just as the Raj of another dynasty had used to meet on the cricket pitch in Malabar.' But in this fun game Richler parallels, exposes, criticizes, and ridicules the real life games of these showbiz types—petty betrayals, sequential polygamies, and pathetic pretensions. It's true that some of them yearn for the lost idealism of their politically radical youth. One of them 'still subscribed to *The Nation*; and his spectaculars had content . . . he filled his Roman slaves with anti-apartheid dialogue and sagacious Talmudic sayings.' Another former radical is so proud of the fact that he fought in the Spanish Civil War that he still boasts of the shrapnel wound hidden under the elastic bandage on his leg, bringing to mind Gorky's comment that 'to ridicule professional martyrs is a good thing.'* As for the theme of exile, it is ever present in the longing for the honest cold of the Canadian climate and the reassuring heat of Canadian houses— not to speak of the homesickness for Montreal's smoked meat sandwiches and bagels—but it is dismissed as trivial by one of the players who sums up life in London with the words: 'Look at it this way, it isn't home.'

We meet more former radicals in Helen Weinzweig's 'My Mother's Luck', and Jack Ludwig's 'Woman of Her Age', although generational conflict and women's rights are the real subjects of Weinzweig's story, while Ludwig's Mrs Goffman, in the process of summing up her life, is mostly concerned with the changing world and the loss of continuity of a tradition. A.M. Klein's charming story modernizes the ancient Talmudic legend of the prophet Elijah by transplanting it to Montreal, where it is further transformed by a family's kindness at Passover to a poor half-wit.

---

*Maxim Gorky, letter to Mikhail Zoschenko, in *Letters* (Moscow, 1966).

Sharon Drache also uses traditional Jewish material to weave into her tale about a scribe-turned-painter a criticism of the religious prohibition against graven images.

Families are crucial in many of these stories. Shirley Faessler's 'A Basket of Apples' concentrates on the close family ties in the immigrant milieu of Toronto, where the death of one member strengthens the love among the others. Ted Allan's 'Lies My Father Told Me' recreates a loving relationship between grandfather, grandson, and their horse, which ends in transience and loss. The stories by Rochl Korn and Adele Wiseman are both about families, and both are strongly rooted in the sense of place and climate. The families are very different, however: Wiseman's is close and loving, while Korn's is torn apart by hatred and bitterness. Korn's story, written in Yiddish, takes place against a background of village life in Poland just before the First World War. Her chief character is a Jewish farmer who, determined to acquire some land of his own, divides and destroys his family. Both Korn and Wiseman use the setting and locale of their stories to release inner meaning. Korn's farmer tries to establish permanence against rootlessness and exile through unity with the earth, the countryside, and the wheat fields, where all are enfolded in the rhythms of nature. Wiseman, whose story was written much later, makes palpable a children's prairie winter, full of snow and the steam of wet woollen clothing, which contrasts with the warmth and cheerful poverty inside the house. The climate, pure and without ambiguity, becomes a metaphor for the child's clarity and innocence that heals an emotionally sick woman.

I suggested earlier that acceptance of difference, of the other, was an essential condition of being Canadian, but I didn't expect to find it expressed so clearly in no less than five stories—by Henry Kreisel, Norman Levine, Chava Rosenfarb, Naim Kattan, and J.J. Steinfeld—in addition to my own. We see in them a recurring motif that is not to be found in either American Jewish or British Jewish stories—acceptance of and reconciliation with the other, sometimes even with the enemy. In Kattan's story the narrator visits Dachau in the company of a casually encountered American traveller who is not a Jew. They share the same experience, but from two very different spiritual locations. Yet they take leave of each other knowing they have made a deep connection, which will last a lifetime. Steinfeld's story about the friendship between the child of survivors and a former Nazi is more complicated. It deals with suffering and guilt, with love and hate, but the love between the Jewish boy and German ex-officer is the compass that draws the story to its centre. Rosenfarb's story ends in an epiphany for the protagonist when the kindness and interest of a French Canadian girl in a garment factory transforms a hostile environment. In my own story, the alienation and fear on the part of a Canadian woman in Israel is resolved by a chance encounter with an Arab watchman.

But the two stories that best exemplify the essence of a Canadian Jewish story are Norman Levine's 'By A Frozen River' and Henry Kreisel's 'The Almost Meeting'. Levine's narrator is an expatriate Canadian writer who feels homesick for winter. Levine gives us winter with all its Canadian associations of isolation, beauty, stillness, and the sense of imminent awakening. In this arrest of time, this winter pause, he accidentally discovers two other Jews—one is transient but the other is the last Jew in the town and the only one to pray in the synagogue. He faithfully carries on the tradition of Friday night prayers and the Sabbath meal, and the narrator joins him, thus affirming his own Jewishness that was, until then, unimportant to him. That is the major theme of the story. A minor one is the intermarriage of a Jewish woman and an itinerant French Canadian photographer. In a reversal of the usual stereotypes, the Christian husband supports and loves his wife despite the suffering she causes him.

Henry Kreisel's story is equally haunting. Its Jewish resonances are too many to enumerate, but its Canadian realities of place and person are familiar to us all. The story concerns the elusiveness of an old and famous Canadian Jewish writer, David Lasker, and the pursuit of him by a young, non-Jewish Hungarian writer, Alexander Budak. 'Lasker had given a voice to the immigrants who had come to Canada in the early years of the century . . . His first book presented a . . . gallery of Jewish immigrants . . . but then he had gone beyond his own community and had written . . . about the immigrants who had come to the city after the Second World War . . . he gave voice to the voiceless.' Kreisel's Lasker is reminiscent of the *lamed vovniks*—the thirty-six wise men who magically hold up the world but who are completely anonymous even to themselves, since they do not know they are *lamed vovniks*. (Kreisel's story also reminds us of A.M. Klein's classic novel *The Second Scroll,* where the search for Uncle Melach proves so fruitless.) Lasker's unwillingness to meet the younger writer has to do with his own reluctance to supply answers—he believes there are many answers and at the same time, there are no answers. Each one must find his or her own way.

Finally, each reader will have to find personal answers to the questions raised earlier about what is Canadian and what is Jewish in a Canadian Jewish story. Perhaps the answers are not as important as the search for them. All of these stories tell us something new about people we know, and perhaps if we are lucky, we will also find in the story-teller 'the figure in which the righteous man encounters himself.'*

My thanks to Richard Teleky, Sally Livingston, Phyllis Wilson, and Jaye Mastalerz of Oxford University Press for their unfailing patience and help.

---

*Walter Benjamin, 'The Story Teller', in *Illuminations,* edited by Hannah Arendt, translated by Harry Zohn (London: Fontana, 1973).

ROCHL KORN · 1898-1982

Earth

I

It wasn't easy for Mordecai to find a second wife. Behind his back, people in the surrounding villages whispered that he had worked his first wife to death the same way he had his horses. In the forest nearby there was a deep hollow pit, and almost every spring, when the ploughing was over, Mordecai would harness his team to a new corpse and drag it off to the forest. The next day, on their way to pasture, the cows would stir up the powdery dust and reveal the long narrow furrows made by the ribs of the dead horse.

When Mordecai had the hardest of the spring work behind him, and only part of one hill was left to plough, the last of the three new horses he had bought to work alongside his stallion toppled over in the midst of the ploughing. Mordecai tugged at its tail and put a prod under its stomach. A tremor ran through the chestnut, which lifted its head and rose up on its front legs. But soon its knees buckled, its head dropped to one side and only its large gentle eyes followed the movements of the man who was applying the whip and prod to its dying body. 'Come on chestnut, whoa there, whoa!'

Seeing that nothing was to be done with either kindness or cruelty, Mordecai finished the ploughing with the stallion. The horse now stood on trembling legs while his whistling breath filled the evening air. As Mordecai surveyed his field, a stray smile hovered and was lost in his thick round beard; then he doffed his cap, bowed three times and gave thanks to the stallion in a loud voice: '*Jancoyen tzi bulanki.*' Three days later Mordecai was dragging the stallion's corpse into the forest.

When the spring sun began to drink the moisture from the earth, and the first violets poked out of their leaves like timid question marks, a putrid smell rose from the forest. The peasant women who came to gather herbs scattered and fled to the other end of the woods. They held their noses and joked, '*Konsco smert* has opened his treasure box again.' The Jews simply gave him a nickname; they called him the *Malakh Hamoves*, the Angel of Death.

Everyone in the surrounding countryside also knew that Mordecai was courting Zisha's daughter Sima. On Saturdays after supper he went into the village to sit with Zisha in front of his house. He would throw covert glances at Sima, who sat on a bench with her two sisters and their friends—Yona's daughter, Eli's son, and the steward's son. The latter could never keep a job and came home every other month. The boys kept moving closer to the girls and touching their new dresses while pretending to test the quality of the material. From time to time Zisha would turn his long thin neck towards the young people and say: 'What's going on there? Why don't you go chattering some place else? This isn't a café!' Mordecai understood that Zisha wanted to establish his daughter's respectability, so shrugging and smiling grudgingly he said: 'Oh leave them alone Zisha! They're like young colts when you turn them loose in their first pasture!'

Ever since Mordecai began his visits, Zisha did not have to worry about ploughing his bit of meadow. Mordecai did it for him. When Zisha pretended to offer to pay, Mordecai smiled and answered blithely, as if every one of his words was bestowing good luck on the whole world, 'We'll settle it all later—with happy celebrations!'

Sima pretended she didn't understand Mordecai's glances, which crawled over her body like insects. She never interrupted her work during Mordecai's visits, but when she saw him approach with his heavy swaying walk, she would quickly put on a fresh blouse or a fancy crocheted shawl. She couldn't depend on the steward's son who had been courting her for the last three years without purpose or plan.

II

But things turned out differently, and not at all as Mordecai had imagined. One evening when he had unharnessed the horses, his son Yankel came walking towards him on the path behind the stable. Mordecai's look contained a question about his son's sudden and unexpected return from the village. Later, when Mordecai came into the house, he found Yankel sitting on a bench with his long legs stretched out in front of him. His hands were in his pockets and he was poking his fingers through the holes in his worn-out trousers:

'Father, I need new pants, I'm ashamed for people to see me.'

He drew his words out as if he wanted to taste the flavour of his father's future anger ahead of time.

Mordecai's voice left nothing to the imagination. 'Who's telling you to go where people will see you? Can't you stay home like me and work? Who's going to get up at dawn tomorrow to do the ploughing? Who's going to drive the horses into the forest and stay there overnight with them? It's always me, me, me! And when it comes to work—there is no one. All you want is to feed at the trough!'

This time Yankel did not oppose his father or even bother to reply. He simply shrugged his shoulders. Mordecai sensed that there was something in his indifference, something elusive, something odd, that at an inconvenient moment would turn nasty, like a snake on the forest path. Silence descended in the house like a thick mist through which it was difficult to breath. Yankel kept playing with his clothes, as if afraid that his hands might be forced to do some kind of work if he stopped. He straightened his vest and turned to his sister.

'Ita, have you bought a new dress yet? You'll soon be a bridesmaid.'

Without curiosity, with the hopelessness of one who expects nothing from life, Ita asked: 'Who are you talking about?' And while Yankel told her about Zisha's daughter becoming engaged to the steward's son, he gave his father a look that repaid him for the torn pants, for being wakened in the middle of the night to go to work, and for all the verbal jabs that had mocked him and shattered his hopes. Mordecai was stunned by the news. His legs suddenly felt heavy, heavy as two logs. He banged his fist on the table and then the choked-back sarcastic laughter that everyone feared filled the house.

'Ha, ha! You'll dance too! Dance in your torn pants, you! Your mother's youngest brat!' Then he walked to the threshold and slammed the door. A tall shadow flickered outside the window and mingled with the sound of horses' hooves and the shrill tune of a village song. Mordecai whistled between his teeth as he drove the horses to their far-off pasture in the woods.

III

Now old Kopel began to visit. He and Mordecai whispered in corners, but when Ita came into the room they stopped and Kopel began to tell little stories. Whenever he hit on a juicy phrase, the lines on his face would dissolve into a broad smile.

Because of his visits, Ita would put on a white blouse, but Kopel didn't even notice. He frowned, and under his thick eyebrows his eyes became narrow slits.

'It's hot in your house.'

He turned to Mordecai in order to avoid Ita's glance as she stubbornly sought out his eyes, reminding him that not so long ago he used to visit here because of her. In those days her mother was still alive. Maybe Ita hadn't yet forgotten that dark young man, Berl's son, whom Kopel had once brought to meet her. He could see well enough, even through his squinting eyes, how her hands trembled as she removed the plates from the table, and how she tried to hide the shame and vulnerability of her lumpy, graceless body.

After Kopel had signalled to her father and both had gone outside, Ita took off the white blouse and, along with it, her smile. Her cheekbones stood out under her eyes naked and knotted.

Mordecai's married daughter, Hassia, must have heard about these goings on, because she stopped by one market day, having gotten a lift on the village elder's cart. Her hungry brown eyes roamed into every corner as they counted every new pot, every new dish, every egg on the shelf. Her pregnant stomach was just as greedy as her eyes, and so as not to lose any time a new child was added to her family every year.

'So, father, you raised a daughter, may no harm befall her! Well then, have you thought of arranging a marriage for her?' And

Hassia began to list all the good points of her father-in-law's son. Maybe fate would still favour Ita with unexpected good luck, maybe even with a rich broad-shouldered cattle merchant. If only her sister hadn't demanded her inheritance the day after their mother's death! Two strings of pearls, a diamond ring and earrings! Mordecai did not even bother to answer Hassia. He simply smiled while his eyes ran around like squirrels in a narrow cage. Ita, who knew—and dreaded—that smile, quickly grabbed the hoe and ran out into the garden. She could hear them quarrelling; her sister's thin high voice grated like a saw against the hard substance of an unbending will, while her father's bass voice sounded like the heavy blows of an axe.

Through the tangled mish-mash of incoherent words Ita realized that her fate and her hopes for the future were retreating further and further from possibility. Suddenly Hassia ran out of the house, her face flaming, holding a bag in her hand. She fell on Ita's neck with long wailing cries. 'Oh our poor mother! We have no mother, our mother's gone!' Her sister's tears tickled Ita's neck and she was revolted by the sweetish odour of mould which came from Hassia's black knitted shawl.

The two sisters had not talked to each other lately. Ita was longing to ask what Hassia's brother-in-law looked like. Perhaps a bit like Berl's son? But Hassia quickly bade her sister good-bye and hurried off to the village to rent a cart to take her home. As she was leaving she turned around once more and said, loud enough for her father to hear: 'You can tell him that I'm going to send my husband, Chaim, to speak to him, and if he refuses to give you a dowry my husband knows what to do!' Ita knew that Chaim was afraid to raise his voice in his own home and that he wouldn't dare come to Mordecai to collect his mother-in-law's jewellery. She gazed after her sister until she had disappeared behind the trees. Then she began turning the earth, breaking it into lumps with such force and energy that as it crumbled it spurted around her feet like a heavy black rain. When she stopped digging for a moment and straightened her back, she suddenly felt such a heaviness in her knees, such a weariness through her whole body, that she thrust the spade into the hard ground and leaned against a tree. Never had the young grass smelled so fresh as today. Its fragrance assaulted her nostrils with a moist sweetness that made her feel as dizzy as if she had been drinking wine. She dropped to the ground and stretched out. In every pulse she suddenly sensed the rhythm of the ripening, awakening earth as it answered the wild beating of her own heart. A sob, passionate and poignant as the mating call of water birds in the short summer nights, escaped her. Then her body dissolved and her spirit was released into a quiet weeping.

IV

On this day Mordecai awoke earlier than usual. When he led his horses out to pasture the first wind of dawn parted the mists between day and night. The money that Mordecai had readied for the squire, which he kept under his pillow, burned a hole in his mind and wouldn't let him sleep. The money reminded him that the field he had worked day and night was not his own, and because of a loophole in his contract he might have to move and abandon everything. Mordecai remembered that only a few years ago a dense forest had covered his plot, shutting the sun out on the sunniest day. He remembered when the squire first began cutting down that forest. At the beginning only coarse brush grew there but soon the squire found a tenant to watch over it. The next morning the tenant appeared with a waxen face and, crossing himself, said the following: 'I wouldn't stay there another night for any money. There's something evil in that place . . . It's unclean.' From that time on everyone in the village had avoided the logged-over forest, even in daylight.

The clearing was quite far from the squire's estate, and before his peasants came with their horses and ploughshares the sun was already high in the sky. Not having a foreman over them, the peasants didn't hurry, and every half hour they stopped working, lit their cigars, and told stories about Preussen in Germany, where half the village intended to immigrate. The whole business scarcely merited the squire's interest. At one point he had Mordecai brought before him.

'I want to rent that site, that clearing behind the forest. Find me a tenant who understands how to run a farm and who knows how to pay on time.'

'Well squire, it's going to be hard.'

'Why hard?' The squire jumped up from his chair.

'Well, people say there is something frightening there.'

'Nonsense, the devil's not going to grab them.'

'Well, I'll ask, I'll ask around, squire. And how much of the harvest will you take?'

'A ton and a half of corn. Just to be rid of it.'

'A ton and a half of corn or wheat for a distant field like that isn't exactly cheap. Not everybody will want to rent such a small holding.'

Mordecai thought about the matter all day. The idea of renting the field and the old clearing gave him no peace. He busied himself with his pots of sour cream, figuring and figuring the whole time. He didn't even hear what his wife, sitting in her corner, was saying to him. He was tired of his rickety old wagon, tired of driving around to the houses of the rich day in day out with a rusty milk can and a litre measure. More than once, in winter, his fingers had frozen to the metal of the can and his skin had peeled down to the raw flesh. Now Mordecai began to feel that all those years when he had been delivering milk, in the deepest corner of his heart, there had been the longing for some land of his own, like the farm they used to have at home, before his father had wasted it all in litigation with his own brother.

Mordecai went ahead and rented the clearing from the squire for a period of twelve years, even though his wife filled every corner of the house with her wailing, bemoaning her fate to all the neighbours.

'Where's he dragging me to? Where? How does he expect me to live in the backwoods, where you never see another living soul? And besides, they whisper that there's a . . .'

And she would put her hand up to her mouth, choking back the words. 'May it wander without rest through the desolate forests and fields.'

She even sent Reb Yanzia's wife to try to talk him out of it. But in vain did Zissel of the wide hips make the whole floor shake: Mordecai had answered her quietly and reasonably while smiling his mocking little smile—the smile that was so familiar to his family, who knew how much anger was hidden in it.

'Since you have taken the trouble to come, Zissel, sweetheart, tell my Hannah from me that I, for one, am not staying here. Let her do what she likes. Let her stay here and deliver the milk herself to those rich little madams in town, why not?'

No one had slept that first night in their new home. It was the end of March and a northwest wind kept rattling the roof and the eaves. Part of the time it sounded like people in bare feet cavorting in the attic. The children dragged themselves around all day, pale, tired, and listless. They kept their eyes on the sun, jealously hoarding the hours before dark. His wife had gone about her chores red-eyed, lamenting her fate and that of the children. But Mordecai had refused to budge:

'I'm staying here, and that's that.'

And he had his way. And not only when it came to staying. On the meagre, neglected plot of land he had cultivated twelve acres with one pair of horses. In the barn he had five cows and two calves. Mordecai begrudged himself a single free minute, and the same was true for his wife, his children, and his horses.

'For the time being I'm a tenant; I have nothing of my own. When I own the land we'll all be able to take it easy, and even eat challah on weekdays.'

The peasants, on their way to church from one village to the next, stopped to look at his fields. They pulled the broad green ribbons of wheat through their fingers, saying:

'When a field falls into the hands of a good owner, it rewards his hard work with interest. Doesn't it brother?'

The Jews in the village began to whisper among themselves that Mordecai was planning to buy the whole field from the squire, and that he had already saved up enough to buy half of it.

'If a man doesn't allow himself even the smallest luxury and lives poorer than the poorest peasant, why shouldn't he have money? But just wait and see. His daughter will be an old maid. He'll never give her a dowry.' With such talk those who envied him consoled themselves.

Whenever Mordecai was at home he kept fingering the money in his breast pocket, and although he spent more and more time rejoicing at the rustling of his paper notes, he still needed something to which he could attach his anger.

Ita had guessed that on this day her father was taking his instalment payment to the squire, and she did her best to avoid him. But he stopped in front of her in the corner where she was churning butter while chasing away the flies.

'Lazer-Nota is wondering why you bring him so little butter and cheese these days.'

Ita knew that whatever she said now would only serve to feed his anger. Nevertheless she tried to answer. 'Father, you know that two of our cows are about to calve.'

'That's just an excuse. Everyone eats too much, and there's no housewife looking after things. You'll make me go begging in my old age! I know that's what you want—you and your brother! He's busy in the village chasing girls and playing cards! Don't you ever dare to let him into this house, do you hear?'

He took the churn from Ita's hands, and as if it might pacify him, began turning it. From time to time he shook the churn and listened to its contents as if the fragments of butter were calling to him. Afterwards he removed the butter, washed off the whey, and locked it in a cupboard, hiding the key in the purse where he kept his money. Only then was he at peace. Satisfied with himself at last, he took his stick, and with a heavy tread started out on the most difficult road of all, the road that led to the squire's where he would have to pay the semi-annual instalment of his rent.

v

One time Kopel, the matchmaker, stayed overnight. Ita prepared a bed of straw for him in the middle of the house, and all night long the old man groaned and muttered so that no one else could get a wink of sleep. Several times he woke up, rubbed his eyes and called to Mordecai. 'Reb Mordecai, reb Mordecai, is it time yet?'

At dawn while the dew lay on the ground like a net of sparkling spiderwebs, Mordecai harnessed the horses and drove off with Kopel. No one knew where he was going or for how long, but when Ita went to take the little mirror off the shelf, she saw that her father's phylacteries were missing.

On the same day Yankel learned from a cattle dealer of a neighbouring village that his father was visiting Chaim-Leib, and that Kopel was arranging a match with his daughter. Yankel came home that evening and reported to Ita with an I-told-you-so smile.

'Didn't I tell you, Ita, not to work so hard, not to kill yourself—none of this is for you! That devil will take it all! Didn't I warn you?'

Ita shook her head in disbelief. 'Go on—people like to talk. If you aren't busy working there's always some nonsense to fill your time.' All the same she decided to air out her mother's things. But the cupboard was locked and the key, which was usually kept in an old bucket beside the stove, was gone.

Three days later, after Ita had finished milking the cows, Mordecai drove up with his new young wife. She was sitting in the back seat of the wagon, her hands folded in her lap. Mordecai unharnessed his horses who were champing at the bit, and asked: 'Why don't you come down off the wagon, Bailtsche?'

Bailtsche remained seated, taking in the freshly patched roof and the forest surrounding the house and field like a black frame that separated it from the rest of the world. The rays of the setting sun swept over the stalks of wheat and gilded their heads. A greenish mist of pollen from the blooming corn hung over the fields, and there was no human sound anywhere. Everything around seemed dead. Bailtsche shuddered. The Turkish shawl slid down from her shoulders, and her narrow, freckled little face peered out from under the black headscarf like a newly hatched egg in a bird's nest.

Mordecai held out his hand to help Bailtsche off the wagon, but soon he dropped it, feeling ashamed. He imagined that his daughter was spying on him from a crack in the stable door.

VI

After Mordecai's marriage, Yankel stayed at home more. There was more to eat, his stepmother lit the stove three times a day, and his father stopped nagging and urging him to go to work. But Mordecai himself worked twice as hard, as if his strength had been renewed. He ploughed both fields and the orchard, and cut and stacked the wheat by himself.

Ita's eyes under her sparse, colourless lashes were now always ringed with red. Since her father's marriage she had begun to sleep on a straw pallet in the lean-to beneath the ladder that led to the attic. Very often she was awakened during the night by the frightened fluttering of hens. And often too in the morning she had to brush the hens' dirt from her face.

Bailtsche soon grew accustomed to her new home. She had been used to living in a different house every few months when she was a maid, and with a housemaid's instinct she soon knew where to find everything. Not once had she asked Ita for anything; right from the beginning she had sensed a bitter enemy in Ita.

She made a face at what she found in the small brown cupboard—four flowered bowls, several tin plates, tall iron pots, and wooden spoons. Every Sabbath she insisted on meat and challah, for Bailtsche had taken on some of the well-fed solidity of wealthy Jewish homes, and she scorned the mean and stingy counting of every mouthful. Even now, Bailtsche secretly added extra fat to her own plate of soup, and often devoured a chunk of cheese in the orchard when no one was looking. The secrecy added an extra flavour.

Sometimes she was seized with a longing for people and the life of the town, as well as with a nameless fear. Her father would often stop by on market days on his way home. He never ceased to praise Mordecai while eating a bowl of cottage cheese with sour cream:

'You've got yourself a diamond of a husband, so look after him! You're hardly worth a man like that, I swear. May I die on the spot if you are. . . .'

Bailtsche was ashamed of her father and thanked God when the old man left. His whiskey-laden breath reminded her of her childhood, and her mother's wild screams when her drunken husband beat her. But even the strongest whiskey couldn't drown out the smell of dead animals; a smell that imbued all his clothing, his hair and his hands. Chaim-Leib was known as the best skinner of hides in the district. He could skin an animal with a single cut of the knife, and he never refused a job. That way he had all the more money to spend on whiskey.

He admired everything in his son-in-law's house, and his eyes always lighted on something he had immediate need of. Sometimes it was a frayed bit of rope, sometimes an odd piece of lumber, a pound of salt, or a bag of feed for his chickens.

After the old man's visit Yankel would puff out his cheeks, half close his eyes, and imitate Chaim-Leib's oafish, stumbling way of talking. And Ita would ask Bailtsche, making sure that her father could hear, if she hadn't seen the hammer with the broken handle, or the little ladder from the stable, or the bundle of flax.

'After all, no thieves come here,' Mordecai would say crossly, 'so where are the things? Why don't you take better care of them?' Ita wouldn't take her eyes off Bailtsche for a second, until the latter could feel her face reddening. But she would merely turn towards the window and say, 'Look Mordecai, it's clouding over.'

The fields unfolded in waves of ripening wheat, as if rivers brimming with sun had flooded the world. The old people in the village could not remember such a plentiful harvest. In the meadows people bowed as if to the gods before the ripening bread. The sickles, like silver crescents, glittered and were extinguished among the thick stands of wheat. The sweetish smell of dry straw mingled with the coolness of the earth while the sun like a heated fireball warmed the bent heads of the wheat. Peoples' bodies dripped with sweat that glued their shirts to their skin and darkened their vision.

Suddenly the news, in the red headlines of distant cities, surrounded the fields with a bloody border. Somewhere someone had started a war. People straightened their backs and searched the skies expecting to find a dark stain shaping the single ominous word: war.

All the more powerfully did the sickles cut through the wheat, and all the louder did the scythes ring in the hands of the peasants. Wives began preparing parcels for the road, and the village chief sent out call-up notices to all the healthy young men in the area.

These days Yankel felt elated. It was as if some long-wished-for happiness had finally come his way and opened a new road to the world. He looked at the village head's letter and read it over at least ten times, laughing with pleasure all the while. When he left home, no one came to the train to see him off, though Ita shed a few tears. Bailtsche waited for him in the orchard, behind the fence, with a small parcel hidden under her shawl.

'Yankel, go in good health. This is from Golda. She came this morning while you were still asleep, but she couldn't wait. She's afraid of your father. Yankel, what message shall I give her?'

He gritted his teeth as if biting on a hard kernel, and waved his hand.

'Say nothing. It's better that way. I'll never come back, whatever happens.'

Before there was time to harvest the crop and store it in the granaries, the hooves of Cossack horses trampled the fields. The nights held up the starry sky with fiery posts. During the day gray ribbons of smoke from burning houses were wafted by every whim of the advancing wind. People fled into the neighbouring forest with crying children in their arms, dragging their cows on ropes behind them. The village emptied as if everyone had died. Chickens were locked in the barns with water and corn in wooden bowls, unchained dogs ran wild with their tongues hanging out, not knowing what to do in their new-found freedom. The sick dragged themselves from their beds and followed the crowd, groaning all the while. Only two people remained in the village— the crippled Hrinka in his daughter-in-law's house, and Mendl Sodevnik's wife who had gone out of her mind from fear. She tore off her clothes and ran naked and shrieking through the crowd of crying children, 'May the devil take Mendl, your father, you bastards!'

Her words were like bandages ripped from a wound that has festered for years. All the helplessness of her prematurely withered body, which had been forced to bring forth a child every year, was now transformed into a wild hatred for the whole world. But primarily for her husband and children. The neighbours chained her to the wall and took away the bawling children.

Mordecai was the last to enter the forest and he had to hunt for a long time before he found his wife and daughter. Little boys who had climbed the trees saw a heavy cloud of dust advancing towards them, with the occasional gleam of a bayonet. People held their breath, and quickly bound up the mouths of the cattle. Mothers forced open their infants' mouths and sprayed milk from their breasts into them to silence their crying. Every leaf that stirred in the wind, every sound of a dry twig crackling pierced their ears and sent their blood pounding.

Only when the last of the dust had settled on the leaves, covering them in grey fuzz, and the sound of horses' hooves had been swallowed up by distance, only then did people push the branches aside and stretch their cramped bodies.

'Did you see?'

'Cossacks.'

'How many can there be?'

'A thousand!'

'Go on, what do you know? You're only good at peeling

potatoes for your mother! Ask me, I'm an old soldier! I cut my teeth on Franz Josef's army bread! I say there weren't more than three hundred.'

The animals were unmuzzled and the horses sneezed; the cows opened their mouths in wide yawns, licking their faces with their hard tongues, while the branches shook with the children's held-back crying.

Hrinka's youngest suddenly appeared, out of breath, and covered with sweat.

'Father, Yantek who lives under the hill is coming here.'

'Which Yantek?'

'The one who went to work on the Krisavitz estate.'

The lad ran forward to greet the newcomer and hung on his coat.

Yantek wiped the sweat from his face and looked around him with wonder.

'What's going on here?'

'Where are you coming from that you don't even know the Russians have invaded us? A while ago three hundred Cossacks rode by with their bayonets.'

'So what? You have something to fear? Let the rich squires and the Jews worry. I've just come from Krisavitz—the Cossacks arrived there yesterday. Did they kill any of you or what? The truth is the landowners have all fled like poisoned rats. Not a single one stayed. But the Russians, good fellows that they are, left their reinforcements to keep our girls company.'

The young men broke into laughter, but the older ones frowned and answered slowly: 'It seems Yantek was right.'

But it was nightfall before people began returning to their homes. Mordecai remained in the neighbouring pasture with his wife, daughter, and cattle waiting to see how things would turn out. But he couldn't bear to be away from his own place for long, so at dawn when Ita awoke she saw that her father was gone. She hunted for him everywhere and woke her stepmother: 'Auntie, Auntie, where is father?'

But Bailtsche groaned crossly and turned over. Ita hurried through the fields to their homestead. Even from a distance she could see her father's massive frame. The lonely figure was walking slowly. His booted legs, knee-deep in ripe oats, stubbornly dug their heels into the earth so as not to yield to the habit and rhythm of the scythe. His arms described large half circles in the air.

Mordecai managed to harvest his late oats. The hard ripe heads of the oats rang like the little silver bells on spice boxes at the least whiff of wind.

Somewhere behind the forest the first rifle shots were heard, as if some wild bloodthirsty beast had been let loose and was attacking the morning.

Ita bound the oats into sheaves and in the wake of her path a trail of low-lying stooks raised their dishevelled blond heads.

IX

Mordecai walked home from the village on the path that bordered the forest. All the talk of the elders in the village chief's house had intoxicated him more than the strongest whiskey. Under his heavy tread the coils of dry leaves crackled and snapped. Violet evening shadows crept out of the forest and, like the hands of a blind man, touched a different part of the meadow each time. The forest that just a few minutes before had risen like a green wave of tree tops was now bending to reveal the naked wounds of its chopped-down trunks, and the first frost silvered the beds of sprouting winter wheat. Soon, Mordecai thought, his sweat-soaked field would belong to him, he would own it all. He wouldn't have to work his horses to death in order to make the earth yield enough for both him and the squire. A good thing he hadn't tried to marry off his daughter. If he had given her a dowry he wouldn't have been able to buy even an inch of land. He would have had to leave this place, to rattle his bones once more on the broken-down cart, delivering cans of milk to the villagers. Someone else would have taken his place and sown the fields that he had ploughed and manured with so much effort.

By the time Mordecai reached his house the lamp was already lit. Bailtsche was just raking some baked potatoes out of the coals and blowing on them as she tossed them from hand to hand.

'Why so late?' she asked without raising her eyes from the fire.

Mordecai seated himself opposite the open kitchen door. The reflection of the fire licked his boots like the red tongue of a dog. He answered her in his thick heavy voice: 'The squire's wife wants to sell the field. She sent the steward to the village.'

Ita was sitting at the table behind the lamp plucking chickens. She sat quietly without talking. That afternoon when no one was in the house she had searched for the white headkerchief. She had found it under Bailtsche's pillow. All four corners were knotted around some folded diapers and lace-trimmed undershirts. She had held the undershirts in her hands, staring at them, while a cold dread crawled up her back. Lace, she thought, where does she get the money to buy lace? He must surely give it to her. He . . . and Ita suddenly remembered how her father had refused to give her mother the money to buy shoelaces for the children. In order to buy them her mother had secretly had to sell a few eggs to the village shop.

The diapers burned her hands and still she could not put them down. The unknown, someone else's secret, that had intruded so suddenly into her life sent the blood to her throat, to her large mouth, to her lumpy cheeks. Now Ita began to observe Bailtsche closely, to notice her slow movements, her freckled face. She would have liked to insinuate herself inside the serene smile that momentarily flared Bailtsche's nostrils as she looked into Mordecai's eyes with the confidence of a wife who knows she is loved.

'Well, that's good—it means we can leave here soon, so let her sell it,' Bailtsche said.

'What are you saying? I intend to buy the field myself.'

'If you want to buy it, then buy. I won't stay here in the middle of the forest in times like these. A person can be killed here without even a rooster crowing.'

Ita read uncertainty in her father's face, an uncertainty that she did not recognize. Her father, who had worked so hard in order to have his own piece of land in his old age, was now ready to ruin everything for Bailtsche's sake. Bailtsche, the intruder, the lazybones who didn't even know how to hold a spade or a hoe! Ita's face, with its white eyelashes, trembled.

She rose from the bench, her eyes narrowed into slits: 'Father, don't listen to anyone, and buy! If you have the money, then don't wait until someone else buys. It will be your own, and wherever you step, it will be your own—'

Bailtsche bent her head as if to avoid an impending blow. Suddenly she felt that the ugly stepdaughter wanted to chain her to the twenty-acre field forever, wanted to enslave her to the land just as she herself was enslaved, just as Mordecai was, just as the tree on the roadside was. And she burst into helpless childish crying.

'So I'll go away by myself.'

Now Ita could no longer contain herself: 'If you find it so awful here, go on! No one is forcing you to stay. Go back where you came from—be a housemaid!'

Mordecai banged his stick against the bench and said in Polish, 'That's my business!'

For him to speak Polish was the sign of deepest anger. It was a thousand times worse than his smile.

'With my money I'll do what I like, and the devil take all of you!'

Ita's head bent still lower and the veins on her neck tightened and throbbed with envy and hatred.

X

From early morning on the jays and crows chattered wildly. Their restlessness foretold snow. The wind lay coiled and tense along the valleys like an animal ready to spring. Later it spiralled into the air, knocking off the dried leaves still left on the trees from the summer.

It pulled the clouds together like balls of cotton wool, trying to stuff them into the space that separates sky and earth. In this the wind succeeded, for soon only a narrow crack between heaven and earth remained—a crack into which the short winter day now crawled to die.

Three men came riding out of the forest dragging several cows tied together with rope. The first to spot them was Bailtsche. 'They look like men from the squire's estate.'

Ita stepped outside and returned with a blanched face and ashen lips.

'Father, the Russians are here again, and they've taken our cows.'

Mordecai fastened the belt of his trousers. 'They have nothing to take from me. I'm not one of your squires, and you women, be quiet!'

They heard the horses on the icy ground beside the well. Two Russian soldiers dismounted and banged on the door with their rifle butts while their three companions guarded the cows who pawed the ground anxiously and, sensing the closeness of the barn, made yearning, homesick noises.

The house seemed to grow smaller. It filled up with the smell of cowhide, sweat, and a vague dull fear.

Mordecai greeted them: 'Good evening! I suppose you're lost, eh? Not surprising in this drizzly fog.'

One of the soldiers, with a fresh bluish sabre cut along one side of his face, burst into loud laughter. 'Just look at him, the clever little Jew! No, we're not lost, sweetheart; in fact we've come especially to pay you a visit, and it's our commander who sent us.'

The whiskers of the other Cossack danced for joy.

'In that case, please sit.'

'No, you'd better lead us to the stable.'

Mordecai's body stiffened.

'Are you coming or should we kick you over there with our boots?'

Ita got up from the bench and threw on her mother's old jacket. 'Come on, father!'

Her eyes were still and their blue-grey nakedness was reminiscent of the frozen little rivers of winter, but her hands trembled as they buttoned the torn jacket. She went ahead, and the Cossacks followed to make sure that no one was hiding. The door to the house remained open behind them.

Bailtsche cowered on the bench. The sharp cold from outside poured a thick white mist which crept closer and closer to her fear-paralysed legs. She couldn't move. Suddenly her ears were assaulted by a knotted tangle of voices. She wiped the film from one of the panes and pressed her face to the window. The two soldiers on horseback were now beside the stable and holding a rope tied to her two finest cows. Mordecai kept pulling on the rope, until one of the soldiers took the rope end and whipped it across his hands. The blow raised a thick purple welt but Mordecai did not let go of the cows. The strain outlined the veins in his neck and forehead.

'These are my cows, my livelihood! I won't give them up. Go to the squire—he has stables full of cattle!'

The soldiers took down their rifles and for a second the metal gleamed thin and sharp as knives.

'For the last time, are you going to let go of the cows or not?'

Mordecai paled. Pearly drops of sweat rolled down his face, but he stood his ground. 'Kill me if you like, but I won't give them up. They're mine.'

Bailtsche watched Ita run forward and seize the soldier's arm. Then a red fog veiled her eyes and hid everything.

Neither did she hear it when the raw healthy laughter of the soldier shattered the strained and breathless silence like a bullet.

'Look at him—this little Jew, this nothing, is opposing the Russian might! If it wanted to, the Russian might could pulverize him, squash him under its heel like a worm, right now, on the spot!'

He laughed as heartily as a child. His laughter was like fresh water rinsing his throat.

And maybe he too would have looked and felt powerless if in his home he had been confronted by German soldiers?

'Well, come along with us to our commander—maybe if you beg and plead he'll let you keep one of your cows. I'll tell him you're a poor Jew. I can't do any more than that. I was ordered to bring the cows, and that's that.'

When Mordecai came into the house to fetch his sheepskin coat, Bailtsche was still sitting where he had left her, her arms and legs stiff and lifeless.

'Bailtsche, what's wrong, Bailtsche?'

She didn't answer. Her lips were pressed tight.

Mordecai called Ita in. 'Rub her chest and temples with snow.'

He himself poured water into her mouth, forcing it between her clenched teeth, until she opened her eyes.

'Bailtsche, darling, do you feel better now?'

She saw that Mordecai was dressed for travel in his sheepskin and that the flaps of his cap were pulled down over his ears; her fingers clutched his arm.

'Where are you going, Mordecai?'

'I'll be back soon. I'm just going to get my cows, that's all.'

'Don't go, Mordecai, don't go! I beg you, wait till tomorrow morning.'

'By tomorrow all that will be left is their hides.'

'I'm so afraid, so afraid—' Her voice was full of tears.

'Go on, don't be silly. Don't act like a child. You won't be alone, Ita is here.' He ran out quickly and kept running on the path through the orchard to catch up with the soldiers who had his cows.

XI

The two women were alone in the house. The lamp threw a patchwork of light over the uneven plastered wall. It was so quiet that you could hear the lamp's wick buzzing as the oil burned.

The wind was howling outside, and it seemed to Ita that she could hear someone crying. She opened her eyes wide and all her senses were on the alert as if to penetrate the surrounding darkness. Soon it began to snow and the hard white grains bounced off the window panes with a glassy ring. Ita's eyes could not break through that thick white blanket, but she could hear a long, drawn-out wailing. She threw on her jacket and went out, carrying the stable lantern.

She returned with a small calf in her arms. When she put it down the calf stood uncertainly on the threshold blinking its round white-ringed eyes. Only when Ita approached the kitchen did the calf follow her on its helpless, splayed-out legs, beginning to wail all over again. Its lonely, orphaned call reached out across the distant fields to the footsteps of the mother cow, footsteps that had long since been covered over by the snow.

Ita lifted a pot of warm whey from the stove and offered it to the calf. But the calf wouldn't touch it and kept tossing its head back. Then Ita dipped her hand into the liquid and put her fingers into the calf's mouth. The calf nuzzled the spread-out fingers and began to suck vigorously. Ita patted its soft trembling body with one hand and laid her head against its warm side. Suddenly a wild inhuman cry broke the silence. It came from Bailtsche. She lay curled up on the bed. The shawl that she had seized to warm her shivering body had slipped down and was hanging from the edge of the bed like the broken wing of a bird. Her belly rose and fell with short jerky movements; it breathed by itself like a separate creature. Ita sat with her hands folded in her empty lap as if to rest them before they were forced to scrub the small white diapers and the dark blood from Bailtsche's sheets.

Bailtsche's broken cries stabbed Ita like so many knives while her hands patted her own narrow hips with vindictive pleasure.

Actually this giving birth was really Ita's. It was here on this bed that she should now have been lying, that she should have been giving birth to her child. And maybe the dark-haired bridegroom from the next village would have been standing beside her . . . but she wouldn't have been shrieking and carrying on like Bailtsche, that intruder. She would have accepted each new pain with joy, knowing it was bringing the ripened fruit closer to the edge of the opening womb. She would have dug her fingernails into the hard wooden frame of the bed and smiled. Just then her head fell to one side and landed on the table, rousing her from her trance.

Bailtsche was now lying stretched out taut as a violin string, with her legs pushing with all their strength against the foot of the bed, readying herself for the next onslaught of pain.

Her tense belly had dropped like a sack with the child's heavings. From time to time the child seemed to be seized by a fit of unexpected shivering. Bailtsche lay there with her eyes wide open, listening to her body, waiting for the next pains which came with merciless regularity, burrowing into her back and thighs, sharp, pointed, and drawn-out.

'Ita, come closer, I want to tell you something.'

And when Ita bent over the bed with suppressed disgust, Bailtsche whispered in an ingratiating tone: 'I beg you—take the lantern and go to the village. Call—you know who to call—the baby is coming too soon—maybe because of what happened.'

Ita sensed the strange woman's shame. It ran through her mind that she should have felt the shame before, with her father. They used to kiss even in the daytime, enough to make people talk. That was all very well. Bailtsche had taken her mother's jewellery, had eaten up the family's hard-earned savings. She had bought lace to trim baby shirts, but when it came to her, Ita, they had refused to let her marry because they didn't want to give a dowry. And now everything really would fall apart. Because of Bailtsche, her father wouldn't buy the plot of land from the squire, he would move to town instead, and spend his old age playing the fool with a gaggle of children. Yes, yes, and she, Ita, would have to go into service, to take the place of Bailtsche, just as Bailtsche had taken hers.

She answered her stepmother with a whisper, full of an odd tenderness. 'Go yourself, auntie. I won't.'

Only then, when Bailtsche looked into her stepdaughter's eyes, did the meaning of those words become clear to her. There wasn't a hint of compassion in those eyes. Bailtsche's body was now covered in a cold sweat. With her last bit of strength she got off the bed, but her legs, filled with pain like two brimming buckets, gave way. She crawled to Ita on all fours: 'Ita darling, I beg you to go—I can't bear it any longer; go, get old Hanka, Ita take pity on me, Ita, it's tearing me apart, I wish I was dead—oh mother!'

She began to kiss Ita's feet feverishly. Only when Bailtsche's next pains came was Ita able to free herself. She grabbed a shawl and went out of the house.

Bailtsche was left all alone in the half-darkened room. A new fear inserted itself between her ribs, and dissolving, spread slowly through her whole body. Her heart wept and she was nauseated by the smell of manure that rose from Ita's barn-soaked boots. She dragged herself to the door. The cold icy air embraced her shivering body. She took a handful of snow and began to eat it greedily. Supporting herself against the wall, she slowly got up. Along her legs she felt a hot sticky flow, and when she looked down she saw that the snow at her feet was red.

It had stopped snowing, and from under the knotted clouds a pale stained moon swam out. Ita was nowhere to be seen. She began to call Ita's name. Her voice fell into the surrounding white silence and was drowned. Suddenly her eye fell on footsteps in the freshly fallen snow along the length of the orchard. The footsteps were black and definite. Bailtsche's knees grew weak with unexpected hope. It meant that Ita had gone for help after all! Her eyes followed the footsteps to the crossroads by the river. Then they opened wide, and grew dark with primitive pain. At the crossroads the footsteps were thick, all in one place, as if the person who had walked there had thought better of it, stopped, hesitated, and returned. From the crossroads the footsteps led in one direction—back into the forest. And now she could see Ita walking fast, almost running. The wind filled her shawl, spreading it open like black wings that carried her high, high into the air.

'Ita, Ita!'

Bailtsche called despairingly. She choked on her own voice. The veins in her throat were tight almost to bursting. For a second she imagined that Ita could hear her, that she had stopped to look back. . . .

But soon Ita's head sunk down into her shoulders and she disappeared among the trees. Only her footsteps were left to darken the endless white of the fields.

Bailtsche's knees gave way. She lay with her eyes closed. From time to time her blood reddened the snow beneath her.

Translated from the Yiddish by Miriam Waddington

A.M. KLEIN · 1909-1972

Prophet in Our Midst: A Story for Passover

I

About six weeks before Passover we began to study the Haggadah. The ordinary curriculum of the *Cheder* was abandoned; the classroom was full of the talk of miracles, and out of the Four Questions a million others bristled. Our days were spent in the calculation of plagues; the Rebbe proved that if the ten plagues were a finger of God, fifty plagues must have been inflicted on the Egyptians when He lifted His right hand, which, explained Leibel, the bright boy of the class, had five fingers; our nights, too, were glorious with dreams of angels and heavenly ministers. At recess periods, while pampered Pee-Wee, the richest pupil in the *Cheder*, could afford to crack nuts as early as three weeks before Passover and while Jeshurun (the Rebbe gave Fatty that nickname because it is written 'And Jeshurun grew fat and kicked')—while Jeshurun already nibbled matzoh, we discussed the Egyptian afflictions, and it is a strange thing that all of us agreed that the slaying of the first-born was the least, and the plague of lice the most terrible of all. I remember very vividly that it was only Mottele the orphan who held the opposite view.

But more fascinating than these arguments about frogs skipping in *Mizraim* and about Moses waving his magic wand over a land of blood, were the tales of Elijah the prophet. When the Rabbi dwelt with glowing picturesqueness and biblical quotation upon the piety and poverty of the man of God, I felt that he was describing my father. It was only when he appended to the description of the prophet a long and flowing beard, that the similarity failed, for my father's beard, alas, has always been shorter in America than in Europe. But even if Elijah did not look like my father, I could still evince an interest in him, so engrossing a character was he . . . Elijah, wandering from town to town, and from village to village, performing miracles here and doing wonders there. Elijah, saving Jews forever hard beset by Jew-gluttons, Elijah bringing splendour to the house of the pauper, and imparting high secrets to the heart of the pious Rabbi,—how we loved him, how gladly, had he appeared in our midst, we would have hailed him! Such a just man was he, we might even have made him referee over all our games!

What intrigued us most, however, was the story that on Passover night Elijah wanders from house to Hebrew house, sipping some wine from the goblet designedly left for him. First of all, we questioned, how could he go to so many places in one night, for, as the Rebbe himself told us, the Jews were scattered in all parts of the world? A little astronomy came to the Rebbe's salvation. He explained that while it was night here, it was day in Palestine, and so Elijah had really two days wherein to do his sipping. But if the wine was sour, how could Elijah drink it? Ready for all occasions, the Rebbe answered, first, that Elijah only sipped a little from each goblet, and second that in the mouth of the prophet all things turn sweet. I always wanted to ask how he kept himself from becoming drunk, after putting his lips to so many cups and after, in going from *Seder* to *Seder*, mixing his drinks. But I was afraid. The Rebbe might become angry at this impertinence and call me 'Shagitz'. The figure of a long-bearded Jew, staggering through ghetto streets, his coat-tails flying behind him in the spring wind, and his silhouette lit up by Passover moonlight, has haunted me ever since.

II

If Simeon the half-wit would have failed to appear on our street about Passover time, the ghetto gossips would have talked about a belated spring. He showed his bearded countenance as regularly as the three maple trees of our ward burgeoned their buds. All winter he retired into a mystical seclusion; he hibernated; but at the earliest twittering of the sparrows, he took up his position at the synagogue doorstep, and dressed in a heavy hat and tattered coat, he dozed away his days. He never worked; he lived upon the compassion and charity of his neighbours . . . 'a screw was loose somewhere,' men said, as they put a finger to their temples. Simeon, for one thing, was obsessed by a mortal fear of blueberries. If you ever wanted to get rid of him, all you had to do was to show him a blueberry. Had he looked at the fact of the Angel of Death himself, he would not have been more terrified. He also had the habit of tying his sleeves to his wrist—he feared that devils would creep into his clothes, and seek shelter in his hairy bosom. And he liked a little drink on any and all occasions. Practical jokers, possessed by a cruel ingenuity, would sometimes treat him to a glass of schnapps but would throw into the red liquid a blueberry. 'Poison! Poison of death,' Simeon would shout, and spit mightily, leaving his benefactors a reward of choice curses.

But he was not dangerous. He was merely a half-wit; doctors said, however, that a great shock at any moment might deprive him even of the last vestiges of sanity. They spoke about chronic alcoholism, and prophesied that his brain would weaken. But he was not dangerous; so, while on a hot summer day, wrapped in a mass of rags, his beard falling over a collarless neck and his mouth open for the exit and entrance of flies, Simeon slumbered away his mad life, Jews passed him by with a shake of the head and a recollection of blueberries.

III

I had finished asking the Four Questions. We were all reading the Haggadah; my uncle outsang my father, my mother outsang them both; amidst the sound of the prayers, I skipped several passages. I could not keep my mind on the Hebrew; either I looked at the pictures in the Haggadah trying to distinguish the different plagues as they were represented in the blurred woodcuts, or I kept a vigilant eye upon the cup of Elijah, to see that its contents did not diminish.

The moment came—my father told me to open the door as he announced the prayer 'Spill Thy wrath upon the heathen, O Lord.' I opened it. The moon was visible, shining over the roofs. On the other side of the street, a shadow stalked. It made its way towards our door. As it approached we could distinguish the tatters, the beard, the rheumy eyes of Simeon; as he entered we heard his adenoidal breathing. 'Elijah, the prophet, as I am a Jew,' laughed my uncle: 'Come in! Sit down! Take a glass of wine, Reb Simeon. "Let all who need, come and eat",' he quoted the Haggadah.

IV

My head was turned at that particular moment so I don't know whether it was really the goblet of Elijah that my uncle gave him. At any rate, Simeon drank. He drank for a legion of Elijahs. My uncle and father insisted, moreover, on calling him Elijahu *Hanavi*. They spoke with him, they argued with him, they convinced him that he was the prophet himself. In the state in which Simeon found himself at the end of the Seder, before the eating of the *Afikomen*, you could have made him believe anything. But the idea that he was Elijah the prophet tickled him particularly . . . Even on that very night, he felt insulted when my mother, forgetting the play for a moment, called him Simeon. 'I am Elijah the Prophet,' he shouted, 'I am Elijah.' And truth to tell, since that night, he has changed his name to Elijah, and as the spirit moves him he indulges in petty prophecies.

When he left our house, I looked through the windows, and in the Passover moonlight I saw the figure of a long-bearded Jew staggering down the street, his tatters playing behind him in the spring wind.

HELEN WEINZWEIG · b. 1915

My Mother's Luck

July 6, 1931

I have decided, my mother said, to go with you to New York to
see you off. Your boat sails a week from tomorrow. In a week you
will be gone; who knows if we will ever see each other again. No,
no, stop it. I can't stand anyone slobbering over me. *Now* what
are you crying for? I thought you wanted to go to your father. I'm
only trying to do what's best for you. You should be happy, going
to Europe, to Germany, travelling in style, like a tourist. Not the
way we came to this country, eh? Steerage, like cattle. Everything
on that boat smelled and tasted of oily ropes. Hardly what you
would call a pleasure trip. But then, how would I recognize
pleasure—how would I know what there is in this world that gives
happiness—when I have been working since I was nine years old.
My feet, my poor feet. I can't remember when my feet didn't hurt.
Get me the white basin, no, the deep one, from under the sink.
And the kettle: the water should be hot enough. Take a chair, sit
down. No, I'll fill it myself. We will have a talk while I'm soaking
my feet. I suppose we should have a talk before you go. I know,
I know; you don't have to remind me; can I help it, the long hours;
you think I like to work so hard? It's not only you I have no time
for: I don't have time to breathe, to live. I said, sit down! What do
you care about your silly girl friends? They'll find someone else
to waste their time with. Jennie? Write her a letter. Ah, that feels
better. My poor feet. I'm looking forward to sitting on the train.
They told me it takes fourteen hours from Toronto to New York.

Just think, I will be off my feet for a whole day.

Why do you look so miserable? I just don't understand you: first you drive me crazy to go to your father and now you sit like at a funeral. Tell you what: in New York we will have a little party before your boat sails. We'll go to a big, fancy restaurant. Sam and me and you. Yes. You heard right. Sam. Are you deaf or don't you understand Yiddish any more? I said, Sam is coming with us. You might as well know: he is moving in with me next week. Your room. No use leaving it empty. There you go again, telling me what I should do. No one tells me what to do. I will stay alone until the Messiah comes, rather than live with another woman. I despise women: they are false and jealous. With a man you know where you're at: you either get along or you don't. They are not hypocrites like women. Marry Sam? What for? To give satisfaction to the old *yentes*, the gossips? I will never marry again: three times was plenty. Get a little hot water from the kettle. Ah, that's better. Now turn low the gas.

So, tell me, have you got your underwear and stockings clean for the trip? Your shoes need a good polish. You don't need everything new. Let your father buy you something, I've supported you for sixteen years, that's long enough. God knows as He is my witness I can do no more. That's what I told your teacher when she came to see me in the winter. She looked around the flat as if fish was rotting under her nose. I couldn't wait for her to leave, that dried up old maid. I told her, I'm an ignorant woman, I'll let you educated people figure out what to do with my daughter. Just one thing you should remember, Esther, it was your idea, not mine, that you should get in touch with your father. Whatever happens, you will not be able to blame me. Of course, you can come back if you want. You have a return ticket. You can thank Sam for that. He said I should let you make up your own mind if you want to live with your father. You don't deserve Sam's consideration. The way you treat him: not talking to him when he greets you on his Sunday visits. He—what? Watch that tongue of yours. I can still give you a good licking if I have to. The smell of sweat is the smell of honest work. I don't like it either, but I've had enough from the educated ones, like your father, who know everything except how to raise a sweat. They all talked a lot, but I could never find out what they wanted from me. I cooked and cleaned and went to work. I tried to please the customers all day and then I was supposed to please them at night.

Like that talmudist, Avrom, you remember him—well, perhaps you were too young. One night I came home from work, tired and hungry, and there he was, exactly where I had left him at eight o'clock in the morning, at the kitchen table. In twelve hours nothing had changed, except there were more books and more dirty plates on the table.—And where, I asked him, am I supposed to eat? He didn't even look up. He raised a white hand.—What means the hand in the air? You think maybe this is Poland and you are the privileged scholar, the permanent guest at my table? In America everybody works who wants to eat. With my arm, like with a broom, I swept clear the table. I waited he should say something, maybe he would realize and say he was sorry he forgot about me, but all he did was look at me like he didn't know who I was. Then he bent down and picked up the books one by one, so slow you would think every book weighed a ton. His face got red like his hair, he was breathing so noisy I thought he was going to bust. Just the books, not the dishes, he picked up. He went into the bedroom and closed the door. All I asked was a little consideration, and for that he didn't talk to me for a week.

So what's the difference to me whether they know enough to take a bath. Sam will learn. He needs a nice home. He's a good man, he works hard, a presser in a factory. So maybe he will be tired at night. And he can pay his own way to New York. A working man has at least his union to see he gets a decent wage. What protection has a scholar got? He leans on the whole world and the world pushes him away. Not that I care about money. I am decent with a man, not taking from him every cent, like their greedy wives. Last week Sam handed me his sealed pay envelope.—Here, he said, take out for New York. Buy yourself a nice coat. Naturally, I wouldn't take his money. So long as he pays the rent, a little for the food, it will be enough. If I was to take his money, next thing he will be telling me what I should do. You can be sure the minute he tries to boss me, out he goes, like the others.

Your step-father, the first one, made that mistake. Max. Tall, the best looking man I ever knew. He worked all night in a bakery and came home seven o'clock in the morning smelling like fresh bread. You two got along well. He made you lunch every day and filled your pockets with bagels for your class. Every Saturday he took you to the show. Remember? When I came home from the store Saturday night, which was his night off, he was ready to step out. I could only soak my tired feet. One day he got a raise.—Lily, he said, you can stop work. Sell the store. Stay home and look after Esther and me. I said,—and suppose you lost your job, what will become of us in this Depression? And suppose your boss gives your job to his brother who came last night from Poland? Max thought we should take a chance.—Maybe someday I will have my own bakery, he said, I want you should stay home like a normal wife. He was not very intelligent: he couldn't get it into his head we would have no security without my beauty parlour. After that, Max was not the same. He talked to me as if I was his servant.—You, he would call me, instead of my name; you, don't make me nothing to eat. I have a bad stomach.—See a doctor.—A doctor won't help. I choke on your meat. He came and went in his work clothes, so that there was flour dust on the furniture. I even paid for the lawyer to get the divorce, just to get rid of him.

What are you sitting like a lump for? Get me a little hot water in the basin. Careful, slow, do you want to burn me! You are such a *shlimazel*! Wipe it up. Are you blind as well? There, over there, by the stove. Ah, that feels good. I hope you will have it easier than me. Maybe your father can give you the education your teacher said you should have. All I have from life is sore feet. My poor feet, look how calloused and shapeless they have become. Once I had such fine hands and feet. The ankles, they used to be so thin. When I was young they said I had the hands and feet of an aristocrat. If you're really so smart as they say you are, you won't have to slave like me. You should have a life like the aristocrats in Europe used to have before the Revolution. I hope you will have a name everyone respects. What a life those fine ladies of Europe used to have: they got married and lived free as birds. Like George Sand or Madame de Staël. Surprised you, eh? I know more than you think. In the papers I recognize names sometimes I first hear in Zürich: Freud, Einstein, Picasso. What's the matter? See, I did learn something from your father. He may tell you I was stupid, he used to tell me I was an ignorant ghetto girl.

Your father taught me to read and write in German. He tried to educate me. So did Isaac. I could always tell there was going to be trouble when they said—Lily, try and understand . . . And then

I'd get a lecture. You would think that after your father I would not again be trapped by fine words. Yet I could not resist a man with a soft voice and clean fingernails. They gave me such fine compliments: how my eyes are the colour of violets; my skin so fair and delicate; how charming my smile; and they quote poetry to add to the feeling. I jump at fine words like a child at candy. Each time I think, this time it will be different, but every man is your father all over again, in a fresh disguise. Talk. Talk. How could they talk. If it wasn't anarchism, it was socialism; if it wasn't atheism, it was religious fanaticism; if it wasn't Moses, it was Marx. Sometimes I wanted to talk, too. Things weren't that easy for me, and I wanted to tell someone about my troubles. They listened for a minute and got a funny look on the face like I remember from the idiot in my village. Once I said to Isaac—That awful Mrs Silberman. Three bottles of dye I had to use on her hair, it's so thick and long. Naturally, I charged her extra. You should have heard her scream blue murder over the fifty cents.—Where you live up the hill, I told her, they would charge you double. I don't make profit on the dye. I called her a cheapskate. Anyway, it was her husband's money not her own she was fighting over. She called me a low-class low-life. I told her never to come back. Isaac didn't say I did right to throw her out. He explained to me about the capitalist class, and I said,—Don't give me the manifesto. You didn't see her ugly expression, I told him. And he said— Her actions were governed by the class struggle: she is the exploiter and you are the exploited. It was nothing against you personally, Lily.—But I'm the one she tried to cheat; I'm the one she cursed, may she rot in hell.—That's an ignorant approach to a classical social problem, Isaac explained—now, Lily, try and understand . . . Still, Isaac and me got along the best. He had consideration. He used to read to me while I was cooking late at night for the next day. On Sundays, we did the laundry together. He couldn't find a job, so he helped me what he could. I found little things for him to do, so he wouldn't feel useless. In the winter he carried out the ashes from the furnace from the store. He fixed the chairs and painted behind the shampoo sink. He was very artistic, the way he fixed up the windows with pictures and coloured paper. He made all my signs, like the 'Specials' for the permanents. I was satisfied. Good or bad, nothing lasts forever.

Isaac decided to go into business for himself. Nobody can say

I stopped him. I gave him the money to buy a stock of dry-goods to peddle on credit. He knew a lot of languages, but that didn't put money in his pocket. He spoke Russian, the customers cried in Russian; he talked in Ukrainian, they wept in Ukrainian; he sold towels in Yiddish, they dried their eyes on his towels. They prayed for help on his carpets; they lay sick between his sheets. How could he take their last cent, he asked me. So he gave everything away. Then he wanted more money for new stock.—I'm not the welfare department, I told him. The way he let people make a sucker out of him, I lost my respect. Then why did I marry him? God knows I didn't want to get married again: twice was enough. The government ordered me to get married.

Oh don't look so innocent. You think I don't know how all that court business started? It was you. You, with your long face and wet eyes, whining at other people's doors, like a dog, as if I didn't feed you right. I can imagine—Come in, come, Esther, sit down and have a piece of cake and tell me all about that terrible mother of yours. Women! Slaves, that's what they are, every one of them; yet if another woman tries to live her own life, they scream blue murder. I can see them, spending their empty nights talking about me, how I live with a man, not married. The Children's Aid wouldn't tell who snitched on me. Miss Graham, the social worker, was very nice, but she wouldn't say either.—I don't like to do this, she said, having to investigate reports from neighbours. Your daughter is thirteen years old and is paying a price in the community because her mother lives in sin. I said,—I am a decent, hard-working woman. See, my rooms are clean, look, my ice-box is full with fruit and milk, Esther is dressed clean, she never misses a day of school. A marriage licence does not make a better wife or mother. She agreed with me, but there was nothing she could do. I had to marry Isaac or they would take away my daughter. I said,—This is a free country, I'll do what I want. So they summons'ed me to Family Court.—Your daughter, the judge said, needs a proper home. I told him,—Judge, Esther has a good home. She has a piano in her room and I pay for lessons. You should hear how nice she plays.—That is not the issue: it is a question of morality.—Judge, I said, I know all about morals and marriage. And what I don't know, the customers tell me. You should hear the stories. Is it moral, I asked him, for a woman to have to sleep with a man she hates? Is it moral for a man to have to support a woman whose face he can't look at?—Come, come, he said, these are not questions for this court to answer. We are here to administer the law. If you do not marry the man you are living with, we will take the child and place her with a decent family. Go fight city hall. So we took out the licence and got married. I have bad luck. Isaac decided to write a book on the trade union movement in the textile industry. He stopped peddling: he stopped helping me. He talked of nothing but the masses: ate and slept the masses. So I sent him to the masses: let them look after him. Just shows how much the law knows what's best.

Love? Of course I loved him. For what other reason would I bother with a man if I didn't love him! I have bad luck, that's all. I attract weak men. Each time I think, aha, this one is different. It always begins with the compliments; it always ends with the silence. After he has been made comfortable in my bed, his underwear in my drawer, his favourite food in the ice-box, he settles down. I rush home from the store, thinking he is waiting for me. But no. He doesn't look up from the paper. He sits. I ask,—Do you want fish or herring for an appetizer? He says to the paper,—It doesn't matter. We eat. He sits. All I ask is a little consideration for all I do for them. Maybe once a week I would like to have a change. I wouldn't mind to pay for a show. I'm not ashamed to go up to the cashier and buy two tickets. Most women would make a fuss about that, but not me—I'm a good sport. I'm not one of your bourgeois women. That was your father's favourite word. Bourgeois. He said the bourgeois woman sold her soul for *kinder, kuchen,* and *kirche.* See, I even remember a little German. That means—oh, excuse me! You know what the words mean—I forgot you are the clever one . . .

Hand me the towel. No, the one I use for the feet, the torn one. You're like a stranger around here, having to be told everything. I'll make a cup of tea. You can stay up a little later tonight: I feel like talking. No, sit. I'll make the tea, then you won't get in my way. What do you want with the tea—a piece of honey cake, maybe?

You and your father will get along, you're both so clever. Words, he had words for everything. No matter what the trouble was, he talked his way out of it. If there was no money for meat, he became a vegetarian, talking all the time how healthy fruits

and nuts are; if he couldn't pay the rent, he spent hours com-
plimenting the landlady on her beauty and charm, although she
was fat and hairy; if I thought I was pregnant again, he talked
about the joys of motherhood. When I cried day and night what
would become of us, he talked the hospital into doing an abortion.
But mouth work brings no food to the table. How was I to know
that, young and inexperienced as I was? When I got married, I
wasn't much older than you are now. I was barely seventeen when
your father came home to Radom on a visit from the university in
Zürich. It was before the war, in 1911. I was only a child when he
fell in love with me. Yet, it can hardly be said I was ever a child:
I was put to work at nine, gluing paper bags. At fourteen, I was
apprenticed to a wig-maker. Every day, as I bent over the wooden
form of a head, my boss would stand and stroke my hair, saying
when I marry and have my hair shorn, he would give me a *sheitel*
for a wedding present if I promise to sell him my hair for the wigs.
My hair was beautiful, thick and silky, and a lovely auburn shade.
I lasted three months, because his wife got jealous and dragged
me back to my father by my silky hair. My father decided I must
have done something wrong and beat me with his leather belt.
What was there for me to look forward to, except more work,
more misery, and, if I was lucky, marriage to a butcher's son, with
red hands?

So you can imagine when your father began to court me, how
could I resist? He had such fine manners, such an educated way
of saying things, such soft hands, he was a man different from
anyone I had ever met. He recited poetry by Goethe and Rilke,
which he translated for me. He called me '*Blume*', which means
flower, from a poem that starts, '*Du bist wie eine Blume*'. He didn't
want a dowry: I wouldn't have to cut my hair. He was a modern
man: his views caused a scandal. Your father wasn't much to look
at—short and pale and poor teeth. You know that small plaster
statue of Beethoven on my dresser? The one you hate to dust? That
belonged to him. He imagined he looked like Beethoven—he had
the same high, broad forehead and that angry look. Still, to me his
pale, shaven face was very attractive compared to the bearded
men of the town. So we were married by a rabbi and I went back
with him to Switzerland. Four years later, just before you were
born, we were married in the city hall in Zürich so you would be
legal on the records.

Let me see, how old is he now? I'm 38, so he must be 48. The *landsleit* say he never married again. I bet he never thought he'd ever see his daughter again. He won't be able to deny you: you're the spitting image. Pale like him. Same forehead, and the same red spots across when you get nervous. I'd give anything to be there when you're both reading and pulling at your hair behind the right ear. You certainly are your father's daughter. Even the way you sneaked around, not telling me, writing to Poland, until you got his address in Munich. I should have known you were up to something: you had the same look of a thief as him when he went to his meetings.

Those meetings! An anarchist he was yet. The meetings were in our small room. Every other word was 'Revolution'. Not just the Russian revolution, but art revolution, religious revolution, sex revolution. They were nearly all young men and women from the university, students like your father. Since he was a good deal older than the rest, he was the leader. They yelled a lot. At first I was frightened by the arguments, until I realized that these intellectuals didn't have anything to do with the things they fought about. It wasn't real people they knew, just names; it wasn't what they themselves did that caused so much disagreement—it was what other people somewhere else were doing. Where I come from, I was used to real trouble, like sickness and starvation and the threat of pogroms. So I didn't pay too much attention until the night we all had a big argument about Nora. First I should tell you about the young women who came to these meetings. They thought themselves the equal of the men, and the men treated them like comrades. Not like in Poland, where every morning of their lives, men thank God for not having been born a woman. In Zürich, the young ladies wore dark mannish suits, had their hair shingled and smoked cigarettes. Beside them, I felt like a sack of potatoes.

This play, *A Doll's House*, shocked everybody. Before you were born, your father sometimes took me to a play. For that, he found money. He called the theatre food for the soul. All such money-wasters he called his spiritual nourishment. I went anyway, because it was nice to sit in a big warm theatre, in a soft seat, and watch the actors. Remind your father about the night we saw *A Doll's House*. About ten of us came back to our room and talked until three in the morning about Nora. For the first time, I was able to join in. I was the only one who sympathized with the husband—he gave her everything, treated her like a little doll, loved her like a pet. This is bad? So they have a little argument, so she says she must leave him and the children. Leave the children! Did you ever hear such a thing!—The servants know how to run the house better than I do, she tells her husband.—Servants! I said to myself, there's your answer—she had it too good. If she had to struggle like me for a piece of bread, she would have overlooked her husband's little fit. She should have cooked him a nice supper, given him a few compliments, and it would have all been *schmired* over, made smooth. Of course, I don't feel like that now, but that's what I thought the night I saw the play. The men agreed with me: it was stupid to leave a good life, even a bourgeois life, to slave for someone else as a seamstress. The women were disappointed in their comrades: couldn't these revolutionaries see that Nora was being exploited by her husband. . . ? The men argued that she was responsible for bringing up her children and should not have left them to the mercy of servants: that motherhood was sacred in all societies. The women said Nora was an intelligent, sensitive human being and was right to refuse to be treated like a possession, like a piece of furniture. Nora had to leave to keep her dignity and her pride. Exactly, the men said, dignity and pride are bourgeois luxuries. In the new society. . . . Back and forth the rest of the night.

All the next day, I could think of nothing but what Nora did. It never occurred to me that a woman leaves a man except if he beats her. From that time on, I began to change. I shingled my hair, I started to sit in the cafés and smoke. When I got pregnant again, I refused to go for an abortion. Four in three years was enough. I don't know why your father, with all his education, didn't know how to take care I shouldn't get in the family way. So you were born. Your father had to leave university and be a clerk in a shoe store. He hated the job: he hated me. You cried a lot. Nothing in your father's books explained why you cried so much. Then your father talked me into going back to work. They were glad to have me back at the beauty parlour. I was a good marceller. It was better to work than be stuck in a little room all day.

And the anarchist meetings started again. While everybody was making plans to blow up the world, I was busy running down the hall to the toilet to vomit. I was pregnant.—Well, look who's back they said at the clinic,—sign here, Lily.—I hope you will have it easier than me. Your father should send you to college. Maybe being educated will help, although sometimes I wonder. I met educated women who never knew what to do with themselves. Once, I remember, I asked one of my customers, Frau Milner was her name,—And how was the march yesterday for getting the vote for women?—It was called off, I couldn't lead the march to the city hall, she said, I got my period, only it was a miscarriage and I was hemorrhaging and couldn't get out of bed.—So you think the world is going to stand still until we stop bleeding?

What finally happened? What do you mean, finally? Things don't happen all at once. You want a drama like in a play, a big fight, with one person wrong, one person right. . . ? Nothing like that. I came back from the warm, clean hospital, where they were so kind to me, they looked after me like a child, I came back to a cold room, and dirty sheets, and our six dishes and two pots sticky with food. There wasn't a penny for the gas and I couldn't heat your milk. You cried, your father yelled he couldn't study. After going to university for four years, I couldn't understand why he still needed to study. I had to get up six in the morning to take you to the crèche at one end of the city and go to work at the other end. You wouldn't stop screaming, and I spanked you, and your father said I was stupid to take out my bad feelings on an innocent child. I sat down, beaten. In that moment I knew I was going to leave. There is a second, no longer than the blink of an eye, when husband and wife turn into strangers. They could pass in the street and not know each other. That's what happened that night.

How did we get here? A good question, but a long story. We've talked enough; I'm tired. What's the difference now. Well, all right. You can tell your father how I did it: I want him to know I was not so stupid. He never knew I was getting a divorce until it was all over and I was out of the country. One of my customers was a very beautiful girl. She had long hair which I used to dye a beautiful shade of red, then I marcelled it in deep lovely waves from top to bottom. She came every Monday morning, and every week she would show me new presents from her lover. She was the mistress of a famous judge in Zürich. Her secret was safe with me: our worlds were miles apart.

One day, instead of going to work, I took you and went to the Court House. You were four years old; the war was over. I wasn't sleeping with your father because I was afraid of getting pregnant; and he wasn't sleeping at home much. At the Court House I bothered a lot of people where is Judge Sutermeister; I found out where he was judging. You were very good that morning while we sat outside on a bench, waiting. People smiled at us and asked you your name, and found things in their purses or briefcases to give you—pencils, paper, bon-bons, a small mirror. About twelve o'clock, when the doors opened and people came out, I stood in the doorway and watched where the judge went. He left through a door at the back. I went in with you, through the same door. He was sitting at a big desk, writing. Oh, he was an elegant gentleman, with grey hair. He looked very stern at me, and I almost ran way. I didn't wait for him to speak. I stood by his desk and told him my troubles, right away I said I wanted him to get me a divorce, and that I knew all about him and Fräulein Olga. He got up, he was so tall, and made such a big scene, like he was on stage; he was going to have me arrested. But I stood there, holding on to you and the desk.—And what will become of her if I go to jail? And what will happen to your career and your sweetheart if your wife finds out her money buys rings and pearls for your mistress? For the next six months, I kept on like usual. Fräulein Olga was the messenger for me and the judge. She didn't mind. She said it gave her something to do, asking me lawyer's questions, writing down my answers, bringing me papers to sign. One Monday morning, Fräulein Olga came with a large brown envelope holding my divorce papers. Inside also was a train ticket and some money. The judge wanted me to start a new life in America. I agreed. I remembered I had a cousin in Toronto. Fräulein Olga was very sad.—Who will do my hair? And she cried.

Two days later, I left our room with you. This time, we went straight to the train in Hamburg. We stayed near the station overnight. I bought underwear for us, a new sweater for me and a nice little red coat for you. We took the boat for New York. A sailor gave you a navy blue sailor hat with the name of the boat, George Washington, in gold on a ribbon around the hat. You wore it day and night, on Ellis Island, on the train to Toronto. It looked nice with the blond curls. I could go on and on. The things that happened, what I went through . . . It's one o'clock already! Let's go to bed. First, wash the cups. Wash them, I said.

I can't stand a mess in the kitchen. Remember, never leave dirty dishes around. Show your father I brought you up right. Which reminds me: did you buy rolls like I told you? Good. Sam likes a fresh roll with lox for Sunday. Just think, in a week you will be on the ocean . . . Go already. I'll turn out the light . . .

TED ALLAN · b. 1916

Lies My Father Told Me

My grandfather stood six feet three in his worn-out bedroom slippers. He had a long grey beard with streaks of white running through it. When he prayed, his voice boomed like a choir as he turned the pages of his prayerbook with one hand and stroked his beard with the other. His hands were bony and looked like tree-roots; they were powerful. My grandpa had been a farmer in the old country. In Montreal he conducted what he called 'a second-hand business'.

In his youth, I was told, Grandpa had been something of a wild man, drinking and playing with the village wenches until my grandmother took him in hand. In his old age, when I knew him, he had become a very religious man. He prayed three times a day on week-days and all day on Saturday. In between prayers he rode around on a wagon which, as I look back, rolled on despite all the laws of physics and mechanics. Its four wheels always seemed to be going in every direction but forwards. The horse that pulled the wagon was called Ferdeleh. He was my pet and it was only much later, when I had seen many other horses, that I realized that Ferdeleh was not everything a horse could have been. His belly hung very low, almost touching the street when he walked. His head went back and forth in jerky motions in complete disharmony with the rest of him. He moved slowly, almost painfully, apparently realizing that he was capable of only one speed and determined to go no faster or slower than the rate he had established some time back. Next to Grandpa I loved Ferdeleh best, with the possible exception of God, or my mother when she gave me candy.

On Sundays, when it didn't rain, Grandpa, Ferdeleh, and myself would go riding through the back lanes of Montreal. The lanes then were not paved as they are now, and after a rainy Saturday, the mud would be inches deep and the wagon heaved and shook like a barge in a stormy sea. Ferdeleh's pace remained, as always, the same. He liked the mud. It was easy on his feet.

When the sun shone through my windows on Sunday morning I would jump out of bed, wash, dress, run into the kitchen where Grandpa and I said our morning prayers, and then we'd both go to harness and feed Ferdeleh. On Sundays Ferdeleh would whinny like a happy child. He knew it was an extra special day for all of us. By the time he had finished his oats and hay Grandpa and I would be finished with our breakfast which Grandma and Mother had prepared for us.

Then we'd go through what Grandpa called 'the women's Sunday song'. It went like this: 'Don't let him hold the reins crossing streets. Be sure to come back if it starts to rain. Be sure not to let him hold the reins crossing streets. Be sure to come back if it starts to rain.' They would repeat this about three hundred times until Grandpa and I were weary from nodding our heads and saying, 'Yes'. We could hear it until we turned the corner and went up the lane of the next street.

Then began the most wonderful of days as we drove through the dirt lanes of Montreal, skirting the garbage cans, jolting and bouncing through the mud and dust, calling every cat by name and every cat meowing its hello, and Grandpa and I holding our hands to our ears and shouting out at the top of our lungs, 'Regs, cloze, botels! Regs, cloze, botels!'

What a wonderful game that was! I would run up the back stairs and return with all kinds of fascinating things, old dresses, suits, pants, rags, newspapers, all shapes of bottles, all shapes of trash, everything you can think of, until the wagon was filled.

Sometimes a woman would ask me to send Grandpa up to give her a price on what she had, and Grandpa would shout up from downstairs, 'My feet ache. The boy will give you a price.' I knew what he offered for an old suit, for an old dress, and I would shout down describing the items in question and the state of deterioration. For clothes that were nothing better than rags we offered a standard price, 'Fifteen cents, take it or leave it.' Clothes that might be repaired I would hold out for Grandpa to see and he'd appraise them. And so we'd go through the lanes of the city.

Sometimes the women would not be satisfied with the money Grandpa had given me for them. Grandpa would always say, 'Eleshka, women always want more than they get. Remember that. Give them a finger and they want the whole hand.'

My Sunday rides were the happiest times I spent. Sometimes Grandpa would let me wear his derby hat which came down over my ears, and people would look at me and laugh and I'd feel even happier feeling how happy everyone was on Sunday.

Sometimes strange, wonderful smells would come over the city, muffling the smell of the garbage cans. When this happened we would stop Ferdeleh and breathe deeply. It smelled of sea and of oak trees and flowers. Then we knew we were near the mountain in the centre of the city and that the wind from the river was bringing the perfumes of the mountain and spraying it over the city. Often we would ride out of the back lanes and up the mountain road. We couldn't go too far up because it was a strain on Ferdeleh. As far as we went, surrounded on each side by tall poplars and evergreens, Grandpa would tell me about the old country, about the rivers and the farms, and sometimes he'd get off the wagon and pick up some black earth in his hands. He'd squat, letting the earth fall between his fingers, and I'd squat beside him doing the same thing.

When we came to the mountain Grandpa's mood would change and he would talk to me of the great land that Canada was, and of the great things the young people growing up were going to do in this great land. Ferdeleh would walk to the edge of the road and eat the thick grass on the sides. Grandpa was at home among the trees and black earth and thick grass and on our way down the mountain road he would sing songs that weren't prayers, but happy songs in Russian. Sometimes he'd clap his hands to the song as I held the reins and Ferdeleh would look back at him and shake his head with pleasure. One Sunday on our ride home through the mountain a group of young boys and girls threw stones at us and shouted in French: *'Juif. . . . Juif. . .!'* Grandpa held his strong arm around me, cursed back muttering 'anti-Semites' under his breath. When I asked him what he said he answered, 'It is something I hope you never learn.' The boys and girls laughed and got tired of throwing stones. That was the last Sunday we went to the mountain.

If it rained on Sunday my mother wouldn't let me go out, so every Saturday evening I prayed for the sun to shine on Sunday. Once I almost lost faith in God and in the power of prayer but Grandpa fixed it. For three Sundays in succession it rained. In my desperation I took it out on God. What was the use of praying to Him if He didn't listen to you? I complained to Grandpa.

'Perhaps you don't pray right,' he suggested.

'But I do. I say, Our God in heaven, hallowed be Thy name, Thy will on earth as it is in heaven. Please don't let it rain tomorrow.'

'Ah! In English you pray?' my grandfather exclaimed triumphantly.

'Yes,' I answered.

'But God only answers prayers in Hebrew. I will teach you how to say that prayer in Hebrew. And, if God doesn't answer, it's your own fault. He's angry because you didn't use the Holy Language.' But God wasn't angry because next Sunday the sun shone its brightest and the three of us went for our Sunday ride.

On weekdays, Grandpa and I rose early, a little after daybreak, and said our morning prayers. I would mimic his sing-song lamentations, sounding as if my heart were breaking and wondering why we both had to sound so sad. I must have put everything I had into it because Grandpa assured me that one day I would become a great cantor and a leader of the Hebrews. 'You will sing so that the ocean will open up a path before you and you will lead our people to a new paradise.'

I was six then and he was the only man I ever understood even when I didn't understand his words. I learned a lot from him. If he didn't learn a lot from me, he made me feel he did.

I remember once saying, 'You know, sometimes I think I'm the son of God. Is it possible?'

'It is possible,' he answered, 'but don't rely on it. Many of us are sons of God. The important thing is not to rely too much upon it. The harder we work, the harder we study, the more we accomplish, the surer we are that we are sons of God.'

At the synagogue on Saturday his old, white-bearded friends would surround me and ask me questions. Grandpa would stand by and burst with pride. I strutted like a peacock.

'Who is David?' the old men would ask me.

'He's the man with the beard, the man with the bearded words.'
And they laughed.

'And who is God?' they would ask me.

'King and Creator of the Universe, the All-Powerful One, the Almighty One, more powerful even than Grandpa.' They laughed again and I thought I was pretty smart. So did Grandpa. So did my grandmother and my mother.

So did everyone, except my father. I didn't like my father. He said things to me like, 'For God's sake, you're smart, but not as smart as you think. Nobody is that smart.' He was jealous of me and he told me lies. He told me lies about Ferdeleh.

'Ferdeleh is one part horse, one part camel, and one part chicken,' he told me. Grandpa told me that was a lie, Ferdeleh was all horse. 'If he is part anything, he is part human,' said Grandpa. I agreed with him. Ferdeleh understood everything we said to him. No matter what part of the city he was in, he could find his way home, even in the dark.

'Ferdeleh is going to collapse one day in one heap,' my father said. 'Ferdeleh is carrying twins.' 'Ferdeleh is going to keel over one day and die.' 'He should be shot now or he'll collapse under you one of these days,' my father would say. Neither I nor Grandpa had much use for the opinions of my father.

On top of everything, my father had no beard, didn't pray, didn't go to the synagogue on the Sabbath, read English books and never read the prayer books, played piano on the Sabbath and sometimes would draw my mother into his villainies by making her sing while he played. On the Sabbath this was an abomination to both Grandpa and me.

One day I told my father, 'Papa, you have forsaken your forefathers.' He burst out laughing and kissed me and then my mother kissed me, which infuriated me all the more.

I could forgive my father these indignities, his not treating me as an equal, but I couldn't forgive his telling lies about Ferdeleh. Once he said that Ferdeleh 'smelled up' the whole house, and demanded that Grandpa move the stable. It was true that the kitchen, being next to the stable, which was in the back shed, did sometimes smell of hay and manure but, as Grandpa said, 'What is wrong with such a smell? It is a good healthy smell.'

It was a house divided, with my grandmother, mother, and father on one side, and Grandpa, Ferdeleh, and me on the other.

One day a man came to the house and said he was from the Board of Health and that the neighbours had complained about the stable. Grandpa and I knew we were beaten then. You could get around the Board of Health, Grandpa informed me, if you could grease the palms of the officials. I suggested the obvious but Grandpa explained that this type of 'grease' was made of gold. The stable would have to be moved. But where?

As it turned out, Grandpa didn't have to worry about it. The whole matter was taken out of his hands a few weeks later.

Next Sunday the sun shone brightly and I ran to the kitchen to say my prayers with Grandpa. But Grandpa wasn't there. I found my grandmother there instead—weeping. Grandpa was in his room ill. He had a sickness they call diabetes and at that time the only thing you could do about diabetes was weep. I fed Ferdeleh and soothed him because I knew how disappointed he was.

That week I was taken to an aunt of mine. There was no explanation given. My parents thought I was too young to need any explanations. On Saturday next I was brought home, too late to see Grandpa that evening, but I felt good knowing that I would spend the next day with him and Ferdeleh again.

When I came to the kitchen Sunday morning Grandpa was not there. Ferdeleh was not in the stable. I thought they were playing a joke on me so I rushed to the front of the house expecting to see Grandpa sitting atop the wagon waiting for me.

But there wasn't any wagon. My father came up behind me and put his hand on my head. I looked up questioningly and he said, 'Grandpa and Ferdeleh have gone to heaven. . . .'

When he told me they were *never* coming back, I moved away from him and went to my room. I lay down on my bed and cried, not for Grandpa and Ferdeleh, because I knew they would never do such a thing to me, but about my father, because he had told me such a horrible lie.

MIRIAM WADDINGTON · b. 1917

Breaking Bread in Jerusalem

I

Her father had Anglicized the family name when he came from Russia, but Hannah Sayers still felt very Jewish and longed to feel even more so. When she had passed her forty-fifth birthday without marrying again she decided to go to Israel. There she hoped to find a new direction for her life, and at the back of her mind was the vague thought that she would stay forever. Developers rebuilding Toronto were glad to buy her weaving studio on Gerrard Street. Her brother, a dentist, invested the money in first mortgages. She stored her looms, her furniture, her fur coat, and her car, locked the door of her Spadina Road apartment, and for the first time in twenty years, felt free. Her parents were dead, her husband so long ago divorced as to be almost forgotten, and she had no children.

Hannah had no plans, no address to go to, hardly a definite destination. She flew directly to Ben Gurion Airport and from there taxied to Jerusalem, impatient to begin her new life. For the first few weeks she stayed at the King David Hotel, but realizing that unless she got a place of her own she would remain a tourist forever, she began to study the personal columns in the *Jerusalem Post*. Eventually she found a third-floor apartment in Beit Hakerem which she rented from a young couple who had moved to Beersheba.

At first she pored over maps and guidebooks and spent her days wandering around Jerusalem. She was unprepared for the beauty and depth of the city which lay like a lion asleep across its legendary mountains and valleys. When she stepped into the street, it seemed to her that the lion awoke and gazed at her out of golden eyes, blinding her with love. Her body was filled with a weightless power. Even in the recklessly-driven city buses, she had the feeling of being both in the city and suspended above it.

Jerusalem acted on her like a drug. She was full of expectation, yet felt confused, apprehensive and empty, as if waiting for a lover. Every morning the sun was harsh and hot, the cats lay in the shade of shrubs and fences, but by noon, the city rose from its bleached terraces and hung drowsily from layers of stone.

It was now November and night came early. By four o'clock it was dark with a finality that sealed the streets. At such times, if she happened to be in the old walled city she was beset by vague fears. She heard the ghostly voices of the dead, the cries and quarrels of all the Jews who had walked through these stone alleys. Their murmurings dragged her back into shadowy nether worlds.

Where had she heard those voices, seen those apparitions? More than once she ran, terror-stricken, through the tangled maze of lanes escaping from the soft voices of the Arab shopkeepers, avoiding their sexual glances, desperately trying to keep her balance against the pull of the city's buried years.

For the first time in her life Hannah began to sleep badly. She would awake exhausted, knowing she had dreamed, but could not remember about what. She had never cared for jewellery, but now she bought herself a Bedouin necklace of old coins, and earrings set with ancient seals. She found a gaily coloured straw mat which she hung on the wall above the chest of drawers in her room, and to her key-ring she attached a cheap plastic ornament containing the words, *Remember Jerusalem.*

One day without thinking she folded her girdle into eight neat little squares and pushed it to the back of a drawer along with her pearls, her lipstick and her hair dryer. Letters came from her brother about her mortgages and mail, from her best friend in the throes of a marriage crisis, and from her favourite niece. She could not bring herself to answer any of them, dismayed at her own paralysis.

In this mood Hannah's eye was one morning caught by a poster outside a travel agency on Jaffa Road. Without knowing how it happened, twenty minutes later she found herself with an air ticket to Eilat and coupons for a five-day stay at Coral Sands Hotel.

She had expected Eilat to look like the tropical resorts in Florida and the Bahamas. The plane landed in an Eilat that was raw and ugly. Huge mountains of gravel—or coal—sat on the beach waiting to be shovelled onto the freighters anchored in the harbour. A few dispirited trees drooped against shapeless buildings. The road along the beach leading out to the desert was criss-crossed with railway tracks and flanked on either side by oil storage tanks. The whole thing resembled a hastily thrown-together theatre set.

Coral Sands turned out to be a one-storey structure that unfolded its twenty motel units along the highway a few miles south of the town. The taxi deposited her in a courtyard where two camels and a donkey were tied up beside a battered old Mercedes. An Arab workman in a red and white keffiyeh was silently spraying flies with a can of Flit.

In the office Hannah handed her travel coupons to a swarthy young man who surprised her with his perfect English.

'You're an American,' she offered. 'Where from?'

'From Chicago.' He was utterly indifferent.

Had she come all the way to Eilat to meet grudging Jews from Chicago?

The clerk handed her a key. 'There's a bus into town every half hour. You'll find the post office, drugstore, and two movie houses in the square. But there aren't many tourists around this time of the year. Eilat doesn't fill up till January. Dinner's at one, supper at seven.'

Hannah found her room and saw at a glance that it was a total loss. There was no reading lamp, not even a wire hanger for her clothes. She unpacked her few things, hung them across the back of the single chair, and crossed the road to the beach.

Like all northerners, Hannah loved the sea. She thought of it as something huge and comforting, with long surfy tides. But as she now realized, the Mediterranean is not an ocean. The water of Eilat lay pale and inert with dark shaded areas where the coral reefs grew.

While she stood there a girl came out of the water holding her foot and crying. Blood was pouring from her wound. The shore was so thickly littered with broken glass and garbage that there was no place to sit. Hannah picked her way along the beach to the hot dog stand. There were a few tables with young people drinking cokes and playing checkers. Their sleeping bags lay among eggshells, broken glass, and grapefruit rinds. An air of transience hung over everything, and despite the heat, a breath of something wintry. The uneasiness in her heart sharpened and again she felt a stab of fear. This wasn't the place she had seen photographs of in the tourist brochures. Where were all the white hotels, the blue lagoons?

She walked further along the beach. A sign in Hebrew and English informed her that she was now in a national park where it was unlawful to litter or camp overnight. She was still picking her way through the broken glass when she heard someone speak to her in a slow blurry English. Minutes ago there had been nothing but sun and sand, and now there suddenly stood before her a man in a black hat and a faded close-fitting jacket. He was addressing her.

'You like Eilat? You like Israel? Will you come perhaps into my house and drink with me some coffee?' He pointed to a canvas hut a little way up the beach. Seeing her hesitate, he repeated, 'Yes, you will come. You like to her Israeli songs? Or maybe we talk about the life.' He pronounced it 'zee life'.

She fell into step with him. Outside his tent he pointed to a couple of old tires and motioned her to sit.

'You are American?' His accent was the deep guttural one of the Middle East.

It had always irritated Hannah to be taken for an American—as if her country was of so little account that no one knew about it, much less could anyone come from it. But now she answered with lazy indifference.

'No, I'm Canadian.'

'So? From Canada?' he stretched it out, 'and I, I come from Egypt. Yacob. And how are you called?'

'Hannah.' In this place her name danced, resonated.

'A good name, Hannah, very brave. And we are both of us in the Bible.' Yacob laughed showing missing teeth.

Hannah felt suddenly ashamed; for herself that she didn't remember the story of Hannah and for him because of his missing teeth. Also for the stains on his shirt. What was worse, as he busied himself with making coffee on the little primus stove, she saw that he limped. A cripple.

Conversation was easy between them. They talked and fell silent and talked again. He asked why she had come. She told him she was searching for something, she didn't know what. He sighed and nodded, said everyone comes for the same reason, everyone expects the impossible. Miracles. He too had come expecting a miracle.

The only son of a widow, he came to Israel after his mother died. He had some sort of technical training, something to do with repairing agricultural machinery—but there was no place for Jews in Egypt, and in Israel the machinery he knew was outdated. So he had worked in the kitchens of the big hotels in Tel Aviv—that's where he learned English.

As he talked, he began to cough, apologizing for his weak lungs. That's why he lived here in the desert; the air was dry, it helped his lungs. Also, he told her, two years ago he had a dream. He was walking through a walled city and suddenly the walls turned to fire and a voice spoke to him saying that all those who lived in cities would be destroyed. The voice commanded him to go into the desert. Then, giving her a sly look he added, 'Wait, you will see for yourself, everyone who comes here serves this country's purpose.'

He offered her coffee, spooning it out of a jar of Nescafé. She drank it slowly thinking about what he had just said. He started to cough again, reached into his tent and brought out a bottle of brandy. He offered her a swallow and took two or three big swallows himself.

The brandy filled him with contentment. He gazed lovingly at the bottle, and caressed it. Brandy was cheap here, but not cheap enough. If only his mother were still alive she would take care of him, she understood everything. Hannah took some Israeli pounds out of her handbag, smiled, and saying that the next bottle of brandy was on her, departed.

As she walked away she thought how everything balances out. The heartsick idle rich and the heartsick idle poor. She could have met Yacob anywhere—in Jamaica, Mexico, or Crete, but having met him here in Israel made it different. The conjunction of Hannah and Jacob, their lives in legend were somehow dear to her. Personal. Perhaps her meeting with Yacob had a meaning deeper than she understood?

She continued her walk—past the one-storey agricultural station, past the litter on the beach until everything was at last clean and empty. She walked until she was tired, then she turned, found the highway and went back to Coral Sands. Tomorrow, she decided she would take a bus trip up the coast to an island called The Castle.

II

They called it The Castle, because of the rock formation that looked like a turreted castle. 'It's very romantic,' the desk clerk had assured her, 'go. You'll enjoy it.' He saw her hesitate and added, 'what can you lose? You don't even need a taxi. Just get on a bus outside the door and ask to be let off at The Castle.'

Yes, what could she lose? Her will seemed to be elsewhere, locked away with her furniture in a Toronto warehouse. Besides, there was no other way to use up the days until she could return to Jerusalem. So Hannah rose early, dressed quickly and went out to the highway to wait for the Sharm-el-shek bus.

The driver was a youngish man with a profile out of an Egyptian frieze. There were only two other passengers besides herself, and one of them wasn't really a passenger. He sat beside the driver holding a rifle across his knees. Perhaps later he would take a turn at driving the bus. Beside him sat an Israeli official with a briefcase on his lap. He looked like the manager of a supermarket, but was probably a major, or a colonel, this much Hannah had already learned about the deceptive appearances in Israel. None of the three paid any attention to her. They talked to each other in rapid Hebrew, only stopping to point out landmarks along the way.

When she got on the bus, Hannah had asked to be let off at The Castle. The driver spoke no English, but seemed to understand. The official explained that The Castle was about ten miles up the road. Through him she tried to find out at what time there would be a bus back, but the driver was vague. Hannah put aside her anxieties, determined to enjoy the trip.

The desert was not sand at all, nor was it flat the way she had imagined it. It was stony, huge, and mountainous. In the Bible it was called the wilderness, and now she understood why. It was to such country, harsh and treeless, that the prophets had gone to meditate. Among these giant piles of stone, little Elijah had fed the birds.

Mostly the stone was rosy, or it was golden and diaphanous, yes, almost gauzy. Could you drape stone, gather it, fold it, bunch it, pleat it? The hand of some wonderful weaver must have spun tons of variegated quartz into these fine and subtle layers of gold and brown and pink. And some other huge hand, of a housekeeper perhaps, must have taken the immense bolts of stone cloth afterwards, and rolled them up, unrolling a bit here, folding back some there, pinching a few pleats in one place, taking up tucks in another.

This was the landscape of Sinai, its rosy folds glittering with silence. Here and there in its folds and pockets she could see a few scattered sheep, the occasional black tent of the Bedouins and the figure of a shepherd.

At one point, the bus stopped to take on one of these Arab tribesmen, a boy no more than fifteen. He flashed a brilliant smile at the bus driver, then hitched up his tangle of stained, sunburned skirts and capes, and from some inner region produced a coin for the fare. There was laughter and badinage, and as he passed her, Hannah caught a whiff of desert smell, a goaty smell of oil, rubber, sand, sweat, and sheep.

Before she realized it, the road had curved around to where the sea flowed into a horseshoe-shaped bay. A little way out was an island, with rocks growing out of it shaped like a medieval castle. The Israeli official turned to her: 'Well, here you are. This is your stop.'

Hannah watched the bus disappear. She felt small and abandoned. What if the bus back didn't get here before dark? She studied the timetable she had picked up at the hotel desk. At the very latest, she assured herself, the bus would have to pass here at four o'clock. There was no other road to Eilat. It would have to pass.

She turned and looked down at the sea; on the beach below someone had pitched a tent. It seemed very far away. She could just make out the figure of a girl in white shorts. An old car with the hood up stood beside the road near the bus stop. At least she was not completely alone here.

Her relief did not last. She walked down the steep, winding path to the sea, passing close to the campers. The girl in shorts was washing clothes and stared at Hannah without replying to her greeting. The sun lay like lead against the motionless sea. Though the sky was clear the air was so dense that the castle seemed carved out of the haze. On the other side of the bay, Hannah reminded herself, lay Egypt. Swan boats and Cleopatra. Grapes and adders. Pharaoh, why didn't your people think of planting trees? And why, Moses, did you choose this awful geography? The rhythms of my voice falter here; my language sickens and dies.

Then she saw an Arab coming down the path. He was dressed in the black robe and white headdress of the Bedouin, and carried a rifle across his shoulders. 'What is an Arab doing here?' was her first panicky thought.

He drew nearer. He stared at her, and spoke some words in greeting, whether in Arabic or Hebrew Hannah couldn't make out. Occasionally she recognized a Hebrew word in his flooding speech. Then he suddenly smiled, and she dared to look at him. His face was burnt, weathered, and he had the strong hooked nose of the Jews. She was still afraid.

She did not smile but she nodded. His dark figure against the sunlight and sea reminded her of something. After he had gone, she suddenly thought: why didn't I marry again?

There was doubtless some flaw in herself, some demand that had made it impossible for her to connect with a man. Maybe she had come to Israel to discover that flaw—after all didn't people come here, Jews and Christians alike, to find themselves? And maybe that's what was frightening her; the chance that she would find part of herself which she had long ago consigned to darkness.

She believed that things and people repeat themselves to return in other guises. She thought of her husband. They had only lived together for two years, but they had been stormy ones. He had a job on a Toronto newspaper and was writing a novel. She worked at the Children's Aid and was saving to buy her own loom. They lived in an attic apartment where she had to wash the soot off the window sills every day. A skilful weaver, she dreamed of designing tapestries. Her mind was crammed with textures and colours, and their apartment was crowded with geraniums of all shades, and others that did not flower but smelled of mint or lemon. They were happy—at least so Hannah thought. After all, they had known each other through high school, and had been drawn together by their common interest in art, their difference from the others. He was a handsome man, but distant. And he was vain.

It must have been hard to resist the girls who listened to every word he said as if to an oracle. And now that she thought of it, there had been an unending stream of such girls trooping through their apartment. All her unmarried friends visited. She had cooked hundreds of spaghettis, made a thousand salads, opened endless litres of wine, while Josh White's records sang union songs into the summer evenings of their living room.

It was all pleasantly cluttered. Until, coming home one evening she found Annette's name underlined in the phone book, and an unfinished letter on the kitchen table.

'Hey, what's this, Max?'

'On, nothing; just part of my novel.'

'How come she's called Annette?'

'My God, you're a nag, aren't you.'

Sullen silence from him, and in her, a large nameless fear, like the fear that had flooded her just now when the Arab passed.

Well, she had been injured, she supposed. Max was weak, and she was worse—not only weak, but dumb. Of all three, Annette was the one who had known her own mind. When Hannah said choose, it was Annette and not Max who had answered, 'He's coming with me.'

Of course, Annette wasn't Jewish. Maybe that was part of it. A lot of Jewish men were like Max; they didn't like Jewish women. Incest taboo? Jewish women were serious, always expected marriage, nagged, reminded them of their mothers. Or, as Hannah thought now, in a more subtle way it was their fathers they were really running away from, rebelling against. Or then again maybe they were just paying back old debts. Hadn't Abraham sent Hagar and Hagar's child away? His sons would therefore right old wrongs and marry her daughters. Interesting how history turns on itself chasing its own tail.

Of course not all Jewish men were busy paying off old debts. There was her accountant, Morris Denny, for instance. He believed in owing rather than being owed, killing rather than being killed. He liked to have affairs only with Jewish women. He was a good Jew himself, and insisted on always sinning comfortably in congenial company.

For a time, he had brought brief consolation to Hannah's life. After Morris there had been one or two disappointing flurries and then no one important. There were trips: Greece, with her college friend Eileen, some conferences having to do with her work, buyers and visiting colleagues from abroad, and before she knew it, twenty years flew by.

Where does all lost time go? Her soul, and the very substance of her body, had been taken up and woven into her cloth, imperceptibly absorbed into the linen and wool of her tapestries, the goldfinch feathers and grasses of her hangings. Her very essence had been boiled dry, dyed with roots of orris, coloured by the juices from the stems of aster and astilbe.

The sea was hypnotic. Hannah lay back on the beach and let the heat from the earth rise up and flow through her body. First she felt drowsy, then she slept. She dreamed, and images rocked to and fro in her mind like boats anchored close to shore. There were a lot of boats from somewhere, and they were all rocking gently, rocking her all the way back to Jerusalem.

It is morning, brilliant and fresh. She is waiting for a bus across from the supermarket in Kiryat Yovel. It is Friday so she carries a bunch of flowers in her hand for the Sabbath. Beside her, also waiting for the bus, is a wrinkled old grandfather with a long, white beard, wearing a skull-cap. She turns and speaks to him in Yiddish, surprises herself by saying, '*Zayde*, tell me a story.' He looks back at her blankly; he is from Morocco, and doesn't understand Yiddish. And she doesn't know Hebrew. She draws back disappointed and lapses into silence.

Another image. She is living in London on the fourth floor of an old house in the Marylebone district. She has visited some married friends in Hampstead and just manages to catch the last bus home. She is the only passenger. The driver is a black man. The bus waits for other passengers but none arrive. She imagines his life: soon he will go home, his wife will be waiting, their two children will be asleep. He will say, 'How did things go?' and she will tell him what the children did, what they said. They will kiss, she will make him a cup of tea, they will go to bed. Everything will be warm and close between them.

Suddenly as the bus is starting, she hears herself call out, 'Take me home with you!' The driver does not hear. He is busy manoeuvring the bus, so she calls to him again, but pleadingly this time, 'Won't you please take me home with you?' But he neither hears nor turns around, and they go driving into the dark London night, past all the familiar landmarks, Belsize Gardens,

Camden Town, Regent's Park, until at last they come to Baker Street, where she gets off. In the dream, she sees her own figure, receding down Baker Street wrapped in loneliness.

Loneliness wraps her round like a cape, laps her round like a sea, until she becomes a boat herself, anchored close to shore, rocking, gently rocking, until she rocks herself home to Winnipeg. Now she's in her parents' big house on St John's Avenue, the one her father built on four lots. The house is unchanged, but somehow, instead of being on four lots in the city, it's built on the seashore. The room is as she remembers it. There is the same oblong oriental rug in blues and browns covering the floor. The brass samovar her mother brought from Russia shines beside the fireplace. There is the same grand piano with a silk fringed shawl draped over it, and the vase of overblown roses standing on top of it. A life-size portrait in pastels of the Yiddish writer, Peretz, hangs on the wall above the piano.

But something is odd, different. The room is empty. She looks at the piano, knows she cannot play it. Then she remembers she is waiting for someone to come in and play. At last a man comes in—he looks familiar but she doesn't know him, can't recognize him. He sits down and plays the Moonlight Sonata, then some Grieg and finally he begins to play Yiddish folk tunes. He even sings the words of a very old song: *A malach veynt, a malach veynt, un begisst die Groz mit toi; liebster meiner, liebster meiner, o, ich benk noch dir azoi.* (An angel weeps, and angel weeps, and covers the grass with dew; beloved mine, beloved mine, how I long for you.)

In her dream Hannah sits back and listens to the song, remembering her grandmother who used to sing it. She feels a smile spreading over her face. Then the music stops and the man walks over to where she is sitting. Her eyes close. She is full of the warmth and sweetness of the song when she feels her face being covered with little kisses. A thousand little kisses are raining down on her, embracing loving little kisses. First on her eyes, then on her forehead, then her cheeks, her chin, her lips, and then all over again. Kisses.

She awoke and found herself gazing into the eyes of a large German shepherd. The dog was standing over her and licking her face with a hundred friendly licks. The feeling of surprise left her. It went away slowly but the feeling of the dream was still light and happy within her. A few yards away, sitting with his legs crossed under him, was the same Arab with the rifle who had passed her an hour ago. He sat there now drinking coffee out of a red thermos flask and eating bread and cheese from a paper bag. And he was smiling—just like his dog.

She looked at him; she was no longer afraid. Gazing directly into his eyes she saw that his face was neither young nor old, neither mild nor stern. It was the face of a watchman. Their looks met. Hers was friendly; so was his. He spoke a few words, then pouring some coffee from the thermos into a paper cup, he held it out to her. Without taking her eyes from his smiling face she stretched her hand out, took the coffee and drank. It was warm like the sun.

She nodded to him that it was good. He laughed and patted his dog.

A group of young people came scrambling down the path. Their cries rebounded from the mountains filling the cove with splinters of laughter, light, and youth. Hannah drank her coffee. She forgot about miracles. What was it Yacob had said? Everyone who comes here serves the purposes of this country. But what were its purposes, and how could you find out about them? Maybe only through other people. Or through a tapestry woven out of radiant premonitions. Or, and this was a new idea to her, even through kisses. Kisses from a thousand strangers, the living and the dead.

She would go back to Jerusalem. She knew that no matter what should befall her there, the light from its towers would warm her through all the winters she had ever lived or ever would.

SHIRLEY FAESSLER · b. 1921

A Basket of Apples

This morning Pa had his operation. He said I was not to come for
at least two or three days, but I slipped in anyway and took a look
at him. He was asleep, and I was there only a minute before I was
hustled out by a nurse.

'He looks terrible, nurse. Is he all right?'

She said he was fine. The operation was successful, there were
no secondaries, instead of a bowel he would have a colostomy,
and with care should last another—

Colostomy. The word had set up such a drumming in my ears
that I can't be sure now whether she said another few years or
another five years. Let's say she said five years. If I go home and
report this to Ma she'll fall down in a dead faint. She doesn't even
know he's had an operation. She thinks he's in the hospital for a
rest, a check-up. Nor did we know—my brother, my sister, and
I—that he'd been having a series of x-rays.

'It looks like an obstruction in the lower bowel,' he told us
privately, 'and I'll have to go in the hospital for a few days to find
out what it's all about. Don't say anything to Ma.'

'I have to go in the hospital,' he announced to Ma the morning
he was going in.

She screamed.

'Just for a little rest, a check-up,' he went on, patient with her
for once.

He's always hollering at her. He scolds her for a meal that isn't
to his taste, finds fault with her housekeeping, gives her hell
because her hair isn't combed in the morning and sends her back

to the bedroom to tidy herself.

But Ma loves the old man. 'Sooner a harsh word from Pa than a kind one from anyone else,' she says.

'You're not to come and see me, you hear?' he cautioned her the morning he left for the hospital. 'I'll phone you when I'm coming out.'

I don't want to make out that my pa's a beast. He's not. True, he never speaks an endearing word to her, never praises her. He loses patience with her, flies off the handle and shouts. But Ma's content. Poor man works like a horse, she says, and what pleasures does he have. 'So he hollers at me once in a while, I don't mind. God give him the strength to keep hollering at me, I won't repine.'

Night after night he joins his buddies in the back room of an ice-cream parlour on Augusta Avenue for a glass of wine, a game of klaberjass, pinochle, dominoes: she's happy he's enjoying himself. She blesses him on his way out. 'God keep you in good health and return you in good health.'

But when he is home of an evening reading the newspaper and comes across an item that engages his interest, he lets her in on it too. He shows her a picture of the Dionne quintuplets and explains exactly what happened out there in Callander, Ontario. This is a golden moment for her—she and Pa sitting over a newspaper discussing world events. Another time he shows her a picture of the Irish Sweepstakes winner. He won a hundred and fifty thousand, he tells her. She's entranced. *Mmm-mm-mm*! What she couldn't do with that money. They'd fix up the bathroom, paint the kitchen, clean out the backyard. *Mmm-mm-mm*! Pa says if we had that kind of money we could afford to put a match to a hundred-dollar bill, set fire to the house and buy a new one. She laughs at his wit. He's so clever, Pa. Christmas morning King George VI is speaking on the radio. She's rattling around in the kitchen, Pa calls her to come and hear the King of England. She doesn't understand a word of English, but pulls up a chair and sits listening. 'He stutters,' says Pa. This she won't believe. A king? Stutters? But if Pa says so it must be true. She bends an ear to the radio. Next day she has something to report to Mrs Oxenberg, our next-door neighbour.

I speak of Pa's impatience with her; I get impatient with her too. I'm always at her about one thing and another, chiefly about the weight she's putting on. Why doesn't she cut down on the bread, does she have to drink twenty glasses of tea a day? No wonder her feet are sore, carrying all that weight. (My ma's a short woman a little over five feet and weighs almost two hundred pounds.) 'Go ahead, keep getting fatter,' I tell her. 'The way you're going you'll never be able to get into a decent dress again.'

But it's Pa who finds a dress to fit her, a Martha Washington Cotton size 52, which but for the length is perfect for her. He finds a shoe she can wear, Romeo Slippers with elasticized sides. And it's Pa who gets her to soak her feet, then sits with them in his lap scraping away with a razor blade at the calluses and corns.

Ma is my father's second wife, and our stepmother. My father, now sixty-three, was widowed thirty years ago. My sister was six at the time, I was five, and my brother was four when our mother died giving birth to a fourth child who lived only a few days. We were shunted around from one family to another who took us in out of compassion, till finally my father went to a marriage broker and put his case before him. He wanted a woman to make a home for his three orphans. An honest woman with a good heart, these were the two and only requirements. The marriage broker consulted his lists and said he thought he had two or three people who might fill the bill. Specifically, he had in mind a young woman from Russia, thirty years old, who was working without pay for relatives who had brought her over. She wasn't exactly an educated woman; in fact, she couldn't even read or write. As for honesty and heart, this he could vouch for. She was an orphan herself and as a child had been brought up in servitude.

Of the three women the marriage broker trotted out for him, my father chose Ma, and shortly afterward they were married.

A colostomy. So it is cancer. . . .

As of the second day Pa was in hospital I had taken to dropping in on him on my way home from work. 'Nothing yet,' he kept saying, 'maybe tomorrow they'll find out.'

After each of these visits, four in all, I reported to Ma that I had seen Pa. 'He looks fine. Best thing in the world for him, a rest in the hospital.'

'Pa's not lonesome for me?' she asked me once, and laughing, turned her head aside to hide her foolishness from me.

Yesterday Pa said to me, 'It looks a little more serious than I

thought. I have to have an operation tomorrow. Don't say anything to Ma. And don't come here for at least two or three days.'

I take my time getting home. I'm not too anxious to face
Ma—grinning like a monkey and lying to her the way I have been
doing the last four days. I step into a hospital telephone booth to
call my married sister. She moans. 'What are you going to say to
Ma?' she asks.

I get home about half past six, and Ma's in the kitchen making
a special treat for supper. A recipe given her by a neighbour and
which she's recently put in her culinary inventory—pieces of
cauliflower dipped in batter and fried in butter.

'I'm not hungry, Ma. I had something in the hospital cafeteria.'
(We speak in Yiddish; as I mentioned before, Ma can't speak
English.)

She continues scraping away at the cauliflower stuck to the
bottom of the pan. (Anything she puts in a pan sticks.) 'You saw
Pa?' she asks without looking up. Suddenly she thrusts the pan
aside. 'The devil take it, I put in too much flour.' She makes a pot
of tea, and we sit at the kitchen table drinking it. To keep from
facing her I drink mine leafing through a magazine. I can hear her
sipping hers through a cube of sugar in her mouth. I can feel her
eyes on me. Why doesn't she ask me, How's Pa? Why doesn't she
speak? She never stops questioning me when I come from hospital, drives my crazy with the same questions again and again. I
keep turning pages, she's still sucking away at that cube of
sugar—a maddening habit of hers. I look up. Of course her eyes
are fixed on me, probing, searching.

I lash out at her. 'Why are you looking at me like that!'

Without answer she takes her tea and dashes it in the sink. She
spits the cube of sugar from her mouth. (Thank God for that; she
generally puts it back in the sugar bowl.) She resumes her place,
puts her hands in her lap, and starts twirling her thumbs. No one
in the world can twirl his thumbs as fast as Ma. When she gets
them going they look like miniature windmills whirring around.

'She asks me why I'm looking at her like that,' she says,
addressing herself to the twirling thumbs in her lap. 'I'm looking
at her like that because I'm trying to read the expression in her
face. She tells me Pa's fine, but my heart tells me different.'

Suddenly she looks up, and thrusting her head forward, splays
her hands out flat on the table. She has a dark-complexioned

strong face, masculine almost, and eyes so black the pupil is indistinguishable from the iris.

'Do you know who Pa is!' she says. 'Do you know who's lying in the hospital? I'll tell you who. The captain of our ship is lying in the hospital. The emperor of our domain. If the captain goes down the ship goes with him. If the emperor leaves his throne, we can say good-bye to our domain. That's who's lying in the hospital. Now ask me why do I look at you like that.'

She breaks my heart. I want to put my arms around her, but I can't do it. We're not a demonstrative family, we never kiss, we seldom show affection. We're always hollering at each other. Less than a month ago I hollered at Pa. He had taken to dosing himself. He was forever mixing something in a glass, and I became irritated at the powders, pills, and potions lying around in every corner of the house like mouse droppings.

'You're getting to be a hypochondriac!' I hollered at him, not knowing what trouble he was in.

I reach out and put my hand over hers. 'I wouldn't lie to you, Ma. Pa's fine, honest to God.'

She holds her hand still a few seconds, then eases it from under and puts it over mine. I can feel the weight of her hand pinioning mine to the table, and in an unaccustomed gesture of tenderness we sit a moment with locked hands.

'You know I had a dream about Pa last night?' she says. 'I dreamt he came home with a basket of apples. I think that's a good dream?'

Ma's immigration to Canada had been sponsored by her Uncle Yankev. Yankev at the time he sent for his niece was in his mid-forties and had been settled a number of years in Toronto with his wife, Danyeh, and their six children. They made an odd pair, Yankev and Danyeh. He was a tall two-hundred-and-fifty-pound handsome man, and Danyeh, whom he detested, was a lack-lustre little woman with a pockmarked face, maybe weighing ninety pounds. Yankev was constantly abusing her. Old Devil, he called her to her face and in the presence of company.

Ma stayed three years with Yankev and his family, working like a skivvy for them and without pay. Why would Yankev pay his niece like a common servant? She was one of the family, she sat at table with them and ate as much as she wanted. She had a bed and even a room to herself, which she'd never had before. When Yankev took his family for a ride in the car to Sunnyside, she was included. When he bought ice-cream cones, he bought for all.

She came to Pa without a dime in her pocket.

Ma has a slew of relatives, most of them émigrés from a remote little village somewhere in the depths of Russia. They're a crude lot, loudmouthed and coarse, and my father (but for a few exceptions) had no use for any of them. The Russian Hordes, he called them. He was never rude; any time they came around to visit he simply made himself scarce.

One night I remember in particular; I must have been about seven. Ma was washing up after supper and Pa was reading a newspaper when Yankev arrived, with Danyeh trailing him. Pa folded his paper, excused himself, and was gone. The minute Pa was gone Yankev went to the stove and lifted the lids from the two pots. Just as he thought—*mamaliga* in one pot, in the other one beans, and in the frying pan a piece of meat their cat would turn its nose up at. He sat himself in the rocking chair he had given Ma as a wedding present, and rocking, proceeded to lecture her. He had warned her against the marriage, but if she was satisfied, he was content. One question and that's all. How had she bettered her lot? True, she was no longer an old maid. True, she was now mistress of her own home. He looked around him and snorted. A hovel. '*And* three snot-nosed kids,' he said, pointing to us.

Danyeh, hunched over in a kitchen chair, her feet barely reaching the floor, said something to him in Russian, cautioning him, I think. He told her to shut up, and in Yiddish continued his tirade against Ma. He had one word to say to her. To *watch* herself. Against his advice she had married this no-good Rumanian twister, this murderer. The story of how he had kept his first wife pregnant all the time was now well known. Also well known was the story of how she had died in her ninth month with a fourth child. Over an ironing board. Ironing his shirts while he was out playing cards with his Rumanian cronies and drinking wine. He had buried one wife, and now was after burying a second. So Ma had better *watch* herself, that's all.

Ma left her dishwashing and with dripping wet hands took hold of a chair and seated herself facing Yankev. She begged him not to say another word. 'Not another word, Uncle Yankev, I beg you. Till the day I die I'll be grateful to you for bringing me over. I don't know how much money you laid out for my passage, but I tried my best to make up for it the three years I stayed with you, by helping out in the house. But maybe I'm still in your debt? Is this what gives you the right to talk against my husband?'

Yankev, rocking, turned up his eyes and groaned. '*You* speak to her,' he said to Danyeh. 'It's impossible for a *human being* to get through to her.'

Danyeh knew better than to open her mouth.

'Uncle Yankev,' Ma continued, 'every word you speak against my husband is like a knife stab in my heart.' She leaned forward, thumbs whirring away. '*Mamaliga?* Beans? A piece of meat your cat wouldn't eat? A crust of *bread* at his board, and I will still thank God every day of my life that he chose me from the other two the *shadchan* showed him.'

In the beginning my father gave her a hard time. I remember his bursts of temper at her rough ways in the kitchen. She never opened a kitchen drawer without wrestling it—wrenching it open, slamming it shut. She never put a kettle on the stove without its running over at the boil. A pot never came to the stove without its lid being inverted, and this for some reason maddened him. He'd right the lid, sometimes scalding his fingers—and all hell would break loose. We never sat down to a set or laid table. As she had been used to doing, so she continued; slamming a pot down on the table, scattering a handful of cutlery, dealing out assorted-sized plates. More than once, with one swipe of his hand my father would send a few plates crashing to the floor, and stalk out. She'd sit a minute looking in our faces, one by one, then start twirling her thumbs and talking to herself. What had she done now?

'Eat!' she'd admonish us, and leaving table would go to the mirror over the kitchen sink and ask herself face to face, 'What did I do now?' She would examine her face profile and front and then sit down to eat. After, she'd gather up the dishes, dump them in the sink, and running the water over them, would study herself in the mirror. 'He'll be better,' she'd tell herself, smiling. 'He'll be soft as butter when he comes home. You'll see,' she'd promise her image in the mirror.

Later in life, mellowed by the years perhaps (or just plain defeated—there was no changing her), he became more tolerant of her ways and was kinder to her. When it became difficult for her to get around because of her poor feet, he did her marketing. He attended to her feet, bought her the Martha Washingtons, the Romeo Slippers, and on a summer's evening on his way home from work, a brick of ice cream. She was very fond of it.

Three years ago he began promoting a plan, a plan to give Ma some pleasure. (This was during Exhibition time.) 'You know,' he said to me, 'it would be very nice if Ma could see the fireworks at the Exhibition. She's never seen anything like that in her life. Why don't you take her?'

The idea of Ma going to the Ex for the fireworks was so preposterous, it made me laugh. She never went anywhere.

'Don't laugh,' he said. 'It wouldn't hurt you to give her a little pleasure once in a while.'

He was quite keen that she should go, and the following year he canvassed the idea again. He put money on the table for taxi and grandstand seats. 'Take her,' he said.

'Why don't you take her?' I said. 'She'll enjoy it more going with you.'

'Me? What will I do at the Exhibition?'

As children, we were terrified of Pa's temper. Once in a while he'd belt us around, and we were scared that he might take the strap to Ma too. But before long we came to know that she was the only one of us not scared of Pa, when he got mad. Not even from the beginning when he used to let fly at her was she intimidated by him, not in the least, and in later years was even capable of getting her own back by taking a little dig at him now and then about the 'aristocracy'—as she called my father's Rumanian connections.

Aside from his buddies in the back room of the ice-cream parlour on Augusta Avenue, my father also kept in touch with his Rumanian compatriots (all of whom had prospered), and would once in a while go to them for an evening. We were never invited nor did they come to us. This may have been my father's doing, I don't know. I expect he was ashamed of his circumstances, possibly of Ma, and certainly of how we lived.

Once in a blue moon during Rosh Hashanah or Yom Kippur after shul, they would unexpectedly drop in on us. One time a group of four came to the house, and I remember Pa darting around like a gadfly, collecting glasses, wiping them, and pouring a glass of wine he'd made himself. Ma shook hands all around, then went to the kitchen to cut some slices of her honey cake, scraping off the burnt part. I was summoned to take the plate in to 'Pa's gentlefolk'. Pretending to be busy, she rattled around the kitchen a few seconds, then seated herself in the partially open door, inspecting them. Not till they were leaving did she come out again, to wish them a good year.

The minute they were gone, my father turned to her. 'Russian peasant! Tartar savage, you! Sitting there with your eyes popping out. Do you think they couldn't see you?'

'What's the matter? Even a cat may look at a king?' she said blandly.

'Why didn't you come out instead of sitting there like a caged animal?'

'Because I didn't want to shame you,' she said, twirling her thumbs and swaying back and forth in the chair Yankev had given her as a wedding present.

My father busied himself clearing table, and after a while he softened. But she wasn't through yet. 'Which one was Falik's wife?' she asked in seeming innocence. 'The one with the beard?'

This drew his fire again. 'No!' he shouted.

'Oh, the other one. The pale one with the hump on her back,' she said wickedly.

So . . . notwithstanding the good dream Ma had of Pa coming home with a basket of apples, she never saw him again. He died six days after the operation.

It was a harrowing six days, dreadful. As Pa got weaker, the more disputatious we became—my brother, my sister, and I—arguing and snapping at each other outside his door, the point of contention being should Ma be told or not.

Nurse Brown, the special we'd put on duty, came out once to hush us. 'You're not helping him by arguing like this. He can hear you.'

'Is he conscious, nurse?'

'Of course he's conscious.'

'Is there any hope?'

'There's always hope,' she said. 'I've been on cases like this before, and I've seen them rally.'

We went our separate ways, clinging to the thread of hope she'd given us. The fifth day after the operation I had a call from Nurse Brown: 'Your father wants to see you.'

Nurse Brown left the room when I arrived, and my father motioned me to undo the zipper of his oxygen tent. 'Ma's a good woman,' he said, his voice so weak I had to lean close to hear him. 'You'll look after her? Don't put her aside. Don't forget about her—'

'What are you talking about!' I said shrilly, then lowered my voice to a whisper. 'The doctor told me you're getting better. Honest to God, Pa, I wouldn't lie to you,' I whispered.

He went on as if I hadn't spoken. 'Even a servant if you had her for thirty years, you wouldn't put aside because you don't need her any more—'

'Wait a minute,' I said, and went to the corridor to fetch Nurse Brown. 'Nurse Brown, will you tell my father what you told me yesterday. You remember? About being on cases like this before, and you've seen them rally. Will you tell that to my father, please. He talks as if he's—'

I ran from the room and stood outside the door, bawling. Nurse Brown opened the door a crack. '*Ssh*! You'd better go now; I'll call you if there's any change.'

At five the next morning, my brother telephoned from hospital. Ma was sound asleep and didn't hear. 'You'd better get down here,' he said. 'I think the old man's checking out. I've already phoned Gertie.'

My sister and I arrived at the hospital within seconds of each other. My brother was just emerging from Pa's room. In the gesture of a baseball umpire he jerked a thumb over his shoulder, signifying OUT.

'Is he dead?' we asked our brother.

'Just this minute,' he replied.

Like three dummies we paced the dimly lit corridor, not speaking to each other. In the end we were obliged to speak; we had to come to a decision about how to proceed next.

We taxied to the synagogue of which Pa was a member, and roused the *shamus*. 'As soon as it's light I'll get the rabbi,' he said. 'He'll attend to everything. Meantime go home.'

In silence we walked slowly home. Dawn was just breaking, and Ma, a habitually early riser, was bound to be up now and in the kitchen. Quietly we let ourselves in and passed through the hall leading to the kitchen. We were granted an unexpected respite; Ma was not up yet. We waited ten minutes for her, fifteen—an agonizing wait. We decided one of us had better go and wake her; what was the sense of prolonging it? The next minute we changed our minds. To awaken her with such tidings would be inhuman, a brutal thing to do.

'Let's stop whispering,' my sister whispered. 'Let's talk in normal tones, do something, make a noise, she'll hear us and come out.'

In an access of activity we busied ourselves. My sister put the kettle on with a clatter; I took teaspoons from the drawer, clacking them like castanets. She was bound to hear, their bedroom was on the same floor at the front of the house—but five minutes elapsed and not a sound from the room.

'Go and see,' my sister said, and I went and opened the door to that untidy bedroom Pa used to rail against.

Ma, her black eyes circled and her hair in disarray, was sitting up in bed. At sight of me she flopped back and pulled the feather tick over her head. I approached the bed and took the covers from her face. 'Ma—'

She sat up. 'You are guests in my house now?'

For the moment I didn't understand. I didn't know the meaning of her words. But the next minute the meaning of them was clear—with Pa dead, the link was broken. The bond, the tie that held us together. We were no longer her children. We were now guests in her house.

'When did Pa die?' she asked.

'How did you know?'

'My heart told me.'

Barefooted, she followed me to the kitchen. My sister gave her a glass of tea, and we stood like mutes, watching her sipping it through a cube of sugar.

'You were all there when Pa died?'

'Just me, Ma,' my brother said.

She nodded. 'His kaddish. Good.'

I took a chair beside her, and for once without constraint or self-consciousness, put my arm around her and kissed her on the cheek.

'Ma, the last words Pa spoke were about you. He said you were a good woman. "Ma's a good woman," that's what he said to me.'

She put her tea down and looked me in the face.

'Pa said that? He said I was a good woman?' She clasped her hands. 'May the light shine on him in paradise,' she said, and wept silently, putting her head down to hide her tears.

Eight o'clock the rabbi telephoned. Pa was now at the funeral parlour on College near Augusta, and the funeral was to be at eleven o'clock. Ma went to ready herself, and in a few minutes called me to come and zip up her black crepe, the dress Pa had bought her six years ago for the Applebaum wedding.

The Applebaums, neighbours, had invited Ma and Pa to the wedding of their daughter, Lily. Right away Pa had declared he wouldn't go. Ma kept coaxing. How would it look? It would be construed as unfriendly, unneighbourly. A few days before the wedding he gave in, and Ma began scratching through her wardrobe for something suitable to wear. Nothing she exhibited pleased him. He went downtown and came back with the black crepe and an outsize corset.

I dressed her for the wedding, combed her hair, and put some powder on her face. Pa became impatient; he had already called a cab. What was I doing? Getting her ready for a beauty contest? The taxi came, and as Pa held her coat he said to me in English, 'You know, Ma's not a bad-looking woman?'

For weeks she talked about the good time she'd had at the Applebaum wedding, but chiefly about how Pa had attended her. Not for a minute had he left her side. Two hundred people at the wedding and not one woman among them had the attention from her husband that she had had from Pa. 'Pa's a gentleman,' she said to me, proud as proud.

Word of Pa's death got around quickly, and by nine in the morning people began trickling in. First arrivals were Yankev and Danyeh. Yankev, now in his seventies and white-haired, was still straight and handsome. The same Yankev except for the white hair and a asthmatic condition causing him to wheeze and gasp for breath. Danyeh was wizened and bent over, her hands hanging almost to her knees. They approached Ma, Danyeh trailing Yankev. Yankev held out a hand and with the other one thumped his chest, signifying he was too congested to speak. Danyeh gave her bony hand to Ma and muttered condolence.

From then on there was a steady influx of people. Here was Chaim the schnorrer! We hadn't seen him in years. Chaim the schnorrer, stinking of fish and in leg wrappings as always, instead of socks. Rich as Croesus he was said to be, a fish-peddling miser who lived on soda crackers and milk and kept his money in his leg wrappings. Yankev, a minute ago too congested for speech, found words for Chaim. 'How much money have you got in those *gutkess?* The truth, Chaim!'

Ma shook hands with all, acknowledged their sympathy, and to some she spoke a few words. I observed the Widow Spector, a gossip and trouble-maker, sidling through the crowd and easing her way toward Ma. 'The Post' she was called by people on the street. No one had the time of day for her; even Ma used to hide from her.

I groaned at the sight of her. As if Ma didn't have enough to contend with. But no! here was Ma welcoming the Widow Spector, holding a hand out to her. 'Give me your hand, Mrs Spector. Shake hands, we're partners now. Now I know the taste, I'm a widow too.' Ma patted the chair beside her. 'Sit down, partner. Sit down.'

At a quarter to eleven the house was clear of people. 'Is it time?' Ma asked, and we answered, Yes, it was time to go. We were afraid this would be the breaking point for her, but she went calmly to the bedroom and took her coat from the peg on the door and came to the kitchen with it, requesting that it be brushed off.

The small funeral parlour was jammed to the doors, every seat taken but for four left vacant for us. On a trestle table directly in front of our seating was the coffin. A pine box draped in a black cloth, and in its centre a white Star of David.

Ma left her place, approached the coffin, and as she stood before it with clasped hands I noticed the uneven hemline of her coat, hiked up in back by that mound of flesh on her shoulders. I observed that her lisle stockings were twisted at the ankles, and was embarrassed for her. She stood silently a moment, then began to speak. She called him her dove, her comrade, her friend.

'Life is a dream,' she said. 'You were my treasure. You were the light of my eyes. I thought to live my days out with you—and look what it has come to.' (She swayed slightly, the black shawl slipping from her head—and I observed that could have done with a brushing too.) 'If ever I offended you or caused you even a twinge of discomfort, forgive me for it. As your wife I lived like a queen. Look at me now. I'm nothing. You were my jewel, my crown. With you at its head my house was a palace. I return now to a hovel. Forgive me for everything, my dove. Forgive me.'

('Russian peasant,' Pa used to say to her in anger, 'Tartar savage.' If he could see her now as she stood before his bier mourning him. Mourning him like Hecuba mourning Priam and the fall of Troy. And I a minute ago was ashamed of her hiked-up coat, her twisted stockings and dusty shawl.)

People were weeping; Ma resumed her place dry-eyed, and the rabbi began the service.

It is now a year since Pa died, and as he had enjoined me to do, I am looking after Ma. I have not put her aside. I get cross and holler at her as I always have done, but she allows for my testiness and does not hold it against me. I'm a spinster, an old maid now approaching my thirty-seventh year, and she pities me for it. I get bored telling her again and again that Pa's last words were Ma's a good woman, and sometimes wish I'd never mentioned it. She cries a lot, and I get impatient with her tears. But I'm good to her.

This afternoon I called Moodey's, booked two seats for the grandstand, and tonight I'm taking her to the Ex and she'll see the fireworks.

HENRY KREISEL · b. 1922

The Almost Meeting

The letter was addressed to Alexander Budak in care of his
publisher in Toronto, and the publisher had sent it on to him in
Edmonton, where he lived. Both the address and the note itself
were hand-written, and Alexander Budak was at once struck by
the unusual way in which the letters had been formed. The writer
had used the thinnest possible nib, and his writing looked like an
intricate web spun by a long-legged spider. At first Alexander
Budak thought that it would be impossible for him to decipher
the writing, but as he stared at it, he could make out a Toronto
address and a date, and then he glanced down the page and saw
the signature. 'David Lasker.' Alexander Budak was intrigued,
even excited. For it was a legendary name. Many people regarded
David Lasker as one of the greatest writers the country had
produced, a great poet as well as a great novelist, who had created
an astonishing body of work, but had then suddenly fallen silent.
During the last ten years or so he had published virtually nothing.
Only once, about two years ago, a new group of his poems had
appeared in the *Canadian Forum*. They were enigmatic utterances, but full of the most striking images, in which the artist
seemed to want to refine himself out of existence, to separate his
fleshly self from the works of his own creation until all that was
bound up with the self was burned away. The poet himself would
become a zero. Only the created work would glimmer and shine
in its anonymity.

It was a far cry from the earlier Lasker, a flamboyant character
who wore outrageous clothes and let his hair grow long when

that was considered offensive, and who delighted to shock and scandalize the respectable middle class of Toronto and of English Canada in general, even the people (particularly the people) who rarely read his serious work, but knew of him only through the stories that appeared in the week-end supplements of the daily papers.

Lasker's writing had a voluptuous quality that Alexander Budak admired. It was full of passion and emotion. Lasker had given a voice to the immigrants who had come to Canada in the early years of the century. His first book of poems presented a marvellous gallery of the Jewish immigrants, the men and women of his parents' generation, but then he had gone beyond his own community and had written some wonderful things about the immigrants who had come to the city after the second world war—the Greeks and Italians and the people from Eastern Europe—and of their impact on what was still a staid and proper puritan city.

Often in his writing people of different nationalities came together and almost touched, only to find themselves pulled apart again. Alexander Budak was hoping that Lasker might have something to say about reconciliation between people, for he had a wonderful gift of moving easily between different ethnic groups and of comprehending and communicating nuances of feeling. But just when it seemed to Alexander Budak that Lasker might hold out the hope that solitudes could touch and intertwine, he had fallen silent, had drawn into himself, and apart from a few enigmatic utterances, had published nothing.

Nonetheless, his achievement stood. He had given voice to the voiceless, had made invisible men and women visible, and when Alexander Budak was driven to write himself, David Lasker's example was of prime importance. He took heart from him when he tried to set down the story that ultimately became his first novel. When he had doubts about what he was doing, he read Lasker, and that gave him courage to go on. His novel began by tracing the life of an immigrant who had come to Canada in the aftermath of the first world war from the border region of Croatia and Hungary. This man, to whom Alexander Budak gave the name of Lukas, had gone first to Ontario, and then had drifted West, worked on farms, and then came to Edmonton, where he found work in a scrap-yard.

There he met Helena, one of the girls who worked in the office, and fell in love with her. She was a vivacious girl who'd come to Canada with her parents when she was a baby. The family came from the same border region as Lukas, but they belonged to a different nationality, and they brought with them all the hostility and all the ancient enmities that were endemic in the border region.

Helena knew that the thought of her having any kind of relationship with Lukas would be unbearable to her parents, and for a long time she resisted his advances. But Lukas was strong and handsome, his eyes glowing like coals, his thick hair black and shiny. She could not resist him.

They began to have their lunch together, sandwiches they had brought from home. Occasionally he dared to take her hand. It was as if an electric current passed through her. Then one day he asked her to have lunch with him in a restaurant. It took her a week to make up her mind because she knew that if she accepted she would have consented to the start of a serious relationship. Although he had not told her, she knew that he was in love with her, and though she did not yet admit it to herself, she was already half in love with him. And so she finally agreed to that innocent lunch in a restaurant.

From then on things moved quickly. She fell passionately in love with him. She could not wait to go to work in the morning because she would see him and at lunch they would be together.

At home, the family noticed the change. One Sunday after they had all returned from mass, her father, his long moustaches bristling, said that she was love-sick. Demanded to know who the man was. She denied at first that there was any involvement with a man, but the family wore her down and she confessed that she was in love. With a man she had met at work. Who was he? they demanded to know. What was his name? Lukas, she whispered. A wonderful man, she said. What was his religion? He was a Catholic. Her mother crossed herself. A burden had been lifted. Thank God, he was not a Lutheran or a Jew.

Her father was not so quickly appeased. Where did he come from, this wonderful man? What wind had blown him here? She mumbled the name of a border town. Her voice was barely audible, but her father's hearing was as sharp as a fox's and he knew at once why she had kept the knowledge from them. He repeated the name of the town in a roaring voice that sounded and resounded through the house. They cowered away from him, the girl and her mother, and her brother and her sister.

No answer was necessary or indeed expected. The name of that town was alone sufficient to proclaim her transgression. How could she do such a thing? How could she bring shame on the family?

Her face became flushed, she felt her anger rising, her hands began to tremble. For the first time in her life she found herself in open rebellion against her father. She had always loved him and had, according to the tradition of her family, obeyed him. But now he suddenly appeared to her as a tyrannous, vindictive man. She was shocked by her own feeling, but she could not suppress it.

This was Canada, she said in a soft voice, and she was an adult now.

He snorted his contempt. She lived in his house, he snarled, she was his daughter, and she would obey. The honour of the whole family was involved.

This reasoning, which only a few weeks ago she would have unquestioningly accepted, now seemed to her absurd. She was defiant. She refused to bend the knee. Instead, she got her coat and rushed out of the house.

She knew the house where Lukas rented a room. He was astonished when she appeared at his door, on a Sunday, in the middle of the day. Under the disapproving eye of his landlady, she slipped into his room. She was agitated and excited. Lukas had never seen her look so beautiful. He took her in his arms and she told her story.

What was she going to do? he asked. It was not what *she* was going to do, she answered without any hesitation, for she had already made the decision, it was what *they* were going to do. They must get married, she said. At once. She was her father's daughter after all, she had his determination and power.

Lukas was quite overwhelmed. He was also afraid. How would they manage? She was not afraid. She felt free, as if shackles had been removed from her wrists. Her heady feeling, her exhilaration was infectious. With a cry he grasped her in his arms and pulled her down onto his bed and kissed her passionately. She did not lose control. She allowed him to touch her breasts and the inside of her thighs, and she responded passionately to his kisses. But then she freed herself from his embrace and said, not yet, not here.

She spent the night in a hotel, alone, and the next day found herself a room and moved out of her father's house. Soon afterwards, they were married, Lukas and she, with only the officiating priest there, and two of their co-workers as witnesses.

Her father disowned her publicly. He would have nothing to do with her, and he forbade her mother to get in touch with her, though occasionally they made contact, but only fleetingly.

Not even the birth of their first child, a girl, changed things. She ached to show the child to her parents, but her father's door remained closed. Once, on a Saturday in the farmers' market on 97th Street, she was wheeling the baby in her carriage, and she saw her mother from afar and her mother saw her. Her mother remained rooted to the spot where she stood and Helena slowly moved towards her. Her mother looked oh so longingly at the baby in the carriage and tears were coursing down her cheeks, but she made no sound, and then Helena saw her father some ten or twelve feet away at a stall where he had just bought potatoes. He looked away sternly—she could see that he was trembling, that it took a superhuman effort for him not to look at his granddaughter—but he would not do it.

It was the most shattering experience Helena had ever had. When she got home she broke down and could not control her sobbing and crying, and it was a long time before she could tell the uncomprehending Lukas what had happened to her.

A few days later she found that she was pregnant again. It was almost more than she could bear, but then the thought came to her that if the new child was a boy, her father would relent. He would not be able to keep away from a grandson.

She gave birth to a son and she was jubilant. But the change she had hoped for did not occur. Her father did not relent. His door remained closed.

In her rage Helena turned against her husband. She blamed Lukas for her despair. The marriage could not stand the strain. Lukas did not know how to handle an emotional situation he could barely comprehend.

One day he did not return from work. He disappeared. No one knew where he had gone. The earth had swallowed him up.

She was deserted and alone and desperate. And only then did her father open his door to her. He had said that nothing good could come of the marriage and now he had been proved right. Now he could take possession of his grandchildren and bring them up and enjoy them. But Helena was defeated and in a sense she never recovered.

The little boy loved his grandfather, and it was not until he was fourteen or fifteen that he began to understand what had happened. His mother told him the story over and over again. His grandfather had robbed him of his father and he had robbed her of her husband. The boy's love for his grandfather turned to something akin to hate. When he was just over fourteen, the boy ran away from his grandfather's house to find his father. He did not know where to begin. After two days the police picked him up and took him back home, and his grandfather punished him. But now his mind was made up and his mother encouraged him because this was a way in which she could have her revenge against her father.

When the boy was seventeen he left his grandfather's house for good and set out to find his father. It was a quest that was to take him across Canada and into the United States. He picked up the trail of his father, and his search took him north to Yellowknife, and then to the East coast and to the West coast, and into California. Twice he almost found Lukas, only to have him vanish before he could meet him face to face.

That was the story Alexander Budak told in his first novel. It was his own story and the story of his family, and he told it with honesty and great power. It had created a stir. And now David Lasker had written to him.

The letter, written in that strange handwriting that looked like the intricate web spun by a long-legged spider, was brief.

'I salute you,' Lasker had written. 'How sad. How sad. How we torture each other. I sense a bitterness in your hero because he cannot find his father. Let him not despair. An almost meeting is often more important than the meeting. The quest is all.'

What did that mean? Alexander Budak sat down at once to answer Lasker. 'You have meant much to me,' he wrote. 'Without your example I could never have become a writer. You gave me courage to write my novel. I'm going to be in Toronto in December and want very much to see you. I have much to ask you.'

Three weeks later Alexander Budak received another letter from Lasker. It contained only one word. 'Perhaps.'

When Alexander Budak came to Toronto in December, sent there by his publisher to promote his novel, snow was already on the ground. His letter to Lasker, telling him when he was coming, had gone unanswered. And when he checked the Toronto telephone directory, Lasker's number was not listed. So it appeared to Alexander Budak that he would not be able to meet Lasker after all.

On the second evening of his stay in Toronto, Alexander Budak had dinner at the apartment of Robert Walker, a writer of Lasker's generation, and once one of his closest friends. Alexander Budak told him of the exchange of letters he'd had with Lasker. He wanted desperately to see him, he said.

'That might be difficult,' said Walker. 'He doesn't see many people any more.'

'Why?' asked Alexander Budak.

'I wish I knew. I could spin some theories, but they wouldn't explain anything. Perhaps he's himself said all that can be said in his last poems. Perhaps the human condition has become too much for him to bear.' He thought for a while. Then he said, 'I haven't seen him for two or three years. But I still have his telephone number. Why don't I phone him? Perhaps he'll see you, since he's obviously interested in your work.'

He left the dining-room to phone and after a few minutes returned. 'He wouldn't come to the phone himself,' he said. 'But I spoke to his wife and she acted as go-between. It was a strange sensation, since he must have been right there. She said he was excited to hear that you were in town. Believe it or not, he said he wants to meet you and he's going to come here. It'll take him a half hour or so. I'm amazed. I didn't think he would actually agree to come.'

They waited, drinking their after-dinner coffee. Alexander Budak felt a growing sense of excitement, as if he expected from Lasker some kind of revelation.

The phone rang and Walker went to answer it. When he came back into the dining-room, he looked puzzled.

'This was the strangest call,' he said. 'It was the man who runs a little grocery store a couple of blocks from here. He said a gentleman was in the store and would like me to come and get him. "Who is he?" I asked. "Can I speak to him?" The grocer said, "That's what I wanted him to do, but he said he didn't want to talk on the phone. He wants you to come down here and fetch him. He says he might get lost." "Is his name Lasker?" I asked. "I'll ask him," said the grocer, and after a moment he said to me, "The gentleman says he might be. He says it's possible." Then he whispered into the phone, "It's weird. You better get here.""

Walker looked at Alexander Budak. 'I'm worried,' he said. 'Let's hurry down. He may not be well. He may need help.'

The snow was coming down hard and it made walking difficult. It took them more than five minutes to walk the two blocks to the grocery store. A little bell tinkled when they opened the door. They shook the snow off their coats. At first they couldn't see anybody, and then they saw the grocer sitting behind the cash register. But there was no sign of Lasker.

'Are you looking for the gentleman?' the grocer asked.

'Yes,' said Walker. 'Where is he?'

'I don't know. I had to go to the back of the store. Then I heard the bell, and when I came back he was gone. I thought you'd come and he'd gone out with you.'

'How did he look?' Walker asked. 'Did he look distraught?'

'Oh, no. He was as pleasant as could be. He just didn't want to talk on the phone.'

'Well, thanks,' said Walker, and to Alexander Budak he said, 'We'd better get back to my apartment. Perhaps he'll show up after all.'

'I had the strangest feeling of déjà vu,' said Alexander Budak as they trudged back through the heavy snow. 'That store looked exactly like a little grocery store up in Yellowknife where I once waited for my father. Someone told me he always came there at a certain time, but he never showed up.'

Back in the apartment, Walker phoned Lasker's house. He hadn't returned. 'Now I got his wife all worried,' he said. 'She said she'd phone when he got back.'

About half an hour later, she phoned. David Lasker had come back. He was terribly sorry, she said. He couldn't wait. Something drove him out of that store. But he did want to see Alexander Budak. Could he come over to Lasker's house next day, around eight in the evening?

Alexander Budak said he would be delighted and Walker passed it on to Lasker's wife.

The next evening was clear and cold. Alexander Budak got a

taxi about a quarter to eight. It took about twenty minutes to get to Lasker's house. When he got out of the taxi and looked at the house, it seemed dark. He paid the driver, but told him to wait.

He walked up to the door and rang the bell. No one came to the door. He rang again, leaving his finger on the button for quite a while. He heard the bell ringing, but there was no answer. He checked to see if he had the right house. There was no doubt. Perhaps he had the wrong address. But no. He'd written to Lasker at that address and his letters had arrived. He rang the bell again. He waited. Nothing moved inside. No light went on. Nobody came to the door.

Slowly he walked back to the waiting taxi. Its running motor was the only noise in the street. 'Nobody home,' he said to the driver. 'Strange. . . . You better take me back to the hotel.'

About ten days after he came back to Edmonton, he got a letter from David Lasker. When he saw that strange, intricate writing, he got very agitated. It took him several minutes before he felt he could open the envelope.

'It was impossible for me to see you,' Lasker had written. 'You wanted to ask me things. I have no answers. But you are in my heart. Let me be in your heart also. We had an almost meeting. Perhaps that is not much. And yet it is something. Remember me.'

JACK LUDWIG · b. 1922

A Woman of Her Age

I

Once a week, even now, Mrs Goffman makes that chauffeur drive her slowly down from the mountain, back to St Lawrence Boulevard and Rachel Street; she doesn't want any old cronies who might still be alive spotting her in that hearse of a limousine, so she gets out a couple of blocks from the Market and walks the rest of the way, not in her Persian lamb or her warm beaver, but in that worn cloth coat she bought at Eaton's Basement years ago, the black one. Long, gaunt as a late afternoon shadow, Mrs Goffman concentrates on smiling. Otherwise she looks like a spook. At seventy-five you can feel warm, sweet, girlish even, but an old old face has trouble expressing soft feelings. Those reddish-brown eyebrows that didn't turn white with the rest of her hair, they're to blame, so bushy, so fierce, with an ironic twist that was snappy when she was a hot young radical, but now, when she's old enough to be a great-grandmother, who needs it?

'Wordsworth', her son Jimmy used to call her. In a drugstore window she sees reflected Wordsworth's broad forehead, deep-set eyes, small mouth, short chin. By God, she tells herself, this is a darned good face. Jimmy had this face. Her father had it too—who knows how far back these purplish lips go, or the dark rings under eyes, or the pale olive complexion? Moses might have had similar colouring. Her nose gives a sly twitch to call attention to itself: Wordsworth's large humped nose she has too, and it deserves the dominant spot it earned for itself on Mrs Goffman's face. She judges everything by its smell. That's why the ambassador's mansion she lives in flunks so badly—it's not only quiet as a church, it smells like a church. Six days a week her nose puts up with that dry lonely quiet smell, does what a nose is supposed to do in Westmount, breathe a little: on St Lawrence Boulevard a nose is for smelling, and Mrs Goffman doesn't miss a sniff. Families are getting ready for sabbath.

Doba, catch that goose roasting, her nose seems to say. Hey, poppyseed cookies! Real stuffed fish! St Lawrence Boulevard, I love you!

II

Mitchell the 'Kosher Butcher' nodded his usual pitying nod as she walked past his full window—fresh-killed ducks and chickens hanging by their feet, cows' brains in pools, tongues like holsters, calves' feet signed by the Rabbi's indelible pencil. Mrs Goffman nodded her black-turbaned head at Mitchell but he'd already given his nod, and only stared back, open-mouthed, his hands pressed against his slaughterhouse-looking apron. Naturally Mitchell has her pegged: doesn't he know this shopping trip is a fake, that Mrs Grosney, the cook, does Mrs Goffman's buying and cooking? Mitchell knows about the Persian lamb coat she doesn't wear to Market. Mitchell knew her dead husband well. Mitchell, like all of Montreal, knows the story of her dead son Jimmy.

When Simon-may-he-rest-in-peace was still alive the Goffmans lived down here, among people, in life. Now life was a novelty to Mrs Goffman. Six days to Westmount, one to St Lawrence and Rachel Street, what idiotic arrangement was that? Some day she'd get real tough with her son Sidney. Marry him off. Make him sell the Ambassador's mansion and lead a normal life.

Her eyebrows went into their ironic arch. You, Doba, they seemed to mock her, when could you get your kids to do anything?

III

In front of Bernstein's Kiddies' Korner a young girl pressed her lovely dark face against the window, her hand nervously rocking a baby carriage. Black hair, heavy lips, nursing breasts, what a beauty of a mother, Mrs Goffman thought; she could double for Jimmy's Shirley! By rights Mrs Goffman should have a grand-daughter this girl's age. One? A dozen!

What would it hurt if she pretended she had come to Kiddies' Korner to buy something or other for her grand-daughter and great-grandchild? The thought made her feel wonderful.

'Dear,' she said, 'good morning, dear. How's baby?'

The girl nodded absently. She had eyes only for a white bunting in the window. If she wanted pink or blue I'd know at least if my grandchild was a boy or girl, Mrs Goffman thought. In her low Russian-sounding voice she cooed at the baby, tried to make her grand-daughter look at her.

'Dear,' she tried again, 'what do you think is nice, eh, dear?'

'That bunting,' the girl said, still not looking at her grandmother, 'but what a high price!'

'Twenty-five bucks! Highway robbery,' Mrs Goffman said in a loud voice, thinking she'd better not ham it up too much. Her purse was lined with dough—a few fifties, four or five twenties, a dozen tens, fives, ones, even a two—Mrs Goffman was never too neat about money. Every handbag was loaded this way, and what Montreal bank didn't have Doba Goffman as an account? Money to her was like a big soup: you cooked it in a vat but then came the problem of how to store it. You pour in one jar, then another, then another—except that with Sidney and Jimmy there was no end to what she had to put in jars. The faster she stored money away the faster they brought her more. No matter what she did to get rid of it—charities, trips to New York every week to see shows, an opera, flights to Israel, Hawaii, buying those bozos Sulka ties at fifty bucks a crack—no matter how fast she gave it, they stuffed her accounts, lined handbags, papered the walls, those successes of hers, those imbeciles!

Bernstein's clerk poked his head out the door.

'Highway robbery, is that what you call it, *babbe*?' he said in a hurt voice. 'Come inside. I'll show you my cost.'

Years ago Mrs Goffman felt offended when people called her *babbe*, grandmother, but not now. She turned her head and gave the man a mirthless smile.

'Honey,' he said to the girl, 'let your *babbe* stay out here with the baby. You come in. I've got a real bargain for the kid.'

The girl didn't seem to hear.

'Go 'head, dear,' Mrs Goffman said warmly. 'I'll rock baby.'

The girl wheeled the carriage around and hurried towards the market. Mrs Goffman followed quickly.

IV

At the corner of Rachel and St Lawrence Mrs Goffman stopped to let a horse-drawn wagon go by. What a wonderful stink an old nag gave off! Wheels creaking was a melody to her deafish ears. Across the way was Simon's store, the 'upstairs' they used to live in. Dimly, like an imagination, Mrs Goffman made out the 'S. Goffman and Sons' which 'J. Olin and Brother' had been painted over. Her nose sniffed at the rubber and leather smell coming from the old store. Those French perfumes Sidney gives her should only smell so nice!

Crossing the street she hurried after her grand-daughter, but, suddenly, without warning, tears gushed from Mrs Goffman's eyes, biting, salty tears mixed in with the heady fish fragrance around the Rachel Street Market stalls. Stop it, old fool, she told herself, but the tears kept running.

She pretended she was buying, dropped her eyes, rubbed a cold slimy fish with her manicured fingernails, poked open a carp's small-toothed mouth, combed its stiff freezing fins with her wrinkled hand. Next to Simon's gold wedding band was the hideous ruby Sidney gave for her birthday last year; above them both was Jimmy's gift, a diamond-studded watch.

'*Babbe, babbe*,' a gentle voice said to her, 'why are you crying?'

She didn't have to open her eyes to know the man was new on the job: everybody on Rachel Street knew why Mrs Goffman cried.

'A cold,' she said.

'In the eyes?' the voice said sceptically. 'Then maybe you shouldn't handle my fish?'

'Listen,' Mrs Goffman said wildly, 'give me two large carp and three nice whitefish!'

'There's an order!' the man clapped his hands together. 'Only your generation, eh, *babbe*? Big families need a full table!'

The girl with the baby wheeled up beside Mrs Goffman, hefted a small pike, looked wistful. Mrs Goffman moved over to give her grand-daughter more room.

'Mister,' she said to the fisherman, 'I've got lots of time. Look after the mother with the baby first.'

The girl had turned around and was poking at the baby's blankets. The fishman grabbed at a floppy-tailed carp beating its fins on the damp wood stall.

'Today's girl,' he laughed, 'can wait longer than you, babbe. Your generation grinds, stuffs, cooks—just like my ma-may-she-rest-in-peace—two dozen people at Shabbes table wasn't too much. But these kids?' He pointed at Mrs Goffman's grand-daughter. 'She'll toss a pike in a frying pan and one, two, it's Shabbes.'

A second carp, big as a shark, fell with a splat against the first; three dancing whitefish got buried in a wad of newspapers.

'Dear,' Mrs Goffman said sweetly, 'he's ready to take your order.'

Again she didn't look up. Mrs Goffman wanted to holler—'Hey, sleeping beauty, can't you even answer when your *babbe* talks to you?'

'*Babbe*,' the fishman said, 'this parcel's too heavy. You live right around here somewheres? St Dominique maybe? I'll deliver you the fish myself.'

'I'm a strong woman,' Mrs Goffman said, holding out her arms.

'I can see, *babbe*. I only wish I should be in your shape at your age,' the man said enthusiastically. 'Have a good sabbath. Enjoy the kiddies. You deserve the best. I can tell!'

'Good-bye, dear,' Mrs Goffman said to her grand-daughter.

'Good-bye, good-bye,' the fishman answered, clapping his hands together. 'Next?'

v

The moment the fish touched her arms they seemed to revive and start swimming—twenty, thirty pounds writhing in her helpless arms! Fish? Who needed fish? When did she cook fish last! That last batch stunk up Sidney's limousine so badly he had to sell it for next to nothing!

The newspaper parcel was leaking all over her coat. Let it bust and she'd be chased by every cat in Montreal! Was she out of her mind? Seventy-five years in this world and still not able to resist the most foolish impulse!

Her arms hurt, her face turned red, her heart beat crazily. Leave it to an old Radical to act like a nut! Two blocks away is that healthy horse of a chauffeur sitting on his fanny and sunning himself. Two blocks? She'd never make it. But where could you dump this useless stuff? In the empty baby carriages scattered around St Lawrence Boulevard? She thought of letting it fall casually on the sidewalk, like a lost handkerchief. Maybe she could slip it into the empty moving van she saw across the street. Who but a woman loaded with money could afford such grandstand plays?

Fish water soaked her gloves, dribbled down her coat front: a bit of fin slipped through the dissolving newspaper, a sappy fish-eye made peek-a-boo. In a shop window Mrs Goffman caught sight of herself—a black streak, a bundle, eyebrows. Get sloppy sentimental and this is the result!

Triminiuk's. She suddenly came up with a brain-wave: Captain Triminiuk would save her! Giggling, panting, giddy, red-faced, she staggered across the street and into Triminiuk's Delicatessen.

The fish hit the counter like an explosion; the whitefish, wild as Cossacks, danced out of their covering.

'Come save an old sap, Gershon,' Mrs Goffman called to the back of the store. 'I overstocked myself with fish.'

She wiped her coat with orange wrappers, fell back, laughing helplessly, into one of Gershon's old chairs. Only Captain Triminiuk's Delicatessen still had these small round marble-top tables with wire legs and matching chairs with backs like wire carpet-beaters. The air inside was like a home-made mist—garlic pickles, pastrami, salami, sauerkraut, fresh rye bread, Triminiuk himself, who smelled like a real smokehouse.

Marching—he never walked—one-eyed Triminiuk came toward her, disapproving, as usual, everything about her. He stood at attention, his black cuff-guards up to his armpits, tieless collar buttoned at the neck, vest unbuttoned, also part of his pants. One of his eyes was almost closed, the other bright as turquoise, his moustache bristly, yellowed with tobacco.

Forty years ago, when she and Simon first met the old bluffer, he was just out of the Russian army, a cook who lost an eye from splattering fat. Since then Triminiuk, in recognition of himself, every ten years or so gave himself a promotion. Now he was a captain. Now the missing eye was a result of a sabre in the Russo-Japanese War.

'Fish?' he sniffed.

'Be a pal. Take if off my hands, Gershon,' she said flirtatiously.

'I need charity, Doba?'

'Don't play poor mouth with me, you bandit,' she laughed. 'You want to be independent, give me a tea with lemon.'

He didn't budge. Long ago she had given up trying to explain things to a stubborn old bluffer like Triminiuk. All he saw was that Doba Goffman, the hot-headed young Radical, became Mrs S. Goffman, prominent member of an Orthodox synagogue, patroness of the foolishness her sons' success brought her. Try to convince Gershon that she'd joined the Orthodoxes in protest against her sons' becoming Anglican-like Reform Jews? If those characters had stayed on St Lawrence Boulevard she would never have set foot in a synagogue. But when they climbed Westmount, bought that enormous mansion from the Ambassador, bragged about looking out on Nuns' Island, took her to Temple where the Rabbi pursed his lips in such a way that everybody should know he learned Hebrew not at home but in a University, then she, in protest, became again a Jew! Gershon should have seen the lousy Jewish-style cooking she, a Radical who had nothing to do with kitchens, forced her big-shot sons to eat—he should only know she got her Jewish recipes from *Better Homes and Gardens*!

Gershon accepted no explanations. He considered her a traitor. Worse. Maybe even a Zionist!

'My tea, Captain,' Mrs Goffman said.

Triminiuk looked toward the door.

A fat woman, hair messy, hands dug deep in the ripped pockets of an old flowered housecoat, drove several kids into the store in front of her, stood for a second sighing, muttering, scratching herself under the pockets. Corns stuck out of her pink-and-aqua wedgies.

'Captain,' she said in a high nasal whine, 'my kids came to eat me up alive again. Let a mouse try to find a crumb by me, let. Herbie's wetters, Gertie's soilers, four five already, and Gertie's carrying again, you've heard about such misfortunes? They act like Westmount millionaires. You can't afford kids, don't have, I keep telling.'

Triminiuk, Mrs Goffman saw, was trying to shut the woman up.

'Lady,' he said in his military voice, 'what can I get for you?'

One of the children, about seven, a girl with black hair, black eyes, front teeth out, stared at Mrs Goffman.

'Ma,' Mrs Goffman's deafish ears heard a whisper, 'why's the old lady all in black?'

'Gimme a couple rye loaves to stop up the mouths quickly,' the woman said shrilly, 'a salami, a few slices lox—'

'Ma,' the little girl stole behind her mother's housecoat and peeked at Mrs Goffman, 'is it a witch?'

'Tammy, stop botherin',' the woman said absently, fingering the fish on the counter. 'Captain, how can you make today's kid stop carrying? It's living here with the French that makes 'em like this, hah?'

'Lady,' Triminiuk snapped, 'is this everything?'

'Ma,' the little girl tugged at her mother's sleeve, 'I'm afraid of her—'

'Let me be,' the woman whined, shoving the child at Mrs Goffman. Hard as Mrs Goffman's old face tried, it couldn't come up with a look to reassure the child.

'You're very sweet, dear,' she said softly.

The child seemed to shudder.

'What did you say?' the woman mumbled.

'She's a very sweet little girl,' Mrs Goffman said.

'Listen, you want her? She's yours, the pest. You can have these others in the bargain,' the woman said without a smile.

'Two dollars and five cents,' Triminiuk all but shouted.

'What's he getting sore for? Don't I pay in time? Here,' she threw down a dollar bill, 'payday I'll give the rest.'

'Gramma,' the smallest kid in the store said quietly, 'can each of us have a sucker?'

'I got no money for suckers,' the woman said nastily, missing with a slap she'd aimed at the kid. Tammy, the little girl, frightened, jumped towards Mrs Goffman, grew more frightened, jumped back, catching her mother's corns with her shoe.

'For godssake, pests!' the woman shouted, slapping Tammy across the cheek. 'Get out of this store!'

'Don't cry, dear,' Mrs Goffman tried to make Tammy hear.

'I'm sorry these crazy kids bothered you, lady,' the woman said as she shooed them out the door. 'With these pests gone you can have peace.'

VI

Triminiuk went to get her her tea.

That kid Tammy was right, Mrs Goffman thought as she caught

sight of herself in Triminiuk's small calendar mirror. A witch, Black. What sentimental soft-headedness made her dress this way? What right did she have to dump her mourning on St Lawrence Boulevard? In her old age was she becoming a professional widow, a dopey eccentric? Tomorrow she'd go down to one of those fancy French shops on Sherbrooke and get gussied up in pink, violet, maybe even yellow.

Sentimentality, respectability, a tough old Radical like Mrs Goffman had been had, by America. How else did a revolutionary become a quiet-spoken tea-sipper dumb with good taste? By God, an old-fashioned St Dominique Street ma would have chased her kids out of the house with a broom, made their lives so miserable they would have to marry, in self-defence. And when Simon died, what stopped her from marrying again? Loyalty. Love. Now, when the time for praying was past and with the lock on the synagogue door, now she realized that love too was smaller than life. A stepfather would have been another way of getting her boys into life on their own. Jimmy had been a bachelor till forty-five, just a year before his death. Poor Sidney, still unmarried, fifty-three, a pill-swallower, complained his way from hotel to hotel crossing three continents.

Waste, Mrs Goffman thought with a sinking feeling, waste is the law of America—too much money, too much talent, even too much fish. Getting stuck with something useless like money and fish was a judgement against her and her sons.

Triminiuk came shuffling toward her, balancing a cup of tea in one hand, a glass in the other. Should she say something? I've done too much damage with silence, Mrs Goffman thought.

'Listen here, Capatanchik,' she said nastily, 'what's the big idea bringing me tea in a cup and yourself a glass?'

'Westmount ladies drink from china cups,' the old bluffer said without batting an eye.

'Turn right around, you pirate, and get me a glass,' Mrs Goffman said, hitting her palm against the marble top. 'To hell with Westmount!'

'I got only one glass,' Triminiuk came back.

'Then it's for me,' Mrs Goffman said in triumph. 'Hand it over.'

To show he was winner, Triminiuk poured his tea into a saucer and sipped noisy, like a roughneck.

'How's the rich son?' he asked. She couldn't tell for sure if he was being nasty.

'Sidney's fine,' she lied. One thing Sidney never was was fine, specially since without Jimmy he was a total loss in the world. He hadn't been with a woman in over a year. Women weren't Sidney's line—his hair was red and thin, his face chubby and round, his eyes watery and always blinking, his lower lip ready to blubber.

But Jimmy!

Elegant, taller than his tall mother, with her face, her colouring, dressed like a British diplomat, smooth with continental manners, chased by every woman in Montreal, and for what, what for? 'Fun', he called it, and what came of his fun? Ashes, dust. The dopiest kid on St Dominique Street had more claim on life than her handsome successful Jimmy. He drove a Bentley, wore a white leather raincoat, a British vest with brass buttons, a Parisian necktie—what he wore Montreal copied, the gals he took out were immediately stamped with approval. 'Lover boy' the high-school year-book nicknamed him. 'Lover man' was what they called him at McGill, and 'Don Giovanni'. Women, women, hundreds upon hundreds of women, affairs without number, and what came of it all? 'Listen to me, bozos,' she had said years ago, when they'd first moved to the Ambassador's mansion, 'let's get down to life now, eh? At sixty I'm *entitled* to grandchildren. Who'll mourn me when I'm dead, our bankers?'

Mrs Goffman's eyes filled, blood rushed to her face, in anger and despair she beat her ringed hand against the marble table. Jimmy, the poor fool Jimmy, marrying at forty-five, and how, with a nineteen-year-old who'd been living with another man since sixteen!

Triminiuk put his hand on her shoulder.

'What are you aggravating yourself for?' His blind eye looked like the dead fish's.

'Gershon, the worst thing is for people to die out of their own generation.'

'If people died neatly,' Triminiuk said, raising his face from the tilted saucer, 'we'd both be long buried by now.'

A little French girl barged into the store, wiggling her hips, pushing out her breasts. Her hair was tight with nasty bobby pin curls that gave Mrs Goffman the pip, her skin was broken out, badly powdered and rouged. She chewed gum with an open mouth. Her arms, though, were lovely and slim, and her legs were shapely. Even you, you tramp, Mrs Goffman thought as she watched Triminiuk give the girl a package of Sweet Caporal, even a gum-chewing slut like you I would have taken for a daughter-in-law at the end, when I saw what the score was.

'Bye, Cap,' the girl said with a wink. Triminiuk dismissed her with a wave.

'What were we saying, Doba?'

'I was being depressed,' she reminded him with a smile, 'and you were trying to snap me out of it.'

'Why should you be depressed?' Triminiuk said after a long slurp. 'The boy died a big success. It should happen to all my grandchildren, such a success.'

All his grandchildren—Gershon, big-shot atheist, lived by 'increase and multiply' the Bible's way. He *was* a success. Eight or nine kids, twenty-five, thirty grandchildren. Jimmy and Sidney took 'increase and multiply' to mean mergers, expansion, deals, transactions. Hundreds of thousands Jimmy left his mother, and bonds, and buildings, and tracts of land—ashes, dust, because neither his loins nor Sidney's produced a child.

She felt the blood rush to her face again. Imbecility, America's imbecility, Jimmy galloping after success while life runs off right under his feet. Mocking, teasing. His Shirley was a born mother, gorgeous, built to bear children. Not Jimmy's, though. On Jimmy's money Shirley, the most beautiful widow in Montreal, married that childhood sweetheart of hers. For him Shirley became a mother.

'Your tea's cold, I betcha,' she heard Triminiuk's voice say gruffly.

'I'll be your guest,' said Mrs Goffman. Triminiuk gave her a searching look, nodded briskly, shuffled with a military swagger to the back of the store.

He understood everything. Sitting with Gershon was comfortable, even in silence. Their conversations were one-quarter open, three-quarters between the lines, as it used to be with Simon. But the other kind of silence, the silence that buzzed in her deafish ears in the Ambassador's mansion, that kind Mrs Goffman couldn't stand. That silence frightened her more than the loudest noise. That silence was the noise of death.

'Gershon!' she called out in spite of herself.

'Look how a madamchikeh can't wait for a glass of tea,' the

old man scolded, but she noticed he was coming back in a big hurry.

'Gershon,' she said as he sat down, 'if we're lucky in life we *see*, if only for a split second. Life *or* death, there's no other issue, Gershon. Jimmy learned it too late. Not till the end could he stop for life, but he had to stop for death.'

'Doba,' Triminiuk said bluntly, 'you're beginning to sound religious.'

'What religious, when religious?' she cried out. 'In those clear moments blindness drops from us, we see and know everything!'

Twice I knew, she thought: once when Shirley's lover turned up at Jimmy's funeral in Jimmy's clothes. The other time too was at a funeral.

'So cut away my blindness,' Triminiuk said gently, poking at his inert gluey eye.

'*Touché*,' she said, hiding her face behind the tea glass. Triminiuk didn't press his advantage.

She glanced quickly at him and imagined him naked. She flushed. His face was weather-beaten, sketched over with tiny red-and-blue blood vessels, but his body would be blue-white, his back rounded, his rib-cage prominent as a starving man's. Mrs Goffman grew conscious of her own body—so long, so gaunt, so like a stranger's now the skin was dry and criss-crossed, now her breasts were flat with colour faded out of the nipples. Her nails didn't grow much, or her hair. Whatever was shrivelled in a man like Gershon was spent, whatever shrivelled on her was wasted.

Wisdom was overrated. It had little to do with life. She was wise, but powerless. When she had power she must have been stupid. Pride, shyness, loyalty to Simon's memory seemed so important years ago. Now Mrs Goffman knew she should have married even a gargoyle of a man, and had more children. But by the time she caught on to what Jimmy's and Sidney's fate was, it was too late for her to do anything for them, or herself. 'Fun', Jimmy said, relying on his mother's Radical tolerance, sneaking beauty after beauty into the house and his bed—for what, what for? All those gorgeous Rachels, but never a fruitful Leah.

'Gershon,' Mrs Goffman suddenly said, 'blaming is for innocents. I don't blame Shirley. I don't even blame Doba Goffman.'

Shirley dressed like a Hollywood star for the funeral—a large black picture-hat, dark glasses, elbow-length black gloves, a clinging sheath dress so open down the front the gravediggers scattered dirt in all directions trying to stay in position to stare at her. Her lover wore Jimmy's black Italian silk suit. They whispered together. Shirley didn't pretend to cry. She didn't even carry a handkerchief.

Sidney, for once in his tired life, got hot, wanted to throw himself at the two of them. Mrs Goffman wouldn't let him. What was Shirley's lower-animal foolishness compared to the horrible truth— Jimmy in the ground without a child to mourn for him! Who was left, Mrs Goffman, an old woman with teeth falling out of her head?

'I get such a cold feeling,' she whispered to Triminiuk. 'We threw life aside like a rag. When we die it's an end—papa's line, Simon's line—a crime, Gershon, a crime against the whole human race.'

Triminiuk nodded stiffly, like an officer commending a subordinate.

It *was* a crime against the whole human race. Life wasn't something to be kicked aside just because you happened to have it. In crowds, on the street, Mrs Goffman felt the difference bitterly—not she alone, not Sidney alone, a whole strain in the human race was dying in them! Simon's stubborn look was finished! Her pa's bass voice. Jimmy's way of greeting you—a *hello*, his arm thrown in front of his eyes as if you were the sun and so brilliant he couldn't absorb you. Jimmy made you feel that you were morning. Even Sidney had qualities the race shouldn't lose. Character, size, shape, all human magnificence, all possibility dying, dying, dying.

Mrs Goffman thought she would pass out.

'Doba, Doba,' Triminiuk's voice sounded urgent in her ear, 'stop aggravating, I said. Look on St Lawrence. The kids are coming home from school.'

He steered her into the doorway, made her look out on the boulevard. Dabs and specks of red, green, blue danced in the distance, faint squeals and shrieks washed terror of silence away from her ears. Gershon knew his onions. Bending down— Triminiuk was the same size as Simon, a peanut—she kissed him on his wrinkled forehead. He shook her off, stood rigid at attention, nodded her away.

'Thanks for taking the fish off my hands,' she said.

'Don't do it again,' he answered gruffly.

VII

Mrs Goffman concluded she would have to change her life, and immediately. She ordered her chauffeur to drive her to Fifi's, Shmifi's—a fancy French place for clothes-horses. It would be a double victory—she'd get spiffed up and stop scaring kids, she'd unload most of the money choking in her handbag.

Not all the perfumes of Paris could overcome the fish smell as Mrs Goffman entered the shop. Only her liveried chauffeur and that funeral car parked in front saved her from being tossed out on her ear. She gave the salesgirls, who sniffed usually just from snobbery, something real to sniff about!

'That coat!' she said, in a voice as military as Triminiuk's.

A salesgirl hid her nose in a useless frilly hankie and came at Mrs Goffman sideways. The coat was a Marlene Dietrich type—magenta. Mrs Goffman made a trade. The girl almost passed out.

'A Gloria Swanson hat—burn the coat, dollie, don't cling to the rag,' Mrs Goffman dismissed the salesgirl who was greenish and crampy-looking from the fish smell. 'Get me a flapper number. And a handbag too.' With one motion she dumped all her money on the counter. The salesgirl's eyes, sick as they had been, bugged with the proper respect money always got.

'I look like a big popsicle, eh Josef?' Mrs Goffman said to her chauffeur. If kids didn't get scared to death by this number, they were still in danger of laughing themselves to death looking at her.

'Take, take,' Mrs Goffman waved the girl onward to the pile of bills on the counter. 'Put what's left in my new bag, dollie.'

Without bitterness Mrs Goffman reflected how easy it was in America to buy everything you don't want.

She left the store, salespeople bowing to her right and to her left as if she were Queen Mary, gave them a queenly wave while her nose triumphantly recorded that in the air, wistful, fleeting, elusive as Chanel Number Five, was Rachel Street Fish.

VIII

Josef put down her arm-rest, adjusted a small reading-light over her newspaper—Sidney's style. Headlines shimmered in front of her eyes, and the usual faces—Khrushchev the hearty liar, Dulles's sour face set permanently in a 'no', Eisenhower with that puzzled look which meant if his press secretary didn't say something fast he was a goner. What was it Jimmy said? Everybody in Eisenhower's cabinet was a millionaire except for Martin Durkin and God Almighty. The headlines recorded imbecile explosions, tests in Siberia, Nevada. Sincere falseness in Ottawa, Washington, false sincerity in Moscow. Idiots! Suckers! At least Jimmy at the end *knew*: these crumbs would never know!

'Josef, go home the long way,' she said gently. Those French put their cemeteries right in the middle of the city—gray crosses stamped on the sky, cold stone saints, wreaths of dark artificial flowers. Silence was loudest near cemeteries.

What the heck was she doing going back up there anyways? Rachel Street was like a wonderful party she couldn't stand to see end. Six more days of nothing was coming.

'Josef, drive your slowest,' she requested.

Every stage in her kids' success mocked her on these trips home. Goffman buildings. Goffman businesses. The banks their money was in. The houses they'd lived in during their climb to the top of Westmount and the Ambassador's mansion. I dragged my feet, Mrs Goffman remembered with sadness, but I didn't interfere. A young Radical became an old dishrag! Good taste left a bad taste in her mouth.

In her small vanity mirror she made a John Foster Dulles face and laughed herself back into a better humour.

IX

The limousine passed the Mount Royal Hotel. Cabs lined up, people were running, some school kids tumbled out of a car and skipped giggling toward St Catherine Street. Mrs Goffman wanted to try her new outfit on a kid and see what the reaction would be. She still felt bad about frightening that young girl Tammy.

Brighten up, sister, she told herself, but the Mount Royal had done its damage already: Jimmy first saw Shirley at a Mount Royal New Year's Eve Frolic—he loved to tell about it, to begin with.

The Mount Royal was Jimmy's home ground, a perfect setting for his style. He had Sally Rossen with him that night—a Toronto deb type, gorgeous, crazy for Jimmy, hot and burning. They danced every dance, drank champagne, moved arm in arm through the ballroom, visiting parties in different rooms, Jimmy in terrific shape, gay, gallant, witty, full of life. Then he saw Shirley. Sally was out.

How his eyes lighted up when he talked about Shirley—her hair he said was like a quiet waterfall in total darkness; her black eyes with that heavy fringe of eyelashes skimmed over Jimmy; she was in white, bare shouldered, proud of her beautiful young full breasts, her sexy body, her slow slow walk. Elegant Jimmy lost his manners. Clumsy as an ox he bumped his way across the floor, leaving Sally standing all alone. Up went Jimmy's arm in that gesture all Montreal knew—Shirley's beauty was blinding, he couldn't look.

Shirley cut him dead.

Sucker! He should have quit! Shirley's lover said something nasty—Jimmy heard—about 'old enough to be your father'. Shirley giggled, leaned on her boy, Maxie, and left Jimmy standing just as he had left Sally! Don Giovanni, huh? Mrs Goffman thought in her agitation. Big shot lover? He couldn't quit.

'My dance, beautiful,' he said, almost chasing after her through the crowd. He gave the old flourish, poured on the charm.

'My card is filled,' Shirley said coldly; they had him.

Like a crack had appeared in a great building. He didn't fall apart then and there, where Westmount society surrounded him, where he was familiar, where his ways could get a gentle response. Later it started, at home, when she caught him in front of a mirror.

'Since when did you pull out grey hair, Jimmy?' she had asked. Jimmy didn't answer.

'Grey hair makes you look distinguished.'

'Distinguished, and old,' Jimmy said with a wink.

Lines on his face from laughing, character lines which made Jimmy the handsome guy he was, he couldn't stand them now. He wanted to rub everything out, be as young-looking as that pimply-faced Maxie who had the only woman who had ever denied Jimmy anything at all. Didn't his mother see Jimmy's reaction? He started to take out younger and younger girls—one was seventeen, not even out of high school! A photographer told him his left side was more handsome than his right, so the dope sat with his right side hidden, as if it had been burned! He sent Shirley flowers, pins, necklaces, phoned her, wired her—what a set-up for those two kids! Jimmy would spend a fortune on Shirley, but Maxie would spend the night!

Mrs Goffman smiled to herself: in a way—if Jimmy's end wasn't so horrible—there was justice in it. The most brilliant lawyer and financier in Montreal getting trimmed down to his BVDs by a couple of snot-nosed kids! Shirley had been sleeping with Maxie for four or five years, but not till her eighth date with Jimmy did she let him so much as peck her on the cheek. Don Giovanni?

Late one night Mrs Goffman had overheard a conversation that made her want to ring bells and blow whistles.

'Jimmy, you, getting married?' Sidney had said—he couldn't have been more shocked if Jimmy had grown sidecurls and turned Hassidic.

'I can't get it from her any way else,' Don Giovanni admitted.

Didn't she know he was going to get trimmed? But what did she care about money by that time? Life—a child—that was at stake, not Jimmy's lousy fortune. Marry even a prostitute for all Mrs Goffman cared by then—but get married. Why, when Marie the upstairs maid got pregnant, didn't Mrs Goffman hope one of her boys had done it? To hell with Westmount's ways! She knew. She had seen the truth by then. So who has to be the knocker-up, this chauffeur Josef!

'Drive more slowly,' she said savagely, thinking how many snot-nosed kids this overgrown squash of a driver must have already brought into the world.

Josef looked back at her, startled.

'Please, I mean,' she added.

A child—she was a lunatic on the subject. After the wedding she nagged, coaxed, threatened, whined. 'Kids, go home early.' 'Shirley, maybe you're late this month, eh, dollie?' Vulgar and rude and coarse—her father's line, Simon's, that's what the stakes were! Sidney was past praying for, she herself couldn't have kids. Everything was up to Jimmy. And he wanted a child too—that was the heartbreaking thing! Jimmy knew, saw, understood everything.

Mrs Goffman felt herself suffocating in the closed car. Her ears pulsed, her heart beat fast, she felt cold all over. Weakly, falteringly, she rolled down the window.

If only a child *had* come out of that marriage. Suffering was a man's lot in life. Everybody suffered, but not senselessly, like Jimmy. His suffering did nothing, made nothing, was worse than death. Noises made him jump. Coffee made him nervous. He began gobbling Sidney's pills. How could a hot-looking girl turn out so cold? He was repulsive, old, a mark, a fool—his nerve went.

Every bourgeois cliché that she as a Radical had scoffed at came thudding home—*you only live once*, what was more ghastly than that realization? *You're not getting any younger*, how that mocked Jimmy! What good was Mrs Goffman to her suffering son? Could she reverse her campaign to make him want a child? Could she destroy what he felt for Shirley just by telling him exactly what he knew anyway—that he was a cinch, a target, a bankroll, but feeling his age, and growing helpless?

Mrs Goffman began to cough, gasp, and with a great effort pushed her face close to the open window.

'Madam, what is it?' Josef said, slowing down.

'I'm all right,' she lied, 'don't stop.'

It was all as if life and time couldn't hold back their revenge. Shirley sneaked ties to Maxie, money, let him put things on Jimmy's charge accounts. Flagrant, open, Jimmy was Montreal's parlour-car joke. And Mrs Doba Goffman watched and waited, hoping hoping hoping.

Shirley never did bear Jimmy a child.

x

The limousine made a sudden swoop, a turn, a halt, then began its progress up the hill. Mrs Goffman craned her head, trying to get a last look at what wasn't Westmount. Her nose behaved like a pair of opera glasses after the opera, folding itself up, awaiting the next liberation. Streets were empty, windows heavily draped so you couldn't see a sign of movement. Closer to the Ambassador's house there were no sidewalks, black limousines sped out of hidden driveways. Like the one, Mrs Goffman thought, sickening.

What a terrible death! Her confident Jimmy, worrying about flat tires all the time, stopping the car a dozen times to make Josef check, or getting out himself. Nothing was ever wrong, only Jimmy's shot nerves—he was half-destroyed when he stepped into the fog on Summit Circle. A limousine crushed him against his rear bumper and finished the job! Upstairs in the Ambassador's mansion Mrs Goffman heard the smash and Jimmy's screams—horrible, horrible!

Mrs Goffman writhed, pinned her new hat against her ears, tears streaming from her eyes. Like a tiny boy Jimmy shrieked for her, screaming, screaming, and she ran into the cold dark mist, barefoot, in her nightgown, seeing nothing, hearing nothing but silence. That silence. Death's.

She'd screamed too—slapped at Josef, called him pig, ingrate, block, crook, shirker—why didn't he get out of the car instead of Jimmy? But now, when everything was past blaming, Mrs Goffman conceded the truth: Josef had more claim to life than Jimmy, much as she loved her son, great as his success had been.

She pulled wet terrified eyes away from the limousine floor and looked out at the houses on Summit Circle.

Right here! On this spot! She closed her eyes again and waited.

XI

You fake, she chided herself. A real Radical would never cry. What a way to louse up this new magenta outfit—streaming eyes, a shiny shnozzola! You'd think she'd spent her afternoon at a Yiddish tear-jerker.

As Josef turned into the driveway Mrs Goffman touched her sulking nose with a powder puff, dried her eyes, made her old face smile. When there was hope it was OK to despair, but now hope was gone, what was the point of it? She winked at herself.

Sidney's worried face peeked out from her heavy drapes, his wristwatch close to his bad eyes. Why depress Sidney? She'd jolly him up a little, tell him how ridiculous she looked carrying the fish, how she stunk up that ritzy dress shop good.

She shielded her eyes, sighed, smiled more broadly, seeing past Josef's shoulder Nuns' Island. It was for sale. A million bucks they wanted.

By rights, Mrs Goffman thought as she looked toward her door, they shouldn't sell it. Nuns should stay on an island.

NORMAN LEVINE · b. 1923

By a Frozen River

In the winter of 1965 I decided to go for a few months to a small town in northern Ontario. It didn't have a railway station—just one of those brown railway sidings, on the outskirts, with a small wooden building to send telegrams, buy tickets, and to get on and get off. A taxi was there meeting the train. I asked the driver to take me to a hotel. There was only one he would recommend, The Adanac. I must have looked puzzled. For he said,

'It's Canada spelled backwards.'

He drove slowly through snow-covered streets. The snow-banks by the sidewalk were so high you couldn't see anyone walking. Just the trees. He drove alongside a frozen river with a green bridge across it. Then we were out for a while in the country. The snow here had drifted so that the tops of the telegraph poles were protruding like fence posts. Then we came to the town—a wide main street with other streets going off it.

The Adanac was a three-storey wooden hotel on the corner of King and Queen. It had seen better times. Its grey-painted wooden verandah, with icicles on the edges, looked old and fragile. But the woodwork had hand-carved designs, and the white windows had rounded tops. Beside it was a new beer parlour.

Fifty years ago it was the height of fashion to stay at the hotel. It was then called the George. The resident manager told me this, in his office, after I paid a month's rent in advance. His name was Savage. A short, overweight man in his sixties, with a slow speaking voice, as if he was thinking what he was going to say.

He sat, neatly dressed, behind a desk, his grey hair crew-cut, and looked out of the large window at the snow-covered street. The sun was shining.

'Well,' he said slowly. 'It's an elegant day.'

His wife was a thin, tall woman with delicate features. She also hardly spoke. But would come into the office and sit, very upright, in a rocking chair near Mr Savage and look out of the window. The office connected with their three-room flat. It was filled with their possessions. A small, bronze crucifix was on the wall. Over the piano a large picture of the Pope. There were a few coloured photographs: a boy in uniform, children, and a sunset over a lake.

I rented the flat above. I had a room to sleep in, a room to write and read, and a kitchen with an electric stove and fridge. To get to them I would go up worn steps, along a wide, badly lit corridor—large tin pipes carried heat along the ceiling. But inside the rooms it was warm. They had radiators and double windows.

I unpacked. Then went to the supermarket, by the frozen river, and came back with various tins, fruit, and cheap cigars that said they were dipped in wine. I made myself some coffee, lit one of the thin cigars, and relaxed.

I saw a wooden radio on the side-table in the sitting-room. A battered thing. I had to put twenty-five cents in the back. That, according to a metal sign, gave me two hours' playing time. But that was only a formality. For the back was all exposed, and the twenty-five cents kept falling out for me to put through again.

Listening to the radio—I could only get the local station—the town sounded a noisy, busy place, full of people buying and selling and with things going on. But when I walked out, the first thing I noticed was the silence. The frozen, shabby side-streets. Hardly anything moving. It wasn't like what the radio made out at all. There was a feeling of apathy. The place seemed stunned by the snow piled everywhere.

I quickly established a routine. After breakfast I went out and walked. And came back, made some coffee, and wrote down whatever things I happened to notice.

This morning it was the way trees creak in the cold. I had walked by a large elm when I heard it. I thought it was the crunching sound my shoes made on the hard-packed snow. So I stopped. There was no wind, the branches were not moving, yet the tree was creaking.

In the late afternoon, I made another expedition outside. Just before it got dark, I found a small square. It began to snow. The few trees on the perimeter were black. The few bundled-up people walking slowly through the snow were black. And from behind curtained windows a bit of light, a bit of orange. There was no sound. Just the snow falling. I expected horses and sleighs to appear, and felt the isolation.

That evening I had company. A mouse. I saw it just before it saw me. I tried to hit it with a newspaper, but I missed. And as it ran it slipped and slithered on the linoleum. I was laughing. It ran behind the radiator. I looked and saw it between the radiator grooves where the dust had gathered. It had made a nest out of bits of fluff. I left food out for it. And in the evenings it would come out and run around the perimeter of the sitting-room, then go back behind the radiator.

Birds woke me in the morning. It seemed odd to see so much snow and ice and hear birds singing. I opened the wooden slot in the outside window and threw out some bread. Though I could hear the birds, I couldn't see them. Then they came—sparrows. They seemed to fly into their shadows as they landed on the snow. Then three pigeons. I went and got some more bread.

On the fourth day I met my neighbour across the hall. He rented the two rooms opposite. He wore a red lumberjack shirt and black lumberjack boots with the laces going high up. He was medium height, in his forties, with pleasant features. And he had short, red hair.

'Hi,' he said. And asked me what I was doing.

'Writing a book,' I said.

'Are you really writing a book?'

'Yes.'

'That must be very nice,' he said.

And invited me into his flat. It was the same as mine, except he didn't have a sitting-room. The same second-hand furniture, the used electric stove, the large fridge, the wooden radio.

I asked him what he did.

'I work in a small factory. Just my brother and me. We make canoes. Do you like cheese?'

'Yes,' I said.

He opened his fridge. It was filled with large hunks of an orange cheese.

'I get it sent from Toronto. Here, have some.'

I met the new occupants of the three rooms behind me next morning. I was going to the toilet. (There was one toilet, with bath, for all of us on the first floor. It was in the hall at the top of the stairs.) I opened the door and saw a woman sitting on the toilet, smoking a cigarette. She wasn't young. Her legs were close together. She said, 'Oh.' I said sorry and closed the door quickly. 'I'm sorry,' I said again, this time louder, as I walked away.

A couple of days later she knocked on my door and said she was Mrs Labelle and she was Jewish. She heard from Savage that I had a Jewish name. Was I Jewish? I said I was. She invited me back to meet her husband.

The people who rented these rooms usually didn't stay very long. So there was no pride in trying to do anything to change them. But Mrs Labelle had her room spotless. She had put up bright yellow curtains to hide the shabby window blinds. She had plastic flowers in a bowl on the table. And everything looked neat, and washed, even though the furniture was the same as I had.

Her husband, Hubert, was much younger. He looked very dapper. Tall, dark hair brushed back, neatly dressed in a dark suit and tie and a clean white shirt. He had a tripod in his hand and said he was going out to work.

'Savage told us you were a writer. I have started to write my life story—What the photographer saw—I tell all. You wouldn't believe the things that have happened to me.'

His wife said that the mayor was trying to get them out of town. 'He told the police that we need a licence. It's because he owns the only photograph store here. He's afraid of the competition. We're not doing anything illegal. I knock on people's doors and ask them if they want their picture taken at home. He's very good,' she said, 'especially with children.'

After that Mrs Labelle came to the door every day. She knew all the other occupants. And would tell me little things about them. 'He's a very hard worker,' she said about the man who made canoes. 'He doesn't drink at all.' Then she told me about the cleaning woman, Mabel. 'She only gets fifteen dollars a week. Her

husband's an alcoholic. She's got a sixteen-year-old daughter—
she's pregnant. I'm going to see her this afternoon and see if I can
help. Be careful of Savage. He looks quiet, but I saw him using a
blackjack on a drunk from the beer parlour who tried to get into
the hotel at night. He threw him out in the snow. Dragged him by
the feet. And Mrs Savage helped.' She complained of the noise at
night. 'There's three young waitresses. Just above me. They have
boys at all hours. I don't blame them. But I can't sleep. I can't wash
my face. It's nerves,' she said.

Then I began to hear Mr Labelle shouting at her. 'God damn
you. Leave me alone. Just leave me alone.' It went on past
midnight.

Next day, at noon, she knocked on the door. She was smiling.

'I found a place where you can get Jewish food.'

'Where?'

'Morris Bischofswerder. He's a furrier. Up on the main street.'

I went to the furrier. He had some skins hanging on the wall.
And others were piled in a heap on the floor.

'Do you sell food?' I said.

'What kind of food?'

'Jewish food.'

He looked me over.

He was below middle height, stocky, with a protruding belly.
A dark moustache, almost bald, but dark hair on the sides. He was
neatly dressed in a brown suit with a gold watch chain in his vest
pocket. He was quite a handsome man, full lips and dark eyes.
And from those eyes I had a feeling that he had a sense of fun.

'Where are you from?' he asked. 'The West?'

'No, from England.'

'All right, come.'

He led me through a doorway into the back and from there into
his kitchen. And immediately there was a familiar food smell,
something that belonged to my childhood. A lot of dried mush-
rooms, on a string, like a necklace, hung on several nails. He
showed me two whole salamis and some loose hot dogs.

'I can let you have a couple pounds of salami and some hot
dogs until the next delivery. I have it flown in once a month from
Montreal.' He smiled. 'I also like this food. Where are you staying?'

'At the Adanac.'

His wife came in. She was the same size as Mr Bischofswerder but thinner, with grey hair, a longish thin nose, deep-set very dark eyes, the hollows were in permanent shadow, and prominent top teeth.

'He's from England,' he told her.

'I come from Canada,' I said quickly. 'But I live in England. The place I live in England doesn't have snow in winter. So I've come back for a while.'

'You come all the way from England for the snow?'

'Yes.'

They both looked puzzled.

'I like winters with snow,' I said.

'What have you got in England?'

'Where I live—rain.'

'Have you got a family?' Mr Bischofswerder said, changing the subject. 'Is your mother and father alive?'

'My mother and father lived in Ottawa, but they moved to California eight years ago.'

'I bet they don't miss Canadian winters,' Mrs Bischofswerder said.

'We have a married daughter in Montreal and five grand-children,' he said proudly, 'four boys and one girl.'

'Sit down,' Mrs Bischofswerder said. 'I was just going to make some tea.'

And she brought in a chocolate cake, some pastry that had poppy seeds on top, and some light egg cookies.

'It's very good, isn't it?' she said.

'I haven't had food like this since I was a boy,' I said.

'Why are you so thin?' she said. '*Eat, Eat.*' And pushed more cookies in my direction.

'I wonder if you would come to shul next Friday,' Mr Bis-chofswerder said.

My immediate reaction was to say no. For I haven't been in a synagogue for over twenty years. But sitting in this warm kitchen with the snow outside. Eating the food. Mrs Bischofswerder making a fuss. It brought back memories of my childhood. And people I once knew.

'I'll come,' I said.

'Fine,' he said. 'If you come here around four o'clock we'll go together. It gets dark quickly.'

That night the Labelles quarrelled until after two. Next day, at noon, Mrs Labelle knocked on the door. 'He didn't turn up. This woman was holding her children all dressed up. I told her to send them to school.'

'Is this the first time?'

'No. It's only got bad now. He's an alcoholic.'

She began to weep. I asked her inside. She was neatly dressed in dark slacks and a small fur jacket. 'My sisters won't have me. They say I've sown my wild oats.'

'Would you like some coffee?'

'Thanks. We had a house in Toronto. I have in storage lots of furniture—a fur coat—real shoes—not shoes like this. And where would you see a woman of my age going around knocking on doors? I'm sure I'm going to be killed. He calls me a witch. I found a piece of paper with a phone number. And a name—Hattie. I called up and said to leave my husband alone. I found another piece of paper. It said Shirley. They're all over him. He's a good-looking guy. And when he's working—these women are alone with him. You know—'

That afternoon, while I was writing, the phone went. It was Mrs Labelle.

'I'm in someone's house waiting for him to come and take the picture. Can you see if he's in. He hasn't turned up.'

I knocked on their door. Mr Labelle was sitting on the settee with a middle-aged man in a tartan shirt, and they were both drinking beer out of small bottles.

I said she was on the phone.

'Say you haven't seen me,' he said.

'Yes,' the other man said. 'Say you haven't seen him.'

But Labelle came after me and stood by the open door. 'Why don't you just say hello?' I said.

He went in and I could hear him saying, 'I'm not drunk. I'm coming over.' He hung up and closed the door.

'I'll tell you,' he said. 'Man to man. I'll be forty-one next month. And she's fifty-eight. We've been married fifteen years. I didn't know how old she was when we married. Then she was seven months in a mental home. I used to see her every day. At two. I had to get my job all changed around. But I'll tell you what. I knocked up a woman two years ago. And she heard about it. The child died. She can't have children. She won't give me some rein. I've had her for fifteen years. Don't worry,' he said. 'I won't leave her. You may hear us at night. I shout. I'm French Canadian. But I'll look after her.'

He went back and got his camera and tripod. And he and the other man went down the stairs.

Ten minutes later she rang up again.

'Is he gone?'

'Yes,' I said.

That evening around nine, there was a gentle knock at the door. It was Mrs Labelle, in a red dressing-gown. 'He's asleep,' she said. 'Thank you very much. He hasn't eaten anything. I make special things. But he won't eat.'

It was quiet until eleven that night. I could hear them talking. Then he began to raise his voice. 'Shut up. God damn it. Leave me alone. You should have married a Jewish businessman. You would have been happy.'

On Friday afternoon I put on a clean white shirt and tie and a suit. And went to call on Mr Bischofswerder. He was dressed, neatly, in a dark winter coat and a fur hat. We walked about four blocks. Then he led me into what I thought was a private house but turned out to be the synagogue. It was very small. Around twenty-four feet square and twenty feet high. But though it was small, it was exact in the way the synagogues were that I remembered. There was a wooden ark between a pair of tall windows in the east wall. A few steps, with wooden rails, led to the ark. The Ten Commandments, in Hebrew, were above it. A low gallery extended around the two sides. In the centre of the ceiling hung a candelabra with lights over the reading desk. There were wooden bench seats. Mr Bischofswerder raised one, took out a prayer book, and gave the prayer book to me.

'Shall we start?' he said.

'Aren't we going to wait for the others?'

'There are no others,' he said.

And he began to say the prayers to himself. Now and then he would run the words out aloud so I could hear, in a kind of sing-song that I remembered my father doing. I followed with my eyes the words. And now and then I would say something so he would hear.

I had long forgotten the service, the order of the service. So I followed him. I got up when he did. I took the three steps

backwards when he did. But most of the time we were both silent.
Just reading the prayers.
    Then it was over. And he said,
    'Good Shabbes.'
    'Good Shabbes,' I said.
    On the way back, through the snow-covered streets, it was
freezing. Mr Bischofswerder was full of enthusiasm.
    'Do you realize,' he said 'this is the first time I've had someone
in the shul with me at Friday night for over three years.'

For the next seven Friday nights and Saturday mornings I went
with Mr Bischofswerder to the synagogue. We said our prayers in
silence.
    Then I went back with him to his warm house. And to the
enormous Sabbath meal that Mrs Bischofswerder had cooked. Of
gefilte fish with chrane, chicken soup with mandlen, chicken with
tzimmes, compote, tea with cookies. And we all talked. They
wanted to know about England. I told them about the English
climate, about English money, English society, about London,
Fleet Street, the parks, the pubs. How I lived by the sea and a
beautiful bay but hardly any trees.
    And he told me how the trappers brought him skins that he sent
on to Montreal. That he was getting a bit old for it now. 'Thank
God I can still make a living.' He told me of the small Jewish
community that was once here. 'In 1920 when we came there
were ten families. By the end of the last war it was down to three.
No new recruits came to take the place of those who died or
moved away. When we go,' said Mr Bischofswerder, 'all that will
be left will be a small cemetery.'
    'Have some more cookies,' his wife said, pushing a plateful
towards me. 'You have hardly touched them. You won't get fat.
They're light. They're called nothings.'

Mrs Labelle knocked on my door. She looked excited. 'I'm selling
tickets,' she said. 'The town's running a sweepstake—when will
the frozen river start to move? Everyone's talking about it. I've
already sold three books. Will you have one? You can win five
hundred dollars.'
    'How much are they?'
    'Fifty cents.'

'I'll have one,' I said.

'Next time you go to the supermarket,' she said, 'you'll see a clock in the window. There's a wire from the clock to the ice in the river. As soon as the ice starts to move—the clock stops. And the nearest ticket wins.'

She gave me my ticket.

'Good luck,' she said. And kissed me lightly on a cheek.

She looked, I thought, the happiest I had seen her. My ticket said: March 26th, 08:16:03.

That night I noticed the mouse had gone. No sign of it anywhere. It was raining. The streets were slushy and slippery. But later that night the water froze. And next morning when the sun came out it was slush again. The snow had started to shrink on the roofs; underneath the edges I could see water moving. I walked down to the river. It was still frozen, but I saw patches of blue where before it was all white. Crows were flapping over the ice with bits of straw in their beaks. The top crust of the river had buckled in places. And large pieces creaked as they rubbed against each other. Things were beginning to break up. It did feel like something was coming to an end here.

Next day, just before noon, Mrs Labelle came to the door. She looked worried. 'Savage told us we have to leave. I went to see him with our week's rent in advance. But he said he didn't want it. He said we were making too much noise at night. The waitresses make noise, but he doesn't mind them. I don't know where we'll go. We've been in Sudbury, in Timmins, in North Bay—'

'It's OK,' Mr Labelle said, coming to the door. 'We'll be all right,' he said to her gently. And started to walk her back toward their door. Then he called out to me. 'If we don't see you, fellah, good luck.'

'Same to you,' I said.

'But where will we go Hubert?' Mrs Labelle said, looking up to his face.

'There's lots of places,' he answered. 'Now we got some packing to do.'

After the Labelles had gone, it was very quiet. I had got the reminders I wanted of a Canadian winter. I had filled up three notebooks. It was time that I left. I went down to the office and told this to Mr Savage. He suggested that I stay until the ice started to move.

But I left before it did.

I took a light plane, from the snow-covered field with a short runway. From the air, for a while, I could see the small town. But soon it was lost in a wilderness of snow, trees, and frozen lakes.

CHAVA ROSENFARB · b. 1923

The Greenhorn

'Why are you standing there dumb as a post? The cat got your
tongue? If you want the job, fine. If not, get moving. These days
there're plenty others looking for work.'

That's how the foreman speaks to Baruch while dialing a
number.

'Yes I want the job.'

The foreman doesn't hear. He's talking into the mouthpiece.
His English sounds like a juicy Polish Yiddish. He finishes his call,
puts down the receiver, and scrutinizes Baruch.

'Well?'

'Yes.'

'All right. Punch the clock. Your card's for ten o'clock.'

Reaching down under a counter improvised from rough
plywood, the foreman removes a pen from behind his ear and
starts to write.

'How do you sign yourself?'

Baruch gives his name.

'How old are you?'

'Forty-one.'

'Any wife, children?'

'I had, once.'

'All right. Go punch your card.' Baruch stares, not understanding. 'Punch your card. There, under the clock . . . haven't
you ever punched a card?'

'No, never.'

The foreman walks with him to the clock and punches the card.

'Your number's sixty-one. Your card stays here. You punch it four times a day. What did you do before this?'

'I just arrived three weeks ago.'

'I mean over there.'

'In Warsaw I was a typesetter for a Polish newspaper.'

'Well go hang up your coat. I'll put you on pressing. Have you got any idea how a press works?'

'None.'

'All right then . . . François!'

The foreman's voice cuts through the noise of machines while somewhere in the depths of the shop there's a shimmer of red shirt. A thin fair-haired youth emerges from among the racks of coats. He looks about sixteen. His hair clings to his damp forehead while he wipes the sweat from his face.

'*Montrez garçon* pressing,' the foreman points to Baruch.

Baruch smiles and follows François through the shop, past the racks of finished coats and rows of clattering machines. Here and there some of the workers look up with an indifferent stare while others regard him with frank curiosity. The indifferent glances come from the men. The curious ones, from the women. The men at the sewing machines are middle aged; most of them bald. The women are nearly all young and pretty. French. Take that little one who's sewing on buttons. She has such nice sympathetic eyes. And her curly hair is fine and so transparent that the light from the lamp shines right through it.

But now they've reached the place. Eight presses are arranged in a square. In front of each one stands a tousled half-naked youth. Clouds of steam rise from the press and the heat pummels Baruch.

'Speak English?' François asks, smiling.

'No, French. A little.'

'Are you French then?' François wonders.

'No, but I lived in Paris.'

'Ah, Paris!' Baruch feels the respect in the other's voice.

The work, it seems, is not too hard. One just has to lay out the pockets and lapels on a board and then lower the press. The first few pieces aren't very good, François tells him, but he'll learn. Of course he'll learn. If only it wasn't so unbearably hot. The fans in the windows are humming—surely there ought to be a breeze, even a little one. So why is it so hard to breathe? One has to take off one's tie, unbutton one's shirt and roll up the sleeves. Maybe it will be more comfortable that way. But in a little while Baruch feels the sweat running from his ears down to his neck. His shirt sticks to him and ribbons of moisture tickle his back. He'll get used to it, he tells himself—it's all a matter of habit, but a thousand hammers are hammering inside his head and his legs are buckling under him.

A bell? Why the sudden ringing of a bell? Like magic all the machines suddenly stop. The shop catches its breath in the momentary silence. Of course, it's the lunch break. Twelve o'clock. Baruch stands at his machine feeling lost and watching the others as they hurry past. Nobody pays any attention to him. And then, from nowhere, a pair of warm eyes appears. The girl who sews buttons is beside him.

'*Comment ça va?*'

For the first time it seems to him that Canadian French possesses all the charms in the world. He smiles at her, at the same time feeling that his smile is foolish and out of place.

'*Vous êtes Parisien—n'est ce pas?*'

How does she know? Baruch wonders.

'Yes, well not exactly,' he stammers, and tells her he only lived in Paris for a year.

'Oh, as a tourist!'

'No, as a DP.'

'Oh.' She gives him a questioning smile and he guesses that she has no idea what that means.

'Have you punched your card yet?'

'No.'

'So come on.'

He follows her to the clock and puts his card in upside down.

'No, not that way.' She takes it from him and does it properly. She has small white hands and they look even whiter against the bright red of her painted nails. Her smile is friendly.

'Don't you go home for lunch?'

'I have no home.'

'So where do you sleep? On the street?'

'I have a room. It's rented. But I don't have a home.'

She finds that funny, bursts into laughter and gives him a playful slap on the back.

'Let's go eat. You can get a Coke outside at the buffet. *Bon appétit.*'

He watches her walk down the length of the shop to her table. Her high-heeled shoes strike the floor with a cheerful wooden sound. Her white nylon blouse trembles against her skin and the big flowers of her colourful skirt are like a bouquet, alive and dancing against her legs. The girl possesses a carefree naïve joyousness and Baruch suddenly feels the heavy and oppressive burden inside himself.

Baruch looks around the shop. Here and there someone sits at a machine absorbed in eating.

A group of older Jews has gathered under the window to talk. The smoke of their cigarettes hovers above their heads. On the other side of the room girls and youths sprawl across heaped-up bolts of cloth, whistling and laughing. Those are the French. Why, thinks Baruch, doesn't a Jewish girl approach me? He looks around. Where are the Jewish girls? Are they everywhere else then, except here in this gloomy shop? Do they work in offices? Or study? Or are they at home, the mothers of little Jewish children?

He thinks of his own two children. They're dressed in their best clothes, seated on a high sofa. They're gazing into the photographer's camera waiting for the little bird to appear.

Baruch walks slowly to the window. Nearby, on a long table, the *Forward** is spread out and a young man, bespectacled, dark, and unshaven, looks up at Baruch.

'Is it today's?' asks Baruch.

The young man nods and goes on reading his newspaper. Baruch looks at the headlines and listens to a group of Jews arguing about politics. A Jew in a green sportshirt is shaking his index finger at his listeners.

'You have to be an American to know who MacArthur is. No small thing, MacArthur! A folk hero! What do you know about MacArthur? Listen . . .' and he seizes a listener by the sleeve. But the latter, a fellow with a pointed nose and small merry eyes, laughs and interrupts him.

'Listen, shmissen! When it comes to knowing who the real folk heroes are, better ask us greenhorns! Believe me, mister, the greatest folk hero would be a lot greater if you made him a head shorter. And you'd better stop your song and dance about being an American.'

---

*Jewish daily newspaper published in New York.

'Well then, did I offend your highness by suggesting one ought to be an American?' says the other as he nervously winds his pocket watch.

'God forbid you should offend me! You must really think we greenhorns know nothing. Believe me, you old-timers could learn a lot from us.'

'I'd like to know what, for instance?'

'Little things—such as a bit of human kindness, and a touch of friendliness.'

'Is that all? Not more, not less?'

'You should know,' interrupts a second newcomer, 'that if you had come to us with what we lived through, we would have welcomed you with more kindness.'

One of the listeners sighs, 'For God's sake when will there ever be peace between the old-timers and the newcomers?'

'When Messiah comes,' smiles the fellow with the merry eyes, 'that's when.'

'Do you imagine they'll give the Messiah a better welcome than they gave us? After all, he'll be a greenhorn too.'

'Their Messiah has already come. They don't need anything more.'

'Why are you talking such nonsense?' The anger of the Jew in the green shirt suddenly explodes: 'Of course, as you say, my Messiah must have already come. I've only slaved away forty years of my life at the sewing machine. Forty years! And I'm still at the same stage as you. What do you want from my life? Did I ever take anything away from you, do I owe you something? So what if I like it here in this country . . . what's it to you? You don't like it? So go back where you come from.'

At this there's an uncomfortable silence. The crowd slowly dissolves. Anger and resentment linger in the air.

For the first time someone notices Baruch.

'You're new?'

'Yes.'

'Where are you from?'

'From Paris.'

'A Parisian?'

'No, from Warsaw.'

'Were you in Russia?'

'No, in a camp.'

'Did you meet anyone from Vilna?'
'After the war.'
'Not in the camp?'
'No, not in camp.'
'Did you ever hear of a family called Zlotnik?'
'No, never.'
A new circle forms around them and someone asks, 'Well now, if you're from Warsaw, where in Warsaw did you live?'
'On Krachmalna Street.'
'I'm from Otvotsk. Do you know Otvotsk?'
'What a question—of course.'
'I had a cigarette kiosk on the main street.'
Cigarettes! Baruch is suddenly seized with a desire to smoke. He leaves the group and goes looking for his jacket. He lights a cigarette and inhales with pleasure.
And suddenly here she is again, the little French girl with the warm eyes. A kind of restlessness stirs in him.
'Give me a cigarette!' Her red lips smile. He holds out the package of cigarettes, she takes one and her mouth is close to his. A pleasant coolness flows from her fingers. He's drawn to the happy carefreeness of this girl.
'Did you enjoy it?' she asks as she sits down on a nearby table.
'What?'
'What do you mean what? Your lunch.'
'Oh lunch. Yes, I enjoyed it.'
'Tell me something about Paris. A whole year in Paris! *Mon dieu*, some people have all the luck!'
He looks at her legs dangling from the table. He can see the fine blonde hairs through her nylons.
'About Paris?'
'Yes, Paris.'
Suddenly, the girl disappears. He sees himself in the filthy room of a Paris hotel. He remembers the running around, the reporting to police, the weeks and months of waiting for the 'Joint'*, his worries about papers, visas, booking passage.
'Well, Paris is a beautiful city.'
'Really? Paris is my dream. What did you see there?'
'The Eiffel tower.'

---

*American Joint Distribution Committee. A relief organization founded in 1914 that rescued Jews and assisted displaced persons after the Second World War.

'The Eiffel tower? Did you go to the top?'

He remembers taking a walk on a bright Saturday afternoon. The Trocadéro was bathed in light. The fountains spouted streams of clear water. He didn't have the money to buy a ticket to go to the top of the Eiffel tower.

'Surely you walked along the Champs Elysées?'

'Yes, of course.'

He recalls the magnificent Elysian fields where he walked one summer evening—and how a figure approached, making his heart stand still. At the entrance to the Metro a woman was standing . . . his wife. She had a valise in her hand and was looking around uncertainly. He knew it couldn't be her. He had seen her go to the *umshlagplatz*. Yet he held his breath and broke into a run. She turned around and two strange eyes full of fear met his. . . .

'And how do the women there dress? Elegant, right?'

The girl gazes into his face as if she could read in it all the marvels of Paris—'Why don't you answer? Go ahead, tell me!' And she bursts into laughter, 'Are you a good judge of women's clothes? Somehow you don't look the type . . . I suppose you went every night to the theatre or the opera?'

He remembers the few concerts he went to in Paris, and the nagging loneliness that greeted his homecoming. His wife used to play the violin. When they were herded into the ghetto, she dropped her violin and it was run over by a truck.

'There are wonderful night clubs in Paris, is that true?' The girl is looking at him with her eyes full of longing, 'They drink champagne there like water—there's music—and everyone dances in half-darkness,' she leans towards him, narrowing her eyes, but his desire for her is gone.

'And tell me,' she's not tired of quizzing him, 'surely you visited other countries too?'

He nods.

'As for me, I don't know anything except Montreal and Rivière de Prairie where I was born. If you only knew how much I love to hear about travel in other countries.' Her face becomes childlike and dreamy. He would like to pat her on the head like a little girl. 'So where else have you been? Tell me!'

'In Poland. I was born there in a city called Warsaw.'

'Oh that's far. Warsaw! Did you love Warsaw?'

'Once, long ago, I did.'

'And now?'

'Now I have no feeling for Warsaw.'

'Why? Well, maybe you've been away from it too long.'

'No. I'm still there.'

'What do you mean?'

'My childhood is there and my youth is there, and the dearest things I possessed are there. It's all there, and it's all gone.'

'I don't understand a word you're saying.'

'How can you understand? You were born in Rivière de Prairie.'

'Never mind that stuff. Just tell me about all the places you've been to.'

'I was in Czechoslovakia and Austria. In Germany. Italy too.'

'Jesus Mary! What a world you've seen. Were you rich? I guess you must have been one of the richest men in the world.'

'Actually one of the poorest.'

'A merchant, eh?'

'No, a DP.'

'I don't understand.'

'In English it means "displaced person".'

'Oh, a displaced person! That's what I am too.' And she gives a full-throated laugh.

Her voice is so heart-warming and young. How long it is since he heard such laughter, but he can't laugh along with her. He can't even smile. All at once he feels out of place and anxious. He turns his back to the girl and strides to the door. At the exit, behind the improvised counter, the foreman is drinking a bottle of Coke.

'You there, come over here.'

Baruch's heart leaps. Once another authoritative voice called him in just such a tone.

The foreman eyes him coldly. Another once eyed him that way. He has the distinct impression that this meeting is a repetition of others. . . . Yes, he's in the camp; the selection is imminent, he's in for it. He hears a voice:

'You there, come here!'

In front of him he sees the Jewish kapo. A fist is raised and comes down on his back. He falls into the mud.

'Get up, you'll be cleaning the toilets!' And then it happens that Baruch is overcome with love for the fist that just threw him down.

He's ready to kiss it with gratitude for saving his life.

Well then, he hears the foreman's ironic voice, 'How do you like the job?'

Baruch wakes from his trance—this isn't the camp. This is Canada, the blessed land of freedom.

'I've already told you, I like it.'

The foreman stands up and bangs on the table with his Coke bottle.

'You already *told* me, eh? The question is whether I like *you*, the gentleman with the manicured nails! You've got some nerve!'

Energetically he pulls from under the counter the pieces Baruch finished in the few hours he's worked here; with fussy hands he arranges them on the table. Inquisitive workers holding sandwiches and drinks gather around.

The foreman surveys them and yells self-righteously.

'Nice work, eh? You've spoiled a couple of dozen pockets and lapels.'

Baruch defends himself: 'I told you I had no pressing experience!'

'Again *you* told *me*, eh? All you do is keep *telling* me. Maybe next you'll tell me my job, eh?'

'I don't know what you want from me.'

'He doesn't know what I want from him? Do you hear that, eh? He ruins a few dozen pockets and lapels and the world owes him a living, did you ever hear such a thing? For the last time, I'm asking you do you want the job or not?'

'Yes,' answers Baruch carefully.

'So get this, I'm the boss here, not you. You have to do what I tell you, and do it the way I want. If not, get out.'

Having said this the foreman calms down. Baruch feels his fists clench. With one stride he's in front of the counter, his hot face hard against that of the foreman.

'Don't ever talk to me like that, do you hear!'

But the foreman's eyes have already lost their harshness. He pushes Baruch away mildly, unpacks his smoked meat sandwich and bites into it. Baruch still feels his anger rising and repeats: 'You're not to speak to me that way! This is a free country, understand?'

The foreman goes on chewing, shrugs, and smiles to the little group around him.

Crazy . . .

The others smile knowingly.

'You're not the boss over my life, do you hear? I'm a human being the same as you . . .' Baruch's voice becomes louder and louder and at the same time he feels more and more helpless. 'You're not going to curse me, no! I've had enough of cursing.'

'So go to hell!' laughs the foreman. 'Did you ever hear such talk?' And turning to the others, 'I should talk to him through a silk handkerchief no less. Who do you think you are anyway, you greenhorn? And where do you think you are? At one of Bronfman's receptions? This is a shop, not a salon.'

'Yes a shop,' Baruch's blood is still boiling, 'but a modern shop, not one from a hundred years ago! Those curses may have suited those times, but not any more!'

'You want me to use modern curses? I'm just an old-fashioned foreman.'

'But we're modern workers. We aren't going to allow idiots like you to insult us, we have unions.'

The workers, who all this time are standing around listening, suddenly burst into laughter. One of them gives Baruch a friendly slap on the back.

'This isn't the old country, comrade.'

Another adds with derision: 'This one is really a greenhorn from greenhorn land!'

Baruch feels lost. He's alone in a strange world. Around him people are discussing union matters and wages. The foreman is eyeing him with a mocking expression. He unwraps another sandwich and bites into it. Baruch feels humiliated and wipes the sweat from his face with a dirty kleenex. He doesn't know where to hide.

The bell rings and the workers, still chattering, punch the clock one by one. Suddenly the little French girl is at his side.

'Have a chiclet,' and she stuffs a chiclet into his mouth. Her fingers feel cool and fragrant against his lips.

The foreman yells 'François!'

The skinny youth with the tousled hair appears.

'*Montrez garçon* pressing. Good pressing! Remember, if it's not, may the devil take you, blockhead!'

François nods and smiles, 'Okay boss!' and to Baruch, 'Follow me.'

Baruch longs to flee but the foreman is smiling at him. 'Why are you standing there like a dummy with your eyes popping? Go on, punch your card!' The foreman's voice is fatherly and forgiving.

Baruch goes to punch his card. This time he gets it right, and now he's in front of the press once more. The heat hits him in the face and once again the sweat runs down his back in rivulets, the fans hum and the machines pound rhythmically.

The little French girl is busy sewing buttons somewhere in the depths of the coat racks. Baruch chews his gum. Its sweetness melts in his mouth and flows through his body bringing peace and calm to his entire being.

Translated from the Yiddish by Miriam Waddington

MONIQUE BOSCO · b. 1927

The Old Woman's Lamentations on Yom Kippur

Day of Atonement, when I asked nothing but to meditate, repent.

Day of Atonement, Remembrance Day. They set aside whole days like this for us to clear up our bad accounts, to feel remorse and regret. On this day of silence thunder made a hellish racket all the same, on this September day. I don't even know any more what it was I wanted to forget, erase, blot out, by making this artificial fast so I could be absolved, forgiven.

But I was thirsty.

I did drink, just little sips at first, then big gulps. Once I'd taken a drink—broken the rule of abstinence—my guilt made me ashamed, so I ate too, just to relieve my pangs of anxiety. For a week now I've been scared of these attacks of weakness that come over me and shake me up inside.

Everything has been difficult since . . . since when? To say everything has always been difficult would be more like it.

This tremendous tiredness. I'm getting up. I'm going to get up. I do get up, then crawl right back again under the thick ba-ba-blankets. One more try and . . . I'm senile, you say? Sure, I don't deny it. Age has got nothing to do with it. Neither has the weather. 'Doctor, would you like me to describe my symptoms?' He actually seems to be listening. That's enough to make me keep quiet. I have no idea any more whether I'd want to be like other people, all those people wandering around all over the world. Look at them, energetically coming and going, charging around in sub-ways and buses, criss-crossing the whole island from dawn to dusk. No sooner are these hordes settled in front of the TV, to watch their game or their 'great film', than other hordes start coming out of the woodwork—a different type altogether—full of vitality for going dancing, or gambling, or knocking themselves out all night at porno shows, or simply getting ready to take over at the head of the class, or from yesterday's promotion. Ah! the handsome mahogany desks that have to be freshly polished for the morning!

I feel dizzy, my head is spinning. All these organized people, with their union cards and their daily routines of thinking about what's best. I myself, for months now, for years, have been unemployed.

That, too, has been taken away from me, that one comforting alibi. Comforting for the rest of them, obviously. That's why, when they'd ask about me, I used to make a big show of announcing grandly, 'I'm working, you know. Full time.'

What's to say from now on? 'I'm unemployed. Full time.'

Full time, that's for sure. I have all the time in the world to get upset about the state of the earth, the planet, to take inventory of the disasters, floods, plagues, outbreaks of cholera, that are claim-ing new victims—and that's not to mention AIDS. This way I'll never be idle. I'll make myself a bunch of files on everything. If I had anyone to talk to, I'd be able to provide them with exact references, with up-to-date figures and statistics on the entire universe. It's fabulous, believe me, what goes on. I've got a passion for everything, now that there's never any passion to interrupt my sleep. I sleep all the time, since I can no longer sleep snuggled up, once in a while, beside a living body.

'You're at least eating properly?'

This doctor hears nothing, apparently. I hate the way he looks as much as his voice, when he inspects me this way, skulking behind his white coat. What does he see? My legs, like chicken legs?—one of their famous 'barnyard' chickens, one that wasn't stuffed full of hormones, but scratched frantically in the gravel, crazy with hunger. My arms? Let's not talk about them. Sometimes, when I can't sleep, I get a strange feeling that I've grown old all of a sudden, and find myself rattling around in my casket. Still, very nice that I should have a right to a real pine casket for my 'final resting-place'. I wonder what they'll invent, should it take me a long time, that will be 'durable and economical'. Stainless steel? Sheet metal? I ought to look into that. They're going to make fun of me again. 'Old lady, what's it to you—when, or what kind of saucepan we cook your goose in?' They're right, I don't care. Maybe they've salvaged the old crematoriums, who knows? They let on there was never any such thing.

But there I have to stop.

I dread weeping my eyes out, letting myself stir up the past, raking through the coals and ashes.

My old grandfather, the one on my father's side, the Polish side, when yet one more affliction would strike them, he didn't hesitate to spread ashes all over his face, his clothes. To let out—in public—the most ghastly blood-curdling shrieks. Nowadays we're ashamed of those old people. I miss them. I can't stand the old women my age—the ones of my own generation—with no sense of shame, no religion, yet still terrified of God and the devil. Yes, in the old days they had staying power, something to hold onto. I should have worn a corset, I should have, I should.

He persists: 'Are you really eating properly, Madam?' Don't you know I'm on 'welfare', as they call it? Naturally, I have to watch every penny. I save coupons for 'bargains'. I walk, doctor, regularly, to work up an appetite. I roam the aisles of Steinberg's for hours, keeping an eye out for the stupendous moment when the 'bargains' show up. I never miss one of them. Just try and make a balanced diet when, purely to economize I can assure you, I buy a slightly limp bunch of celery-hearts, or a not-too-fresh cauliflower. The other people go by. They dodge in and out, glide past, bump into me, sometimes they excuse themselves for jostling me—but I can tell that I'm annoying them, there with my little shopping bag that's still good, even though it's been folded a thousand times. As if I'd buy a new one just to please them. Yes, I deliberate over everything, I calculate. I add and add again. No matter what I do, it's thought out, and it's not my fault I've come to this. But the hardest of all is not 'this'.

The hardest of all

Sorrow hidden in the heart, the pit that hides 'way down in the heart of the juiciest peach

The hardest of all is, quite simply, growing old

Where the keynote is less

I see less, I hear less, my hands tremble so much they can't even manage to give a gentle, reassuring little pat to the cheek or the hand of a child.

'Grandmother, why do you have such big teeth?'

The way he used to laugh, little Samuel, when we'd play Little Red Riding Hood together.

He was four then, and I was forty.

Today I'm a hundred, for sure. Pointless to add up the number of years, that's the way I feel, in my bones. A hundred years.

One Hundred Years of Solitude.

'For they are everyone and I am alone,' said the Underground Man. And yesterday when, just to spoil myself a bit, I went out to take a walk up and down Sherbrooke Street—a nice long tour, all the way from Guy to Peel—I got the shock of my life. It was too hot for this time of year. But I was wearing my suit anyway, or, I should say the ex-suit of my cousin Zelda, to be more precise. Zelda's a 'tightwad', but the things she buys for her 'affairs', things that she wants to 'last', as she says, she pays a bundle for. After ten years with this hound's-tooth outfit, Zelda'd had enough of it and handed it down to me. And I wear it whenever I'm really down in the dumps, or for special occasions. Say what you like, having expensive clothes really sets you up. I get the feeling that people bump into me less, and sometimes even absent-minded young people make room for me. Anyway, I was wearing my suit and doing some very careful window-shopping. I was taking in every detail of each display: porcelain from China or Limoges; antiques—easy to call them antiques, they're hardly ever, at the outside, as old as I am; furs: magnificent minks—grey, silver, white. I love Sherbrooke Street—not a price tag in sight to risk spoiling our contemplation. I find that discreet, tasteful. On the other side of the street was the Museum. I wasn't sure whether to cross or not. A tour of the Museum might have been pleasant, and it's free one day a week. But I didn't have enough courage to go and ask what day. So I continued on the same sidewalk. In front of the Ritz I hesitated again. It looked like they'd completely renovated it. The doorman intimidated me. But I made up a little story—a waste of time because I went right in with no trouble at all. I swear, the high ceilings, the rich wall-coverings, and the huge leather chairs took my breath away. I sat in one of them. Nothing happened. No one even noticed me.

So, even an old woman on welfare can have the luxury of watching, in comfort, and, as a matter of fact, for the good of her welfare, the passing scene.

I watched. I listened.

Well—they were an ordinary-looking crowd, very ordinary in fact. Nothing elegant, not the least bit of chic.

Zelda would have been a sensation. Even I, in her old suit, I thought I was pretty elegant, almost dignified.

I probably should have gone to synagogue for Yom Kippur.

To pray with them, for them, to wail and sing with them:

'Next year in Jerusalem.'

No, no Lord, not in Jerusalem,

Next year

No, thank you very much

It's too kind

No thanks, not for me

I beg of you

'Somewhere out of this world' would suit me better.

Translated from the French by Patricia Sillers

NAIM KATTAN · b. 1928

The Pact

I thought I didn't like travelling. As a favour, I agreed to replace
Mr Strong, the head of our company, at the Alpach congress.
There was no question of Linda's coming along; Phil is only three.
They would go to the ocean, to her parents' place at Hyannisport.

'It's a chance to see the Tyrol,' she said, no doubt hoping to
cheer me up.

'Mountains are mountains,' I said. 'And I used to spend all my
holidays in the Laurentians.'

My parents still go there every summer, but since our marriage
we go to my in-laws' at Cape Cod. The day before I left, my
colleagues, all younger than I, invited me to lunch. Their envy
was obvious. To represent the company at a European congress
of economists and financiers is a privilege reserved for the direc-
tor. But Mr Strong was tired and had just got back from Mexico.

'I won't have anything to say,' I objected, when he suggested I
replace him.

'You have a Ph.D. in economics.'

'It's been years since I was at the stock exchange. I've forgotten
everything.'

'There's no paper to present. You won't even have to take part
in the discussions. All you have to do is prepare a report when
you get back. The company has to be represented . . .'

It was no consolation to know how pointless the trip was.

The week at Alpach passed quickly. In the mornings we listened to long speeches on economics and finance, and in the
afternoons went on excursions—Innsbruck, Salzburg. It was a

beautiful early fall, neither hot nor cold. The food was acceptable. And I made friends with a young professor from Los Angeles named Bob Shuman.

'My parents don't approve of this trip,' he said. 'They're still afraid of Germans, even though they've lived in America for forty years. We lost too many uncles and aunts and cousins.'

'It's the same with my parents. They told me the Austrians were the worst Nazis.'

My mother was born in Montreal and my father was eighteen when he left Poland in 1920. A left-wing Zionist, he didn't practise his religion, and neither did we. When I told my parents I planned to marry Linda, their reaction surprised me. 'She's wonderful,' my father said, 'but she isn't Jewish.' Phil's birth swept away their last reservations. It was always Linda who asked them about the war, about the uncles and cousins who died. And when mother would start to cry, my father would cut in abruptly: 'That's all over now, it was a long time ago. And our tears won't bring them back.'

Mr Strong had suggested taking a week's vacation in Europe after the congress. It would be stupid to go so far, for the first time, and see nothing more than a little village in the Tyrol. I wondered if he wasn't trying to get me on a excursion-fare flight and save the company a few hundred dollars. But Linda, who didn't mind spending an extra week with her parents, strongly agreed with him.

I would be alone in Europe for a whole week. Without family or plans. When Bob announced that he was staying longer too, the solution became clear.

'I'm heading for Vienna,' he told me. 'From there, I'll go to Budapest and then Prague.' He wanted to visit the places where his parents were born.

I would be returning to Montreal from Frankfurt.

'You'll have to go through Munich,' said Bob.

He sang the city's praises, and according to him, Frankfurt wasn't bad either. That settled it. An Innsbruck travel agent reserved me a room in Munich right near the station. I wouldn't even have to look for a taxi.

And that was how I found myself one evening at the beginning of September all alone at the Hotel Excelsior. The hotel restaurant looked inviting, so I decided to stay there for dinner.

I slept badly that night. No one in Montreal would understand how I could shut myself up in my hotel room. Neither Linda, nor my colleagues at the office. Early the next morning I made up my mind. Armed with a map of the city, I visited churches and monuments one after the other. The city glowed in soft sunlight. I walked all over the centre of town, and at eleven o'clock found myself with a group of tourists waiting for the clock carillon at the city hall, with its parade of wooden horses and soldiers obeying the magic wand of the mechanical orchestra—marionettes for grown-up children. At a fruit stand I managed to buy some grapes, thanks to my long-ago memories of Yiddish. A rush of excitement came over me. I could be completely alone in a strange city and succeed not only in finding my way but in jabbering a foreign language. What a joy this discovery was! I ate in a restaurant not far from the city centre.

Suddenly I noticed a stela that looked like a large gravestone. Hebrew letters leapt out at me. I pored over the inscription, trying to decipher both Hebrew and German. What elation to succeed. It was there that the great synagogue of Munich once stood. Burned down like all the rest. A feeling of uneasiness gripped me. This city was not foreign; it could not be completely unknown to me if synagogues there had been set on fire and the people inside them burned.

Surrounded with grass and flowers, there was nothing unusual about the monument; people went on their way without stopping. I walked slowly around it, as if it were an animal to be tamed. Here I was, in this city, looking at stones intended specifically for me. I was not some anonymous stranger. The name inscribed in my passport, safely hidden in my pocket, shouted itself to the world. And as if to confirm the disclosure, a man made his way resolutely towards me.

'Are you a Jew?' he asked in English, with an accent I couldn't place.

I stared at him as if the ghosts had materialized.

'Yes,' I said.

'So am I.' His smile hesitated, revealing a toothless mouth.

He was wearing a threadbare sweater and an oversized jacket that emphasized his thinness. With several days' growth of beard, he looked dirty and poor.

'I am a Soviet refugee. It is difficult. I have great difficulty. And you? American?'

'No. Canadian.'

He didn't seem surprised. His continuous smile accentuated both the pathos and the shadiness of his appearance. In this great city, this illustrious capital of Bavaria, this man shrouded in fog was questioning, interrogating me. He could be working for some secret police force, an informer for some invisible gestapo.

'Any spare change?'

I put a few coins in his outstretched hand. As he lifted the hand to his face, his smile became a snigger, as if he were jeering at all the poor innocents who believe that the dead can come back to life. He quickly moved off.

I visited the art museum. Paintings I had so often studied in reproduction were there, present in all their reality, their rarity, and in recognizing them I found many less beautiful, less radiant, than in the books.

Ashamed—no doubt like all tourists—of my ignorance of the city, I asked the hotel concierge to direct me to a typical Munich restaurant. He thought, thumbed through the guidebooks, consulted the cashier, and finally handed me an address. I could get there on foot through the pedestrian district around the city hall.

The restaurant was on the second floor of an old house; two small rooms, one of which served as a bar. A man in shirtsleeves led me to the back of the room, to a table where three men and a woman were already seated. Two men squeezed together to make room for me on their seat. Following the others' lead, I ordered a beer. The three men didn't know each other. The one sitting across from me was squeezing the young woman's shoulder as he talked to her. In her thirties, she was wearing a flowered blouse and a rose in her hair. Too blonde. She must dye it, I thought with regret; otherwise she would be very pretty. Deep blue eyes, nose just slightly upturned, narrow lips. I was famished. I ordered a cheese plate and, embarrassed to eat alone, invited my companions to share it. They all declined, having already eaten, but my neighbour obligingly helped himself. His gestures were precise, mechanical. He had taken off his jacket and loosened his tie. What did he do for a living? The man beside him was silent, raising his glass and drinking without a word or a smile. So I was surprised when he spoke to me, in German, and asked where I came from.

'Montreal?' His face relaxed. 'I have a cousin in Toronto. He's a pharmacist. He has a beautiful house.'

'And you? Are you a pharmacist too?'

He broke into a ringing laugh, though his face remained impassive.

'No, a teacher.'

'I'm an accountant', said my neighbour.

'I work at the stock exchange.'

'You're an accountant as well?'

'Not exactly.'

Suddenly the voices were lowered and silence settled over the room. A man in lederhosen, with an accordion slung over his shoulder, elbowed his way through the crowd, greeting people as he passed, shaking hands and joking. He arranged himself in a corner, bowed to us, and told a funny story about a professor who goes to the wrong restaurant. My companions guffawed and the young woman apologized that she unable to translate. Stories about Amin Dada and the Ayatollah followed, and the room rocked with laughter. Our artist raised his glass and we did the same. The first bars from the accordion brought a burst of applause.

'It's a Bavarian song,' my neighbour explained.

A drinking song. Everyone sang along. The teacher's face was less rigidly fixed, his voice one of the most resonant.

Waving their arms over their heads, two young men were clapping harder than anyone else. The singer bowed to them. One, a scrawny, skin and bones type wearing delicate glasses that contrasted with his heavy features, stood up and called for another song.

'You're a model Prussian,' the singer told him. 'You answer before I even ask the question.'

The young Prussian pounded the table and guffawed all the louder.

'Prussians are conceited,' the young woman explained. 'They know everything.'

'They have no sense of humour,' added my neighbour.

To whoops of delight from the audience, the singer told two jokes about fat-headed Prussians. The two young Prussians doubled over laughing—proof, to them, that they were not afflicted with the slow wit of their countrymen.

'Prussians don't understand us Bavarians,' the young woman

commented, 'how lighthearted we are, our joie de vivre.'

'So those young men come from East Germany?'

'Not necessarily. There are millions of refugees in West Germany.'

Her companion interrupted in a low voice, staring at me.

'My friend wants me to tell you,' she laughed, 'that everyone who isn't Bavarian is Prussian.'

The singer went back to his songs; glasses were raised to his health; our choir accompanied him. People stood by the door and joined in the general amusement while they waited for seats.

'Bavarian beer is the best in the world,' the young woman told me.

'Canadian beer is very good too,' I felt compelled to add.

'Ours is low in alcohol,' her companion said. 'You can drink a lot of it.'

Glasses were emptying faster and faster. The waiter came by and jotted down the number we had consumed.

The young woman got up to go to the washroom:

'I'm Claudia, and that's Hans.'

'I'm Paul,' I said, giving the first name that came to mind.

The teacher raised his glass to Paul and everyone followed suit. We raised them again to salute Claudia's return.

Despite the low alcohol content, I was beginning to feel the effect of the beer. I had the impression I was no longer in control of what I was doing. I heard my own voice, with a will of its own, loudly singing songs I didn't know. And when the singer stopped, the drinkers' discordant voices carried on the quest for a collective joie de vivre. The singer returned, told some jokes, and the frenzied laughter was thunderous, as if through the noise they were chasing after some fundamental refusal, some melancholy inseparable from the soul, some total, pervading negation. I've been in Montreal taverns where the later it got, the more the drinkers, no longer masters of their sorrow, ended up its victims. The laughter is louder, but it's no more than a pathetic sniggering, a hypocritical dumb-show, a recognition of the supremacy of a fate they cannot escape. I laughed without understanding in order to take part in this violent hunt. It was essential that I pass unnoticed. The man in the lederhosen no longer excited hilarity, no longer set the tone. He was beating the rhythm of a march that seemed more and more like a flight. I looked at all those men and women who were so correctly dressed, so polite and courteous; they gave me the impression of plunging headlong into a kind of compensatory disorder, setting up against the refusal an ignominious violence. I was the stranger, the Prussian from far away with no complicity, no tacit recognition to link me with the singing mob. I was afraid and I sang. A Bavarian among Bavarians, I bellowed an illusory joie de vivre to silence a deafening terror. We sang and our glasses were always full and always empty. We had set out on the hunt. Woe to the victim who accepts the role, who offers himself as prey to a craving that nothing can ever satisfy. The faces appeared impenetrable, resolved to meet one refusal with another, more powerful one. I had to leave, flee. The slightest spark, and we would all be swept up in the fire. I rose and hurried awkwardly to the washroom. Then I paid my cheque without smiling at the waiter or saying goodbye to my fellow pleasure-seekers. I was afraid and I fled before they could realize that their hunt had no object, that there was no prey to put an end to it.

Outside I became unknown, anonymous, once more. A cool breeze revived me. The city was lively and indifferent. In the pedestrian district, groups of people gathered around young singers, many of them American, strumming their guitars in shop doorways. I lingered to catch my breath and inhale the city's air again. Already I was becoming used to the landscape. This growing familiarity delighted me. Mute, tamed, recognized, the street did not expose me. I was unknown, a stranger. My name was my possession, a secret I wasn't sharing. I strolled twice through the bright-lit streets as they emptied. Finally I was alone and could safely allow this beauty, a compound of charm and leaden weight, to penetrate me.

When the hotel receptionist handed me my key, I remarked enthusiastically: 'Munich is a very beautiful city.'

In the elevator I gave in to the feeling of well-being. I was light, weightless. I was in a strange city and could experience its beauty. All alone, without a guide, I took what I wanted and the city spread itself before me in complete unconsciousness. While I knew.

The next morning I got up as if I were going to the office. Breakfast in the restaurant, then back upstairs to get my raincoat. At the reception desk I avoided the concierge and spoke to the cashier.

'I would like to go to Dachau,' I said.

Her dark blue eyes showed no surprise.

'Yes. By train?'

The concierge turned to me solicitously.

'You want to visit the camp?'

'Yes,' I said, hesitating between embarrassment and shame.

He gave me precise instructions. Get off at the level for suburban trains. I didn't have to buy a ticket at the counter. Automatic distributors . . . I had the necessary change. I must make sure of the stop. There were many trains.

At the station I followed the signs. Dachau was nothing more than a stop on a line. I had to know which stop. I tried to decipher the information on the timetable board and did not succeed. I would have to ask a more regular traveller for help. Timidly, I approached a woman who was carrying one child and holding another by the hand.

'Dachau? Certainly. It's on my way. I get off at the station after. Just follow me.' A train pulled in. I was about to offer to carry one of the children when a voice stopped me.

'Are you going to Dachau?' I heard in English.

I turned around. A tall boy with a round face, his eyes hidden behind thick glasses.

'I'm going to Dachau too. Would you mind if I followed you?'

'Not at all,' I said as we boarded the train.

A jean jacket and pants, a red turtleneck covering the bottom of his chin.

'I'm American,' he said.

I could have sworn it. Had Dachau become a tourist attraction?

'From where?'

He didn't understand.

'From where in the States?'

'Oh! California. San Diego.'

'I know it. I'm from Montreal.'

'I've never been to Canada.'

He was in his twenties, though his bulk could be misleading.

'You're a student,' I observed.

'Yes, but this year I'm going to work. My father has a bookstore.'

I looked at him, trying to chart a course between indifference and courtesy.

Tacitly, we chose silence. Passengers got on and off at each stop. We remained standing. The woman told us our stop was coming. The next station. I got off the train and the boy followed. On the station wall was a large poster. An invitation to the Dachau Cultural Centre. Courses in drawing, art history . . . I held back my anger. This wasn't the time to squander emotion, to channel it in other directions. A station like any other. Men and women going about their business. Cars stopped and left again . . . I headed for the taxi stand. The boy was still following me.

'Get in,' I said beside the taxi.

Ill at ease in his body, he moved awkwardly. He insisted on paying his part of the fare. I refused. I was taking a taxi anyway.

'I've come here from Paris,' he said.

'Are you spending some time in Germany?'

'No, I get back on the train tonight.'

'And when did you arrive?'

'Today.'

'You mean you came all the way from Paris to . . .'

'Yes, I want to see.'

He spoke without emotion, his eyes obstinate.

'Are you Jewish?' I asked.

'No, but . . .'

'There is no but . . . I wanted to know . . .'

We had arrived. A damp wind was blowing. The sun could no longer penetrate the thickening clouds.

Signs pointed to the chapels, the huts.

'Would you mind if I came along?' he asked in his toneless voice.

'No, except that I may not feel like talking.'

We were following a long path. I quickened my step to get ahead of him. Lawns the same as in all the Munich parks, flowers and trees. We passed two boys and a girl on their way back from the tour. They lowered their voices when they saw my rigid face, but continued their laughing conversation.

It's a park like any other. The grass is closely trimmed, the flowers are carefully tended, the trees . . . Memories crowded my head. The letters announcing the deaths, my mother crying and father trying to calm her, holding back his own tears. The films, the photographs . . . And here I was in a park with the same trees, similar flowers. On the other side, a bus stop, houses, children on their way home from school.

Wooden huts. Wood the same as anywhere else, in cupboards and summer cottages . . . That's all the camps were. Wooden huts, paths in a park, trees and flowers. Familiar, everyday things. Nothing to suggest horror, monstrosity. You take the train and get off in a suburb, you find yourself in a park. There were towers and barbed wire. And green grass. I left the hut. My companion followed a few steps behind. I avoided looking at him. That's all it was? Nothing to provoke anger or tears. Thousands of men, women, and children, in a park, surrounded by flowers and trees.

I walked slowly, my legs numb. A heavy mass weighed down my shoulders. My head sank between them as if to shorten my neck, to make it disappear. I was old, moving one step at a time, under a crushing weight. I was old and small. I tried to bring my shoulders together over my chest to be smaller still, my body bending under the weight.

Here is the oven. Metal, with an opening, a little door . . . An oven like the baker's at Saint-Sauveur, where we used to stop for fresh hot bread. An oven made in a factory, like the baker's. Into this hole they pushed corpses. Men, women, and children . . . I tried to imagine the operation and could not. An ordinary oven, dictating simple, ordinary actions. Outside, my body doubled over under a weight that was growing heavier. My shoulders were collapsing, almost touching one another. My body was a cumbersome, superfluous mass.

On a wall covered with ivy was a notice. Here the firing squads shot. Trees and flowers like everywhere else, damp air in a suburb. Men were lined up against the wall because of their names. They died by the thousands in a park against the ivy wall. I looked quickly through the museum where photographs, newspapers, pamphlets, and books attested that the nightmare was reality. Here already I was back in my own world. Photos and printed pages. The horror was recorded, the terror inscribed. Neither flowers, nor grass, nor wooden huts, nor baker's ovens.

Here we were in the past, in history, and once again I found myself in my memory. My mother's tears burst suddenly into reality. That unknown family swept away in the whirlwind was real. My faraway uncles and aunts had faces. And one fall afternoon they were reduced to memory.

I walked quickly. My legs were weak, as if the springs had broken and I had to hurry to find my body, to take up my weight again. The boy was still following me. Outside, we waited at the bus stop. I looked at his child's face, and for the first time met his eye.

'I don't know what to say.' Embarrassed, I needed to hear my voice, put myself back in the world of the living.

'There's nothing to say.'

'We'll take a taxi if one comes by,' I said.

But the bus arrived first. We sat together.

'I've spent two months in Europe,' he said, and in a neutral, deliberate monotone he started to tell me about his trip.

I listened avidly. What were we trying to exorcise? He belonged to an international exchange club. Girls and boys his own age, from Amsterdam, Paris, Milan, and Frankfurt went to America and stayed with his family. He in turn stayed with their families in Europe.

'One night, in Frankfurt, a man came to dinner with the family of the girl who had invited me. He had only one leg. A war wound. He was nostalgic about the Nazis. It was the first time I ever heard anyone say anything good about Hitler. This man was alive and real. And he was German. Suddenly all the films and books and pictures seemed to have no power. For him, I was an American. What did I know about that time? I wasn't even born. I couldn't leave Europe without coming here.'

'And now you understand,' I said, trying, with difficulty, to smile.

He fixed his eyes on me. He was no longer a well-fed child, but an anxious, troubled man. His body was taking form, as if he were preparing to enter an arena.

'I don't understand anything. I feel American, and that's where I have to start.'

We took the train back to Munich. All the way he talked about his family and I about mine and my wife's. I could not call up my son's face. That seemed a sacrilege. Then at the station, in the turmoil of trains and passengers, I found Phil's picture in my wallet.

'This is my son,' I said, rediscovering his face for myself.

He shook my hand.

'We'll write to each other,' he said, as if to seal a pact.

Translated from the French by Sally Livingston

ADELE WISEMAN · b. 1928

On Wings of Tongue

The winter my father went to Vancouver to look for a job Joe
and I were still too young to go to school. We stayed home and
my mother found things for us to do after Belle and Arty left the
house. In those days the house was full of roomers. You'd be
surprised at how many tenants can be crowded into a five room
bungalow, particularly if the landlady and her four children are
flexible about shifting around to accommodate the guests. For
Mrs Lemon alone we had moved our belongings in turn to every
room in the house. Every time my mother gave in and said, 'All
right, you can come,' we tried to clear out a room other than the
one that she had occupied last time, because my mother wanted
it to be a fresh start each time. She did not want to remind Mrs
Lemon that last time she had moved out because we were piping
poison gas into her room.

Joe was still practically a baby. He missed my father terribly.
Everybody said so, and I could prove it any time. All I had to say
was, 'Where's Daddy? Daddy's gone away.' Fat tears would glaze
his trusting eyes; his belly would heave into some mysterious
preparatory discipline, and from his mouth would burst the
foghorn bass bellow that was the pride of our house. You
couldn't bear to listen for long. Remorsefully, I would yell into
his weeping, 'He's coming! He's coming home!' Joe would
hesitate uncertainly, the sobs clucking and gurgling. I completed
the cure, 'What'll he bring? What'll he bring me?' It was a pleasure
to see the joy spread over his good-natured face. 'What'll he
bring Joe?'

'Me! Me!' chuckled Joe. I played nicely with him for a while after that.

Every morning I took a trip. Sometimes I took Joe. We had our route laid out. To a certain listing, brown-shingled house down the street we went, labouring through unshovelled snow. Up icy front steps we climbed on all fours. Finally we stood rattling the doorknob and banging with our fists on the door. If no one came to the door I would stand back and let Joe holler into the sparkling air. That was when it was good to have him with me. 'Mrs Fi . . . fer!' His powerful roar shattered the air, scattering the billion tiny crystals that darted thick and glittering in the daylight and sending them blinking to hide in the snow. That brought Mrs Fifer running.

Joe got his voice from an uncle on my father's side. That uncle was born with church bells in his chest. An aesthetic priest had gone mad over his voice and had pressed him into the service of the church choir, because there was no one in all Russia who could intone like he could, 'Christ is risen!' Through three successive pogroms his voice had been the salvation of his entire family, and of everyone else who'd had the sense to seek refuge in his house. For when the parishioners ran amok they left his house religiously alone. 'They respect me,' he used to say, with not a little pride.

We all of us in our house had little characteristics that were passed on to us from relatives, some of whom we had never known, so that we grew up with the feeling that we were part of a much larger family than we actually had. They told me that I took after my aunt Yenta, my mother's sister, who lived only a few blocks away. It was because I talked too much. Yenta herself was always the first, though, to accuse me of spreading family secrets. Nobody ever told me why they weren't secrets until I talked about them. They were just things everybody in the house discussed. But the minute they found out I'd told Mrs Fifer they became secrets.

Mrs Fifer was an old lady. She and her husband lived in one of the ground-floor apartments in the ramshackle house right next door to the apartment of my aunt Yenta's best friend, Dvosieh Krotz. She was always wonderfully pleased to see me, and Joe too, though he wasn't much to talk to yet. She loosed our clothing, unwound our scarves, and gave us cookies from a shredded-wheat box.

As we ate Mrs Fifer would ask me all kinds of questions, and I would answer her while my index finger kept the turning crumbs poked back safely in my mouth. Mrs Fifer liked talking to me. She used to tell my mother what a nice little girl I was to come and visit, and how polite I was to spend time talking to an old lady. My mother always smiled in an apprehensive kind of way.

They were not only family things Mrs Fifer asked about, with her intensely interested, kind old face bent forward to hear what I said. She took an interest in our roomers too, what they said, what they did, what my mother thought of them, did they pay their rent on time, which ones were on relief, did any of them have secret jobs the relief didn't know about, was it true this one had fought with that one over a pot on the stove, and so on. I loved to listen to the talk in our house, so I was particularly good at correcting Mrs Fifer when she said, for instance, 'And did your Daddy say so and so?'

'No, he said such and such,' I would reply, proud to be able to set an adult straight.

How did my auntie always know what I'd been saying to Mrs Fifer? I could tell by her preliminary stamping on the ice outside and by the way she slammed into our house, rattling the frosted windows, how serious her visit was going to be in its consequences for me. She would always call out before she was fully over the threshold, 'I'm not staying. Don't make tea.' She kicked off my uncle's old galoshes and came up the five hall steps, bringing the chill of the outdoors into the room with her. Joe, who sat with his flannel kimono loose, shuddered up and down his rolls of baby fat, accompanying his shudders with resonant, self-comforting growls.

'What' cried my aunt, readily indignant, 'is the child doing naked?'

'Don't come near him, auntie,' I said, 'Mama's fixing his combinations. We got the other ones wet outside.'

'You,' said my aunt, 'Leubitchka with the active lips, does Mrs Fifer know that too already? It hurts me for you Rivka,' she turned to my mother. 'This child has a faceful of mouth, a mouthful of tongue, a tongueful of every little thing that goes on in this house, so Mrs Fifer can run and spread it like fire all over the prairie.'

'Mrs Fifer's sick,' I said, 'in an armchair, covered over. I was there with Joe.'

'Not too sick to ask questions,' said my aunt bitterly. 'It hurts me, Rivka. . . .'

'It hurts me,' like 'I'm not staying, don't make tea,' was one of those baffling statements that Yenta made. She always stayed. She always drank tea. And she never told you where she hurt. She always changed the subject in mid-sentence. 'It hurts me your name should be dragged through the mud.'

There was no mud any more. 'Through the snow,' I offered.

'What?' said my aunt.

'Nothing,' I said. Maybe she meant 'It hurts me your name should be dug to the mud.' But why did it hurt? And how did a name get dragged or dug? Anyway, with her dark, flashing eyes and glowing skin, she never looked as though anything was hurting her.

'It's not Mrs Fifer spreads the stories,' said my mother quietly.

'Don't be foolish,' said my aunt heatedly. 'They fly by themselves, all over town.' She looked at me. 'On wings of tongue they fly.'

I laughed. I liked the way my aunt talked. She laughed too. In spite of the things she called me we got along, and it sounded as though it might go easy with me and Mrs Fifer today, though you never could tell. They laughed and laughed and suddenly they jumped you.

'Mama says Mrs Fifer doesn't tell anything,' I said, before I could stop myself.

'Oh she doesn't?' said my aunt. 'So if your mother says she doesn't then she doesn't. Should I argue? When your mother gets stubborn I might as well talk to the walls.' My aunt stopped talking.

My mother, smiling, looked up from her stitching. 'How's your friend Dvosieh?'

My aunt ignored the question and addressed me directly. 'Why do you talk so much? Where do you get your tongue? Why do you tell her everything?'

'She asks me,' I faltered. 'I take after you,' I added quickly.

'Don't be disrespectful,' said my mother.

'But you say so,' I said.

'It's not what you say but when,' explained my aunt, 'that makes respect. Is it true then?' she continued, 'what she told Mrs Fifer? Are you taking Mrs Lemon in again? As if you haven't got enough to worry about. Don't do it Rivka. What do you need her for? Tell her no for a change. Let her find somewhere else.'

'She's here already,' said my mother.

'In the house?' my aunt's voice disappeared suddenly in her lips.

'No, she had to report to the relief,' said my mother. 'But she moved in this morning.'

My aunt frowned. Her eyes seemed to light on me.

'That's what I told Mrs Fifer,' I said.

My aunt shook her head. 'She's getting worse, not better. One day she's fine, talks like anybody else; the next day suddenly, out of nowhere, an accusation you can't make sense of; then locks herself in her room, not a word; then starts to run around to the neighbours. Did you hear what happened? Yesterday she went to her husband's people again and made a scandal. She said they're keeping her husband locked up a prisoner in the TB hospital. She said they're paying the government to put germs in his x-rays to kill him. They wouldn't let her into the house so she went shouting up and down their fancy street.'

'It must be very embarrassing for them,' my mother said. 'The rich are so sensitive.'

'It hurts me for them,' said my aunt in a surprisingly satisfied voice for one in pain. 'They didn't even offer her a glass of tea, not a bite. They tried to give her money to go away, five dollars to ease her pain. She threw it at them. And they from behind closed doors, afraid to let her in, a human being like themselves. She didn't have a mouthful of saliva to chew on all day. She walked from their place to the Hudson's Bay Company in the snow, and fainted twice, once in the notions and the second time when they took her to the restroom. So strangers called an ambulance and took her to the hospital. It's all over town.'

'I know,' said my mother. 'An ambulance brought her this morning.'

My aunt laughed. 'She certainly gets free public transportation. It's always ambulances and police cars.' My aunt could never overcome the suspicion that it was somehow useful to Mrs Lemon to be sick. In spite of her hard talk Yenta had taken Mrs Lemon into her own house three disastrous times already. Things always started off well enough, with my aunt proud of how well she could handle a problem that had once again vanquished my mother, and Mrs Lemon temporarily tranquil because she had once again fought off some obscure threat. Then my auntie's crony, Dvosieh

Krotz, would come over to sit in and give advice, the same crony who lived behind the wall of Mrs Fifer's flat.

Dvosieh advised friendship and reason, and the sane discussion of past delusions in the calm of present clarity. My aunt showed her friendship through the simple means of frequent reiteration. 'I say to her,' she would explain to my mother, 'You see, I'm your friend, Mrs Krotz is your friend. We're all your friends.' And Yenta was not one to be stingy with her sympathy. 'Your poor husband, where is this "san"? Up north? What's up north? The Eskimos! Why would they put a TB san up north? So they can cure him of consumption and kill him with pneumonia?'

Under the stress of reason, advice, and friendship, Mrs Lemon's suspicions were rapidly forced, like monstrous bulbs, in her mind's darkness. By some inspired stroke of malignancy her fits always crystallized around Yenta's most sensitive spot. My aunt is a wonderful cook and a proud one, justly famed in our neighbourhood. Mrs Lemon always ended up by accusing her of poisoning her food. My aunt could not resist taking it personally. She would become incensed and run among the neighbours herself. When my mother tried to reason with her she grew even more irate, 'See here Rivka, listen here. You say it's madness, so let it be an equal madness for everybody. Has she ever told you you poison her food? No!'

'But I've gassed her and drugged her and I whisper in her room at night,' my mother defended herself.

'That doesn't make any difference. Three times she's lived in my house and three times I've poisoned her. It's too much. If at least once I'd gassed her I wouldn't feel so much she was deliberately needling me. She means something by it.'

'She's sick,' sighed my mother.

'You always find something good to say for everybody,' sniffed Yenta.

This time, however, my aunt had a more serious threat to disclose against Mrs Lemon than her own erratic ire. After this last scandal in the south end the in-laws had sworn, in front of witnesses, that if it happened once more, if once more she made trouble, they would have her put away.

'They wouldn't,' said my mother after a silence. 'She's harmless.'

'Oh yes they would,' said my aunt. ' They're out of all patience. Once more and they'll put her away for good. They don't like scandals on the south side.'

'You make money you lose patience,' said my mother.

'Where will they put her away?' I asked.

My mother and aunt looked at each other. 'Nowhere,' said my mother hastily.

'Mrs Fifer has her radio on,' said my aunt, pursing her lips.

'Mrs Fifer hasn't got a radio,' I was happy to contribute.

My mother sighed. 'Just don't repeat everything we've said to Mrs Lemon.'

'All right,' I said. 'I like Mrs Lemon,' I added. 'Joe and I don't want them to put her away. Nor Belle nor Arty neither.'

'Just don't talk,' said Yenta quickly, 'and they won't.'

'She's like you, Yenta,' my mother remarked.

'Like me? How like me? I'm no child. A child shouldn't sell your teeth every time you open your mouth.'

This was the first time I had heard that 'they' could do something dreadful to Mrs Lemon. No wonder she had fits. I could not separate the idea of Mrs Lemon's being 'put away for good' from the memory of the time our dog Rhubarb had to be put away, and the man had come with a closed wagon with a grilled door in back to take her away, and she had stood still behind the grille, and had left us all standing and watching and stained forever with her mute, despairing eyes. Just let them try to come and get Mrs Lemon.

Mrs Lemon played with us, not the way most adults do, always with the end of the game in sight, as though telling themselves approvingly over their impatience, 'now we are playing with the children for a little while.' Rather, she let us play with her. Quietly she sat and stood or turned as we directed her, never imitating us and never rushing us through her time. We usually played in the kitchen those winter afternoons. Sometimes we played in her room, but my mother didn't like that. She said that if Mrs Lemon saw that we kept strictly away from her room there would be less chance of upsetting her. So it was mostly in the kitchen that we had our games, the warm white kitchen with its frost-fuzzed windows, its big grey electric stove, its knife-scarred wooden table covered by a knife-scarred printed oilcloth, and its wooden rung chairs, behind which Mrs Lemon allowed herself to be barricaded while Joe and I pretended we had captured her and had her in our power. She stood quietly, occasionally saying something nice in reply to my mother, like 'No, they're not bothering me.'

I liked the way Mrs Lemon looked. She made me think. She didn't look like a lemon. She was thin and brown. Her hair was black and rolled round and round at the back of her head. Her eyes were big and bugged out a little, with dark brown middles and yellowish white parts. And she was extra brown all around the eyes.

In spite of my mother's instructions Joe and I were not strangers in Mrs Lemon's room. We knew her few belongings well, especially the raddled orange fur collar with the fox's head and its loosely snapping jaw. On her bureau sat a little brown old-country picture of her mother, her father, and two sturdy boys, with a little, big-eyed girl between them I knew was Mrs Lemon long ago. I always wanted to ask her which one was the brother who had dropped dead when they were burying her father; right into the grave he dropped. I knew all about what a sad life she had had that made her go funny sometimes. But I never did. There was another picture, in a small frame, of Mr Lemon. He wore a white collar and looked bristly, and I said like my mother did when she mentioned him sometimes, 'He'll get well soon,' in the same confident voice that pleased Mrs Lemon. The candy was in an almost empty top right-hand drawer, in a box with a gypsy on it.

Sometimes she would say, 'Do you want to take a walk with me?' And my mother would say, 'Mrs Lemon, you shouldn't, they're too wild.' And she would beg and make promises along with us until my mother said, 'All right, but you mustn't buy them anything.' And Mrs Lemon wouldn't say anything and my mother would bite her lip, for fear she had hurt Mrs Lemon's feelings by implying she couldn't afford to spend her relief tickets on us.

They would truss us up and we would move stiffly off between the snowbanks. I slithered around on Arty's old moccasins and screamed into Joe, knocking him over like a kewpie doll, sideways, into the piled-up snow, where he lay, one arm standing straight out, the other buried. His cries shattered the still, needle-charged air. Mrs Lemon dug him out, soothed him, called him 'little snowman', and I magnanimously let him push me back, which he did, chuckling his deep bass chuckle. I flung myself, screaming into the bank, and waited for a panting Mrs Lemon to right me before I flung myself on Joe again. We were snow-plastered and steaming through every layer by the time we reached the corner grocery. Inside it was hot and dingy and glamorous. We consulted with Mrs Lemon for a long time and then she bought us each a string of pink and white crystallized sugar and a flat square package of bubble gum with a hockey picture in it that Arty would be nice for.

'I'm not giving Arty my hockey picture,' I suggested to Joe. Joe gripped his with his mitt against his chest and shook his head fiercely, eyes shining, cheeks fiery, nose running. But I knew very well he would rush, the minute Arty made his noisy, dishevelled entrance from school, with his hockey picture extended, for the immediate gratification of a big brother's thanks. Arty wouldn't win mine so easily. I knew the subtler pleasures of the drawn-out wooing and the gradual surrender 'I have one too, Arty, see? No you can't. What'll you give me? Can I play in your igloo?'

So the winter passed. One day, late in February, my mother was sitting alone in the kitchen, sewing and humming to herself. Mrs Lemon slipped in so quietly my mother didn't even hear her, till the hissing whisper started her out of her chair. 'Do you think I don't know why you're singing? But you won't get me that easily.' My mother got up and made some tea, which they drank in utter silence. After that, Mrs Lemon stopped talking almost entirely. Sometimes she sat in the kitchen without speaking for hours at a time, while my mother did her work, occasionally throwing her an anxious glance. At other times Mrs Lemon stayed in her room. My mother warned us to leave her alone, then, and I heard her tell my sister that maybe if we just kept still too it would blow over.

One day she left the house very early. She spent the whole day wandering among the neighbours and talking to people about her suspicions. My mother knew what she was doing, as she had often received such confidences when Mrs Lemon was living elsewhere. 'Maybe she'll just talk it out of her system,' she told my aunt, who had come rushing over with the news.

'No.' My aunt was triumphantly certain. 'There'll be trouble.'

Mrs Lemon returned home that evening, thoroughly chilled, blue tints frozen into her swarthy skin, and for the next few days she lay coughing in bed. My mother tended to her, talking gently and soothingly, and pretended she didn't notice that she got no answer.

'Maybe the fever will burn it away,' said my mother hopefully.

'No,' said my aunt, 'I tell you Rivka, you won't avoid a scandal. And this time. . . .'

'I'll try to keep her in the house till it blows over,' said my mother.

The coughing ceased and my mother listened anxiously to the silence. She sighed more frequently as she listened, and raised her hand often from her sewing to run it through her softly waving black hair.

Then one day Mrs Lemon, who must have been waiting behind her door for a long time, took advantage of a moment when my mother had gone into her bedroom to slip out of her room, through the kitchen, down the hall steps, and out the side door. Joe and I were playing on the kitchen floor and we called out to her, but she didn't seem to hear our pleased hellos; she was all dug down into her coat. Only the fox winked and snapped at us from her back as she bounded down the steps.

My mother ran out of our bedroom, but too late she scratched at the ice of the window. 'What was she wearing? Was she dressed warmly?'

'Her winter coat and her live fox,' I said. My mother still looked worried. She looked more worried as the day wore on. She talked to my sister in a low voice when Belle and Arty got home from school, and my sister looked worried too. I hung around them and looked worried too, and asked questions that touched on raw worry and was hushed up.

We were eating supper when Mrs Lemon returned. She rushed up the stairs and through the kitchen to her room, still hunched in her coat, and I called after her, but again there was no reply, and my mother shushed me up.

We were still around the table when my aunt came stamping in. She came up the stairs with her coat still buttoned and a very excited expression on her face. 'Is she in?' she nodded in the direction of Mrs Lemon's room, and formed the words through almost silent lips.

My mother nodded.

'You'll have visitors tomorrow,' said Yenta softly, and nodded toward Mrs Lemon's room again. 'Didn't I warn you?' My aunt undid her coat but remained planted in my uncle's old galoshes in the kitchen doorway. 'She went there again, threw herself down into the snow on their lawn, made a big outline, it's still there, for all the neighbours to see, made a scene. . . .' 'She'll catch cold again,' murmured my mother.

'She'll be well taken care of,' said my aunt grimly. She paused and looked anxiously toward Mrs Lemon's room and we all listened with her. 'So . . . that's it. Maybe it's better this way Rivka, though . . . you know . . . somehow . . . it hurts me . . .'

'It hurts me too,' said my mother softly, staring down at Joe's plate. 'It hurts me too.'

The next morning I fought against going out of the house, though a part of me wanted to go and walk to Mrs Fifer. I felt funny-bad all over, and I could tell that my mother felt badly too, though she insisted on sending us out for our fresh air until she realized that there was a blizzard blowing up. I whined about after her all morning, and Joe growled after me. It was out of his range to whine.

By early afternoon the snow was whipping past the windows and piling up against the fences and walls and making spooky sounds all around the house. We had to turn the lights on. Mama began to worry about the children who were at school. I told her not to worry about any little blizzard bothering Arty and Belle.

Suddenly, Mrs Lemon made her appearance in the kitchen. She looked around quickly and without saying anything went to stand at the kitchen window, looking out to where you could see nothing but swirling snow. My mother was looking at her.

'Joe,' I jumped up. 'Let's capture Mrs Lemon!' Delighted, Joe slid off his chair and began to push it toward her, while I began to push my own. 'You're our prisoner!' I shouted out, and rushed to pull another chair to her side. 'Prisoner!' repeated Joe in organ tones.

'Children!' said my mother.

Mrs Lemon had turned from the window and stood looking at us from behind the chairs.

'Children,' said my mother again. 'Come here!' She had risen.

I looked from her to Mrs Lemon. 'She'll be our prisoner,' I cried. 'Then they can't put her away!'

'Leuba!' cried my mother, in a terrible voice.

I started to cry. 'We don't want them to send Mrs Lemon away!'

At the word 'away', Joe cut loose like a trained bullfrog. 'Gone away!' he bellowed, eyes closed, mouth enormous, comprehending in its quivering pink cavern the whole reverberating enormity of deprival. Unable to compete with his mighty gust of expression I contented myself with short, breathy, gasping whimpers and siren whines.

'Children!' my mother implored, 'children!' We pitched on fervently. 'Away!' I prompted as Joe paused for breath. Instantly he exhaled his heartbreak in a fresh gust of shattering sound.

'Children!' my mother's hands were at her ears. 'Children! Children!'

'Children,' said Mrs Lemon suddenly, from behind her barricade. 'Children,' she said in a dazed voice.

I stopped in mid-note, amazed at the first sound I had heard Mrs Lemon utter in days. Joe, unaware of all else but his art, bellowed on. Confused, I forgot how to turn him off. 'Joe,' I yelled. He redoubled his efforts. His face had turned a fierce red that extended all down his neck. My mother, alarmed, started to pat him lightly on the back, murmuring, 'Yosele, what's the matter? Yosele.'

'Shut up!' I yelled, right into Joe's open mouth, so suddenly that he made a gulp and clicking sound and a little 'whirrr', as though his spring had snapped, and he remained voiceless, staring at me with the big, wounded, swimming eyes of one utterly betrayed.

'Leuba!' cried Mrs Lemon, and for the first time ever, other than to help me across the street or to put on my overthings, she laid her hand on me. She had me gently by the shoulder and her voice was dazed and shocked and urgent. 'Never say that to your brother. Never, never say that to your brother.'

I had an awful feeling inside of me, as though I had swallowed a big stone. I started to cry, this time soft, painful tears that wouldn't make a noise but only little groans inside of me. 'I only meant,' I said to Joe, who was also streaming big, sighing tears, 'I only meant, Daddy's coming, honest Joe, he's coming soon,' I bawled. My mother held and rocked us both.

'They miss their father,' said Mrs Lemon. 'Poor children, they miss their father.'

By the time my aunt arrived, all puffy and snowed over, Mrs Lemon was sitting with Joe on her lap, playing tickle with him and receiving raucous response. No blizzard has ever prevented my aunt from just dropping by at the crucial moment of a crisis, and from sitting with her lips all pursed up and her eyes fixed on one or other of us, with an accusing or anticipatory stare. Only this time she quickly became aware that something was amiss. Yenta's glance shot questioningly back and forth from my mother to Mrs Lemon. What had happened? My aunt looked almost indignant. Had Mrs Lemon gone crazy all of a sudden?

'It's a nice blizzard,' said my mother, looking at her. 'If only people who have far to go would have the sense to stay home.'

'Troublemakers should always stay home,' said my aunt, and smiled at Mrs Lemon in the friendliest way.

Suddenly, three more people were huffing and puffing up the stairs into the kitchen, all in enormous, snowed-over coats, all standing and making cold noises and throwing chills around while my mother and aunt helped them off with their overthings, all apologizing because they were dripping on the kitchen floor, as the hall was too small to hold them. Mrs Lemon went and got a chair from her room and my aunt brought another from our room and my mother took her sewing off another chair and pretty soon they were all sitting and blowing on their knuckles and talking about how cold it was and my mother had a fresh kettle on.

Joe had offered himself genially back to Mrs Lemon's arms, and he now sat at princely ease, staring at the visitors from astride her knee. Mrs Lemon started to demonstrate my brother's extraordinary vocal endowments to the newcomers by tickling his belly. The strangers were struck dumb with admiration.

Then the men started to explain how hard it was to drive in a snowstorm, and how they had started out long ago and had stalled twice along the way. The heavy woman who had come with them sat gingerly on her seat and looked all around and finally up and down over her black beads at my aunt, who wore my uncle's old red woollen socks over her shoes, and pulled right up under her skirt, because my uncle is a tall man, with her bloomers tucked into them. They had big yellow and blue darns on them, beautifully sewn, because my aunt is a perfectionist. The lady coughed as she looked, and my aunt spread her knees further apart to give herself purchase, leaned slightly forward, straight of back, folded her arms across her chest, and stared back, with pursed lips and a coldly ironic eye. My aunt is a handsome woman, with a haughty face and thick, straight black hair. She was not going to be stared down on account of her socks.

One of the men, smallish, with a glistening stone in his tie that looked as though it would melt any minute, leaned from his chair and whispered, hesitantly but loudly enough for me to hear, to the beaded lady, 'Er . . . which one?' The beaded lady then introduced Mrs Lemon as her sister-in-law, and all kinds of cross-introductions were made. I stared at her. This was the enemy, on whose lawns the scandals were enacted, and who never even offered a glass of tea, though my mother even now was pouring hers.

I cannot remember in detail exactly what was said during the next little while, but I do remember that I behaved very badly. The kitchen gradually filled and filled and stretched outward with sound, much of it coming from my lips. Numerous faces all turned toward me, with varying expressions of amazement, distaste, disapproval, despair, as I talked, interrupted, contradicted, and mimicked. The rich lady coughed at the smoke from the cigarettes the men had lit, which was mingling with the steam from the kettle to fog up the room. She took noisier and noisier breaths. My aunt told her very kindly that she hoped her brother's ailment didn't run in the family, which made her cough so hard her beads rattled. I started to cough too, and my brother Joe chuckled approvingly at me, adding a stentorian spur to my antics. He thought it was a fine game. My mother pleaded with me in a shocked voice to be quiet, please. I couldn't. I no longer knew how.

Then my aunt and the rich relative got into what seemed to me a traitorously amiable conversation about what an unmanageably talkative child I was, and my aunt told her how I couldn't keep family secrets, and I remember being fiercely hurt that she should sell a family secret of such magnitude to an enemy, and in front of strangers.

Finally, my mother ordered me out of the room and I stood there bawling and insisted that I wouldn't go unless Mrs Lemon came with me. By this time she was the only true ally I had left in the world and I could not leave her to treachery. My last-ditch tantrum was interrupted by loud noises at the door. My brother Arty and my sister Belle were outside quarrelling about who would get into the house first, Belle, with both arms book-laden, with snowpants under her thick coat, besparkled and dishevelled, and chubby Arty, in breeches and high boots and fur-lined jacket, banging his hockey stick against the wall of the house and lashing icicles from the eaves as he argued. There wasn't room for both to squeeze in at once, so meanwhile they held the door open and the blast whipped up blue around the fogged-up kitchen, and everybody shivered.

'I don't care if you are a lady,' challenged Arty, who had wedged his hockey stick in front of Belle so that it suddenly appeared in the kitchen doorway with an ancient pair of razor-sharp skates hanging from knotted yellow laces over its edge.

'Belle! Arty!' boomed Joe joyously, as the skates narrowly grazed his skull. The three strangers exchanged glances as the stick and swinging skates advanced into the kitchen, the blades blinking ferociously and slashing indiscriminately through the air.

'Arty!' cried my mother aghast. 'Belle, shut the door for goodness' sake! We have guests!' she added hopefully.

'I can't,' wailed my sister. 'He won't let me in.'

'Arty, take your skates away!' cried my mother, as the wind howled around the kitchen.

The guests broke for the bedroom. They found their coats. There was confusion in the kitchen for the next few moments, with Belle and Arty getting out of their wet clothes and the guests trying to get into theirs, and everybody exchanging polite 'goodbyes' and 'come agains' and the beaded lady saying something about 'in good hands', and the small man with the pin saying something about 'family atmosphere', as he nodded his way vigorously to the hall. Then they left. Soon afterwards my aunt left, having just remembered she had a word to say to her friend Dvosieh down the street. Mrs Lemon said she was tired, suddenly, she didn't know why, and retired to the quiet of her room.

'What happened?' asked my sister.

'She feels better,' said my mother.

Joe deserted us to go and look at Arty's sled with him in the cellar. Belle and my mother started doing the dishes. My mother said she was afraid supper might be a little late tonight. Everything was flat and quiet suddenly. I picked up the crumbs on the table. 'What can I do?' I asked. My mother came to the table and stood looking down at me. She looked lovely, with her long, fine nose, her delicate skin all pink, her deep-set eyes shining golden brown. 'Aren't you tired?' she asked, as though she really thought I might be, so early.

'No. Can I help you?'

'You know,' said my mother, 'the way you behaved . . .' Suddenly, unaccountably, she grabbed me up, so violently that my curls bounced over my eyes. 'You've helped enough,' she said into my ear, and it felt, from the way her stomach was shaking and from the muffled sounds she was making in my hair, as though she was laughing.

MORDECAI RICHLER · b. 1931

Playing Ball on Hampstead Heath

Drifting through Soho one hot sticky evening in June, too early
for the theatre, Jake stopped at the Nosh Bar for a sustaining salt
beef sandwich. He had only managed one squirting mouthful and
a glance at the unit trust quotations in the *Standard* (S&P Capital
was steady, Pan-Australian was down again) when he was dis-
tracted by an American couple. The bulging-bellied man wore a
seersucker suit and his wife clutched a *London A to Z* to her
bosom. The man opened a credit card-filled wallet, briefly expos-
ing an international medical passport which listed his blood type,
extracted a pound note, and slapped it into the waiter's hand. 'I
suppose,' he said, winking, 'I get twenty-four shillings change for
this?'

The waiter shot him a sour look.

'Tell your boss,' the man continued, unperturbed, 'that I'm a
Galicianer, just like him.'

'Oh, Morty,' his wife said, bubbling.

And the juicy salt beef on rye turned to leather in Jake's mouth.
It's here again, he realized, heart sinking, the season.

At the best of times, American and Canadian show business
plenipotentiaries domiciled in London had many hardships to
endure. The income-tax tangle, scheming and incompetent
workmen, uppity nannies, smog, choosing the right prep school
for the kids, doing without real pastrami, and of course keeping
warm. But come the season, life was impossible. Come summer,
ocean liners and airplanes began to dump clamorous hordes of
relatives, friends of friends, long and better forgotten schoolmates

and army buddies, on London, thereby transmogrifying the telephone, charmingly inefficient all winter, into an instrument of terror. Everyone who phoned, no matter how remotely connected at home, exuded warmth and demanded a night on the town. 'Waddiya say to a pub crawl, old chap?' Or an invitation to dinner at home. 'Well, Jakey, did you tell the Queen your Uncle Moish was coming? Did she bake a cake?' You agreed, oh how many times you agreed, the taxis were cute, the bobbies polite, and the pace slower than New York or, in Jake's case, Montreal. 'People still know how to enjoy life here. I can see that.' On the other hand, you've got to admit the bowler hats are a scream, hotel service is from the stone ages, and the British have snobby British accents. 'Look at it this way, it isn't home.'

Summer also meant, even if you had lived in London for years, though possibly paying your tax in Liechtenstein or Bermuda, being mistaken for a tourist everywhere. Suddenly truculent taxi drivers insisted on larger tips. Zoom went the price of antiques and pornography. The waiters in the Guinea were ruder and more condescending about wines, if possible. It required the sharpest of elbows to get close enough to put down a bet on the roulette table at the White Elephant. Summer was charged with menace, with schnorrers and greenhorns from the New Country. So how sweet and soothing it was for the hard-core show biz expatriates to come together on a Sunday morning for a fun game of softball on Hampstead Heath, just as the Raj of another dynasty had used to meet on the cricket pitch in Malabar.

Manny Gordon drove in all the way from Richmond, clapping a sporty tweed cap over his bald head and strapping himself and his starlet of the night before into his Aston-Martin at nine a.m. Bernard Levine started out from Ham Common, stowing a fielder's mitt and a thermos of martinis in the boot of his Jag, picking up Al Herman and Stan Cohen in Putney and Jimmy Grief and Myer Gross outside Mary Quant's on the King's Road. Moey Hanover had once startled the staff at the Connaught by tripping down the stairs on a Sunday morning, wearing a peak cap and a T-shirt and carrying his personal Babe Ruth bat. A Bentley with driver, laid on by Columbia films, waited outside. Another Sunday Ziggy Alter had flown in from Rome, just for the tonic of a restorative nine innings. Frankie Demaine drove in from Marlow-on-Thames. Lou Caplan, Morty Calman, and Cy Levi usually brought their wives and children, while Monty Talman, ever mindful of his new twenty-one-year-old wife, always cycled to the Heath from St John's Wood. Wearing a maroon track suit, he lapped the field eight or nine times before anyone else turned up.

Jake Hersh, a comparative novice, generally walked to the Heath from his flat in Swiss Cottage with Nancy and the kids; his tattered fielder's mitt, nappies, a baby's bottle, and three enervating bagels filled with chopped liver concealed under the *Observer* in his shopping bag.

Other players, irregulars, were drawn from the directors, actors, writers, producers, and agents who just happened to be in London working on a picture. The starting line-up on Sunday, July 25, 1965, was,

AL HERMAN'S TEAM	LOU CAPLAN'S BUNCH
Manny Gordon, *ss.*	Stan Cohen, *3b.*
Bernard Levine, *2b.*	Myer Gross, *ss.*
Jimmy Grief, *3b.*	Frankie Demaine, *lf.*
Al Herman, *cf.*	Morty Calman, *rf.*
Ziggy Alter, *lf.*	Cy Levi, *2b.*
Jack Monroe, *rf.*	Moey Hanover, *c.*
Monty Talman, *1b.*	Johnny Roper, *cf.*
Sean Fielding, *c.*	Jason Storm, *1b.*
Alfie Roberts, *p.*	Lou Caplan, *p.*

Jake, an unusually inept player, was one of the subs. A utility fielder, he sat on the bench with Lou Caplan's Bunch. It was a fine, all but cloudless, day, but looking around Jake anticipated friction, because some of the players' first wives, or, as Ziggy Alter put it, the Alimony Gallery, was already fulminating on the grass behind home plate.

First Al Herman's Team and then Lou Caplan's Bunch, both sides made up of men mostly in their forties, trotted out, sunken bellies quaking, to take a turn at fielding and batting practice. Last Sunday Frankie Demaine's analyst, walking the dog, had passed accidentally and lingered to watch the game, his smile small but constant, and Frankie had gone 0 for 5; but today Frankie looked his old lethal self. Morty Calman, on the other hand, was in trouble. His first wife, Ethel, had come to watch and whenever

Morty called for a fly ball her sour piercing laughter cut across the field, undoing him.

Nate Sugarman, once a classy shortstop, but since his second coronary the regular umpire, strode on to the field and called, 'Play Ball!'

First man up for Al Herman's Team was small, tricksy Manny Gordon, ss.

'Let's go, boychick!'

Manny, hunched cat-like over the plate, was knotted with more than his usual fill of anxiety. If he struck out, his starlet might glow for somebody else; Lou Caplan, however, who was pitching for the first time since he had signed his three-picture deal with 20th, would be grateful, and flattering Lou was a good idea, especially since Manny had not been asked to direct since *Chase*. *Strike one, called.*

'Atta boy, Lou. You've got a no-hitter going for you.'

If, Manny thought, I hit a single I will be obliged to pass the time of day with that stomach-turning queen, Jason Storm, 1b. *Ball one, inside.* He had never hit a homer, so that was out, but if just this once (*Adonoi, Adonoi*) he could manage a triple, he could have a word with—KNACK! *God damn it, it's a hit! A double!* As the players on Al Herman's bench rose to a man, shouting encouragement—

'Go, man! Go!'

—Manny, suffering under Lou Caplan's glare, scampered past first base and took myopic, round-shouldered aim on second, wondering should he say something rotten to Cy Levi, 2b., who was responsible for getting his name on the blacklist years ago, or should he greet him warmly because after all Cy had married Manny's first wife, the *putz*, and so taken him off the alimony hook. Decisions, decisions. Manny charged into second base, flat feet flying, trying to catch Cy with a belt in the balls. He missed, but beat the throw, grinned, and said, 'Hi.'

'You should come to visit the kid sometimes,' Cy said. 'He asks for you.'

'I'd love to, but I'm too sensitive. If I see him I'll cry.'

Bernard Levine struck out, which brought up Jimmy Grief, who was in a state, such a state. Jimmy had to hit but quickly, urgently, before bigmouth Cy Levi let it slip to Manny, who had not been invited, that the Griefs were giving a cocktail party on Friday.

Jimmy swung at the first pitch, hitting it high and foul, and Moey Hanover, c., called for it and made the catch.

Which brought up big Al Herman, who homered, bringing in Manny Gordon ahead of him. Manny immediately sat down the bench next to Grief. 'Oh, Jimmy baby,' he said, his smile ingenuous, 'I was wondering, I mean if you and Estelle aren't busy on Friday, could you come to dinner at my place?'

'Have to check with Estelle. I'm not sure what we're doing on Friday yet.'

Monty Talman scooped out the last of the Wholefood yogurt, stepped up to the plate, and immediately ground out to Gross, ss., retiring the side. Al Herman's Team, first inning: two hits, no errors, two runs.

Leading off for Lou Caplan's Bunch, Stan Cohen singled to centre and Myer Gross struck out, bringing up Frankie Demaine and sending all the outfielders back, back, back. Frankie whacked the third pitch long and high, an easy fly had Al Herman been playing him deep instead of outside right, where Manny Gordon's starlet was sprawled on the grass. Herman was the only man on either team who always played wearing shorts—shorts revealing an elastic bandage which began at his left kneecap and ran almost as low as the ankle.

'Oh, you poor darling,' the starlet said, making a face at Al Herman's knee.

Herman, sucking in his stomach, replied, 'Spain,' as if he was tossing the girl a rare coin.

'Don't tell me. The beach at Torremolinos. Ugh!'

'No, no. The Civil War, for Christ's sake! Shrapnel. Defence of Madrid.'

Demaine's fly fell for a homer, bringing in a panting Stan Cohen. Morty Calman popped to short and Cy Levi struck out, retiring the side.

Lou Caplan's Bunch, first inning: one hit, one error, two runs.

Neither side scored in the next two innings which were noteworthy only because Moey Hanover's game began to deteriorate. In the second Moey muffed an easy pop fly and actually let Bernard Levine, still weak on his legs after his colonic irrigation and all but foodless week at Forest Mere Hydro, steal a base on him. The problem was Sean Fielding, the young Liverpoolnik who Columbia had put under contract because Hy Silkin's son-in-law Jerry thought he looked like Peter O'Toole. The game had only just started when Lilian Hanover had sat down on the grass beside Fielding, which was making Moey nervy. Moey, however, had not burned his young manhood up at a yeshiva to no avail. Not only had he plundered the Old Testament for his *Bonanza* plots, but now his intensive Jewish education served him splendidly yet again. Moey remembered, *And it came to pass in the morning, that David wrote a letter to Joab, and sent it by the hand of Uriah. And he wrote in the letter, saying, Set Uriah in the forefront of the hottest battle, and retire ye from him, that he may be smitten, and die.* Amen.

Lou Caplan yielded three successive hits in the third and Moey Hanover took off his catcher's mask, called for time, and strode to the mound.

'I'm all right,' Caplan said. 'Don't worry.'

'It's not that. Tell me, love, when do you start shooting in Rome?'

'Three weeks tomorrow. You heard something bad?'

'No.'

'You're a friend now. Remember. No secrets.'

'I've had second thoughts about Sean Fielding. I think he's very exciting. He's got lots of appeal. Real magnetism. He'd be a natural to play Domingo.'

Multi-coloured kites bounced in the skies over the Heath. Lovers strolled on the tow paths and locked together on the grass. Old people sat on benches sucking in the sun. Nannies passed, wheeling toddlers. The odd baffled Englishman stopped to watch the Americans at play.

'Are they air force chaps?'

'Film-makers, actually. It's their version of rounders.'

'Whatever is that enormous thing that woman is slicing?'

'Salami. Kosher.'

'*On the Heath?*'

'Afraid so. One Sunday they actually set up a bloody folding table, right over there, with cold cuts and herrings and mounds of black bread and a whole bloody side of smoked salmon. Scotch. Eight and six a quarter, don't you know?'

'*On the Heath?*'

'Champagne. Mumm's. Out of paper cups. One of them had won a bloody award of some sort. *Look!*'

Alfie Roberts, the next man up, had connected on the first pitch. Only it wasn't a softball he hit, but a cherante melon, which splattered over the infield. A double, Nate Sugarman ruled.

Going into the bottom of the fifth, Al Herman's Team led 6-3.

Cy Levi, first man up for Lou Caplan's Bunch, hit a triple, but heading for third he saw Jimmy Grief, 3b., waiting there with a mean expression on his face, and guessed that Jimmy knew Lou Caplan had hired him to rewrite Jimmy's script and so, instead of pulling up at third, Cy scooted for home and was caught in a run down. Jimmy charged Cy, grinning, actually grinning, as he whacked the ball into his stomach, knocking him down. The two men rolled over in the dirt, where Cy managed to land Jimmy a good one in the nose with his shoe. 'Sorry,' he said.

Sorry? Nate Sugarman, the umpire, who had had nothing but heartache with the Jag he had bought from Cy Levi, waved him out of the game.

Which brought in Tom Hunt, a surly coloured actor, to play second.

Next man up, Moey Hanover, lifted a lazy fly to left field, which Ziggy Alter trapped rolling over and over on the grass, until—just before getting up—he was in a position to peek under Natalia Calman's skirt. Something he saw there so unnerved him that he dropped the ball, turning pale and allowing Hanover to pull up safely at second.

Which brought up Johnny Roper, who crossed his eyes, dropped his bat, knocked his knees together, and did the twist, finally working a convulsed tearful Lou Caplan for a walk.

Which brought up Jason Storm to the delight of a pride of British queers who stood with their dogs on the first baseline, squealing and jumping. Jason hit a line drive to centre and floated down the baseline to second, obliging the queers to move up a base.

With two out and the score tied 7-7 in the bottom of the sixth, Alfie Roberts was unwillingly retired for a new pitcher. It was Gordie Kaufman, a blacklisted writer for years, who now divided his labours between Rome and Madrid, asking $100,000 a spectacular. Gordie came in with the go-ahead run on third and Tom

Hunt stepping up to the plate for the first time. Big black Tom Hunt figured that if he homered he would be put down for another buck nigger, good at games, but if he struck out, which would require rather more acting ability than was required of him on the set of *Othello X,* what then? He would enable a bunch of fat foxy Jews to feel big. Goysy. Screw them, Hunt thought.

Gordie Kaufman was perplexed too. His stunning villa on Mallorca had ten bedrooms, his two boys were boarding at a reputable British public school, and Gordie himself was president, sole stockholder, and the only employee of a company that was merely a plaque in Liechtenstein. And yet—and yet—Gordie still subscribed to the *Nation*; and his spectaculars had content, that is to say, he filled his Roman slaves with anti-apartheid dialogue and sagacious Talmudic sayings. If Hunt touches me for even a scratch single, he thought, I'll come off as a patronizing ofay. If he homers, I'm a shitty liberal. And so with the count 2 and 3 and a walk, the typical social democrat's compromise, seemingly the easiest way out for both men, Gordie, his proud Trotskyite past emerging, threw a burning fast ball right at Hunt, bouncing it off his head. Hunt threw away his bat and started for the mound, fists clenched, but not so hurried that players from both sides couldn't rush in to separate the two men, both of whom felt glowingly emancipated because they had triumphed over impersonal racial prejudice to recognize and hit each other as individuals on a fun Sunday on Hampstead Heath.

Something else of note happened in the sixth.

Going into the bottom of the inning the prime diversion had been Manny Gordon's toreador-trousered starlet. Again and again the men had meandered over, asking if she wanted to catch, a salami on an onion roll, or a drink. Then, in the bottom of the sixth, burly Alfie Roberts had been retired from the mound. He had been humiliated before his wife and children. He had been made to look a zero before hostile agents and producers and, he added to himself, dirtygoyhomosexual actors. Alfie, his last picture still riding in *Variety*'s top money-making ten, walked to his Jag and returned to sit on the grass alongside the third baseline reading a book. A hardcover book. A hardcover book in a plain brown wrapper.

The word leaped from one bench to another, it electrified the field, making it spark with speculation. A hardcover book in a plain brown wrapper meant either Alfie only had an option on the property, and so it could possibly be wrested from him, or, even more intriguing, the property was in the public domain. *My God, my God.* Woody Farber, the agent, strolled down the third baseline to where Alfie sat, his smile open, touchingly honest, only to have the suspicious bastard slam the book shut and sit on it. Next Phil Berger drifted over toward Alfie, forcing him to sit on the book again. Alfie slammed the book shut in Lou Caplan's face. Even Manny Gordon's starlet couldn't get anywhere.

Then, going into the crucial seventh inning, Alfie shook up the infield and was directly responsible for a failed double play, when he was seen to take out a pencil, lick it, and begin to make notes in the margin of his book. Enough is enough. Monty Talman called for time and walked over to confront Alfie. 'Can't you work somewhere else?' he asked.

'Darling,' Alfie said, 'I didn't know you cared.'

Come the crucial seventh, the Alimony Gallery grew restive and began to move in on the baselines and benches, demoralizing former husbands with their heckling. When Myer Gross, for instance, stepped up to the plate with a man on base and his team mates shouted, 'Go, man. Go,' one familiar grating voice floated out over the others: 'Hit, Myer. Make your son proud of you just this once.'

What a reproach the first wives were! How steadfast! How unchanging! Still Waiting For Lefty after all these years. Today maybe necks had gone pruney and stomachs had lowered and breasts had flattened, like yesterday's *latkas*, but let no man say that these ladies had aged in spirit. Where once they had petitioned for the Scottsboro Boy, spit on their families over mixed marriages, packed their skinny scared boyfriends off to defend Madrid, split with old comrades over the Stalin-Hitler Pact, raised funds for Henry Wallace, demonstrated for the Rosenbergs, and never, never yielded to McCarthy . . . today they clapped hands at China Friendship Clubs, petitioned for others to Keep Hands Off Cuba and Vietnam, and made their sons chopped egg sandwiches and sent them marching off to Aldermaston.

The sons. How well and honestly they had raised the sons. When Georgie Gross, for instance, had returned from the hospital after his appendicitis operation and had tried, first morning home, to climb into bed with his mother, she had not rebuffed him with sweet old-fashioned lies. Instead she had said, 'You must understand why you want to get into bed with me. It's because you desire to make physical love to me. You wish to supplant your father.'

Davey Hanover did not have to sit through windy religious instruction at his private school. On the contrary. He had a note which entitled him to leave the classroom for the period and stand alone in the corridor, sometimes, it's true, wetting the floor. When nine-year-old Dickie Herman had put on lipstick and got into his older sister's dress for a hallowe'en party he was told, no punches pulled, all about homosexuality. None of the children played with guns. Or watched violent shows on television. And when ten-year-old Judd Grief rebelled he was taken to see a special screening of a concentration camp documentary so that he could understand clearly where gun-play led to.

Davey Hanover stammered. Dickie Herman suffered nightmares. Judd Grief wanted to grow up to be an S.S. Colonel. But all the children had been honestly brought up and knew there was no God and that all men were brothers and all wars bad.

The wives, nicely alimonied but bitterly alone, had known the early struggling years with their husbands, the rejections and the cold-water flats, but they had always remained loyal. They hadn't altered, their husbands had. Each marriage had shattered in the eye of its own self-made hurricane, but essentially the men felt, as Ziggy Alter had once put it so succinctly at the poker table, 'Right, wrong, don't be *narish*, it's really a question of who wants to grow old with Ana Pauker when there are so many juicy little bits we can now afford.'

So there they were, out on the grass chasing fly balls on a Sunday morning, short men, Jake thought fondly, overpaid men, tubby men, coarse and unprincipled but astonishingly energetic men, all well within the coronary and lung cancer belt, allowing themselves to look ridiculous in the hope of pleasing their new young girls. What appetites, Jake thought, what self-redeeming appetites they had. There was Ziggy Alter who had once directed a play for the Group Theatre. Here was Al Herman who had used to throw marbles under horses' legs at demonstrations and now raced two horses of his own at Epsom. On the pitcher's mound stood Gordie Kaufman who had once carried a banner that read

Non Passaran through the streets of Manhattan and now employed men specially to keep Spaniards off the beach at his villa on Mallorca. And sweating under a catcher's mask there was Moey Hanover who had studied at a yeshiva, stood up to the committee, and was now on a sabbatical from Desilu.

Usually the husbands were able to avoid their used-up wives. They didn't see them in the gaming rooms at the White Elephant or in the Mirabelle or Les Ambassadeurs. But come Brecht to Shaftesbury Avenue and without looking up from the second row centre they could feel them squatting in their cotton bloomers in the second balcony, burning holes in their necks.

And count on them to turn up on a Sunday morning in summer on Hampstead Heath just to ruin a game of fun baseball. Even homering, as Al Herman did, was no answer.

'It's nice for him, I suppose,' a voice on the bench observed, 'that on the playing field, with an audience, if you know what I mean, he actually appears virile.'

In the eighth inning Jack Monroe had to retire to his Mercedes-Benz for his insulin injection and Jake, until now an embarrassed sub, finally entered the game. Jake Hersh, 34 years old, one-time relief pitcher for Room 41, Fletcher's Field High, Montreal (1-4), trotted out to right field, mindful of his disc condition and hoping he would not be called on to make a tricksy catch. He assumed a loose-limbed stance on the grass, waving at his wife, grinning at his children, when without warning a sizzling line drive came right at him. Jake, startled, did the only sensible thing: he ducked. And then outraged shouts from the bench reminded him where he was, in a softball game, that is, and he started after the ball.

'Fishfingers!'

'*Putz!*'

Runners on first and third broke for home as Jake, breathless, finally caught up with the ball. It had rolled to a stop under a bench where a nanny sat watching over an elegant perambulator. 'Excuse me,' Jake said.

'Americans,' the nurse said.

'I'm a Canadian,' Jake protested automatically, fishing the ball out from under the bench.

Three runs scored. Jake caught a glimpse of Nancy, unable to contain her laughter. The children weren't looking at him.

In the ninth with the score tied again, 11-11, Sol Peters, another sub, stepped cautiously to the plate for Lou Caplan's Bunch. The go-ahead run was on second and there was only one out. Gordie Kaufman, trying to prevent a bunt, threw right at him and Sol, forgetting he was wearing his contact lenses, held the bat in front of him to protect his glasses. The ball hit the bat and rebounded for a perfectly laid-down bunt.

'Run you schmock.'

'Go, man.'

Sol, astonished, ran, carrying the bat with him.

Going into the bottom of the fourteenth, Al Herman's Team was leading 13-12. There were two out and a runner on third when Morty Calman stepped wearily up to the plate. If I hit, he thought, sending in the tying run, the game will go into yet another inning, and it will be too late for the pub. So Calman struck out, ending the game, and hollering, 'I say, chaps, who's for a pinta?'

Monty Talman phoned home.

'Who won?' his wife asked.

'We did. 13-12. But that's hardly the point. We had lots of fun.'

'How many are you bringing back for lunch?'

'Eight.'

'*Eight?*'

'I couldn't get out of inviting Johnny Roper. He knows Jack Monroe is coming.'

'I see.'

'A little warning. Don't, for Christ's sake, ask Cy how Marsha is. They're separating. And I'm afraid Manny Gordon is coming with a girl. I want you to be nice to her.'

'*Anything else?*'

'If Gershon phones from Rome while the guys are there please remember I'm taking the call upstairs. And please don't start collecting glasses and emptying ashtrays at four o'clock, it's embarrassing—Bloody Jake Hersh is coming and it's just the sort of incident he'd pick on and joke about for months.'

'I never—'

'All right, all right. Oh, Christ, something else. Tom Hunt is coming.'

'The actor?'

'Yeah. Now listen he's very touchy, so will you please put away Sheila's doll.'

'*Sheila's doll?*'

'If she comes in carrying that bloody gollywog I'll die. Hide it. Burn it. Lock it up somewhere. Hunt gets script approval these days, you know.'

'All right, dear.'

'See you soon.'

MATT COHEN · b. 1942

The Watchmaker

The watchmaker's gold wallet is embroidered and stamped with a picture of the village green. Dense black hair sits on his head in uncombed clumps and there are small tufts from his nose that melt into his moustache. I see him standing outside of his shop, under the awning, his thick arms tapering down into delicate hands that have been shaped by small motions. At times I think he has no face. There is bone and flesh. There are networks of nerves, veins, and arteries that lace through the surfaces. But sometimes he seems to have transformed himself into a blank, a man who sits in the corner and talks to the grandfather clock.

In his coat pocket there is a red satin cushion. This man plays the violin, has small hard calluses on the tips of the fingers of the left hand, is an unbeliever. It would be easy for him to do certain things. He could set all the clocks in his shop to different times. He could grow a beard. He could eat fish sandwiches for lunch or bet on horses. But he restrains himself. He fears that he will reduce his options, lose the mornings under the awning, earn the enmity of his grandfather clock.

His wife would like a new coat. His daughter would like to travel in Europe. He lives in the midst of expectations. So I see him in the summer, under the awning, standing in the shade not even pretending to look for customers. He is pretending he is a shopkeeper. Or he is just letting himself stand blankly for a moment. Perhaps he is unaware of what he looks like. But his wife and daughter must surely catch it sometimes, notice that he has disappeared.

In the winter I sit with him in the corner by the grandfather clock. I try to extract his wisdom, hoping he will dispense it in little lumps.

What is the time? I ask.

Two thirty, he replies. Then he turns to the grandfather clock and points at his huge pendulum. He laughs and drinks his tea. The clock is large and carved; its works shine like gold behind the glass. It ticks off the seconds. I feel that there are some seconds wasted, some in which I should have been doing something else. I fabricate my mortality. I ask him if he ever feels like that, if what he is doing is sitting by the grandfather clock letting his life escape.

Where to? he says. He turns off his face, he is resting his hand on the wooden side. Where to? he says, immensely pleased with his joke, as if it was some profundity he had eaten for breakfast.

All right, I say conclusively, then you can invite me for supper.

It is a disaster. His daughter is unsure if I have been brought for her benefit. She refuses to play the piano. His wife, not knowing what to do, asks him to play the violin. It was unanticipated. He is not the kind of man you ask to play the violin. Still, he does it. He draws the bow out of the case first and meticulously brushes the horsehair with rosin. Then he takes out the violin and tunes it. When everything is ready he gets the cushion from his coat and tucks it under his chin. He stands in front of us, as if we are an audience that must be respected. I shall now play a certain sonata, he says. He nods his head and then begins to play.

Doesn't he play nicely? his wife says. It is as if there were a record on. When he is finished the watchmaker puts everything away and sits down. His wife finds this unremarkable.

He is about forty years old. He came to North America from Europe after the second world war. His accent has intonations of several languages, and when he speaks I feel that everything has been carefully considered in the light of everything. Any man who can survive being turned into a record must know something. What am I going to do? I ask him.

He laughs at me. It doesn't matter.

But, I say, you do something.

Then do something. He pulls out the stool with the chessboard. His hands wrap delicately around the pawns. I wonder if his wife notices it, this delicacy of his hands, or if he is only that way with inanimate things.

From seven to eight every morning I clean his shop. There is a small cupboard with all my appliances. I vacuum the floor, dust off the glass cases, polish the grandfather clock. Then I go home, just before he comes, and stand at the window. The clouds roll by like trains. I stand there invisibly watching the shop. Once a week I stay there until he arrives so he can pay me. In the afternoons I am a visitor, it is different.

Do you have a secret? I ask him point blank. If you don't have one how can you expect me to keep spending all this time here?

Then go, he says. He winks slyly at me and turns to the chessboard. I see, he says, that you will resign in seven moves.

One morning he didn't come to the shop. He was away for two days. Then he came back, sallow and drawn.

Were you sick?

I had a headache, he said. It was clear that there would be no discussion.

A few weeks later he was away again, this time for three days. I had a headache, he said. It was clear that there would be no discussion. But I persisted.

All right, he said. I will tell you why I have the headaches. He leaned back in his chair, put his hand on the clock, and closed his eyes.

It was when I was a boy, he said. During the war. We lived in a town that no longer exists. There was my father, my mother, and myself. They had seen the war coming, heard stories about what was happening, but when the news broke they were thrown into a panic. The house was in an uproar all the time. One day my mother would send me to school early, to get me out of the house. The next day she would make me stay home and hide in the attic. It went on that way for months. At any moment things would fly off in a different direction. Every day it was said there would be an invasion. Finally my father made up his mind. He told me to pack my things in a small suitcase. Then he took me on a journey. We travelled for two days on a train. We came to a town. You are going to stay with my brother, he said. He is the mayor. No harm will come to you.

But, I said, you never mentioned a brother.

Never mind, he said, I was saving it for a surprise.

He took me to the mayor's house. The mayor was a man much different from my father. He was remote and cold. He patted me on the head as if I was a baby. My father knew I didn't like him but he could do nothing. Everything is agreed, the mayor said. Then my father left.

A week later it happened: there were troops everywhere. In tanks, in jeeps, walking up and down the streets looking for someone to fight. They were billeted in the school and in people's homes. We had a captain at our house. He and the mayor would stay up half the night, drinking and discussing the war. People were always disappearing. There was one time when the hostages were shot publicly. The mayor took me to see it. He put his hand on my head and forced me to look. I had no friends except the mayor's wife and there was nothing to do. One day her clock was broken and I fixed it. After that day I fixed clocks and watches. It seemed as if I had always known how. I even fixed the Germans' watches, though somehow I never got them quite right. There was an artillery officer who used to help me when necessary. Eventually the war changed and the Germans left. When the Americans came they didn't want their watches fixed. I asked the mayor when I would be going home.

Your parents are dead, he told me. They were killed two weeks after you came here. So.

And that is why you get the headaches?

No, he said. What I told you was what you expected to hear. If that was enough to give a man a headache the whole world would be in bed. He opened his eyes and patted the clock. The truth is, he said, that it isn't headaches at all. I wake up in the morning and tell my wife to leave the house. I am sick. Then I go back upstairs and lie down on my bed to think. He paused. Don't you want to know what I think about?

Yes, I said.

Good. He leaned back and patted the clock. I will tell you. What I think about is how it happened that my father, a man without a brother, left me at his brother's house. That is unusual, you must admit. It took me a long time to find out but this is what I discovered . . .

It is impossible to imagine what it was like to be young in Europe when my father was young. He came from a family of no wealth. He was a Jew. The old world seemed to be crumbling yet there was nothing, specifically, that he could have. It was after the first world war. He had been brought up very orthodox and was away from home for the first time. He was studying at a university.

But what was he going to do after he studied? Was he going to be a professor? Impossible. A lawyer? How would a man like him, a man of no background, a Jew, get clients? He was a man without a future.

When you have no future the present becomes very important. He met a girl, the daughter of a Jewish merchant. He took her to concerts and had dinner at her house. They went for walks. He felt sorry for himself. He would never be able to afford to marry her. He had a sense that he must destroy something. Yet he was pulled in two directions. The girl was very attractive. She almost loved him. He almost loved her. Perhaps they did love each other. It would be impossible to know; there were other circumstances. They became very involved, going for their long walks in the afternoon. These were secret of course. A respectable girl did not do that in those days, not unless she was engaged. She began to see another man. A man who was older, who would be able to provide her with a house and a life. She felt little for the man but knew that it was inevitable.

My father discovered what was going on. He was young and hopelessly in love with himself, his great despair. The walks grew more frequent. He wrote her passionate letters and said he would kill himself. She was not unmoved by this. They would lie on the grass and my father would describe the various ways in which he might end his life. He would stab himself and shriek her name with his last breath. He would jump off a bridge reciting a poem in her praise. She found this disturbing. It aroused other instincts in her. As he described his suicide my father would caress her, perhaps even kiss her. She would return his kisses.

During this period the other man grew more persistent. He was an established man, a lawyer. He wanted to get married and have children. He couldn't wait forever. He pressed his suit and finally the girl agreed. My father, crushed, did not commit suicide: he left town. A few months later he heard that the man had married—but to a different woman. My father, by now securely in love with his beautiful memory, returned to see the girl. But when he got to the house and knocked on the door, no one answered. Finally he inspected the house. It was clear that no one had been there for months. Everything was out of trim. The curtains were closed.

Disappointed he went to a nearby café to make enquiries. He was told that something terrible had happened to the girl, that the whole family had left town. It was hinted that the girl was pregnant. All suspected that it was the other man. He found out where they were staying and went there. He knocked on the door. The girl's father answered and then, seeing who it was, slammed the door. Finally they let him in. The girl, of course, was pregnant. Everything was arranged and they got married.

And you were the child?

Yes, he said. I was the child. When the news of the war came my father didn't know what to do. He wanted to hide me somewhere but knew nowhere safe. Finally he hit upon the idea of appealing to the other man, the man who had been engaged to my mother, the man who was the mayor. At first my mother refused. But my father pointed out that there were no other possibilities. There was only one problem. How could he persuade the man to accept me?

He devised a plan. He knew that the other marriage had been barren and that the man had wanted a child. Perhaps he could convince him that he was my true father. It would be a flattering suggestion. Memory fades. My father was very pleased with his gambit. He explained it to my mother. She was curiously silent. It wasn't long before he had the whole story out of her: the man had refused to marry her when he found out she wasn't a virgin.

My father went to visit the mayor. He explained that he had discovered that the child was the mayor's. The danger was obvious. Would the mayor protect it? The mayor refused. What if someone found out he was harbouring a Jew? My father pressed his case. Look, he said, who could possibly know?

You could, the mayor said. If the child is not yours you might well want your revenge.

And so the bargain was made. The day the Germans arrived in my father's town they received a message that there were two members of a Jewish organization, at a certain address. When they searched the house they found guns and knives, the handwritten outline for a pamphlet. My father and mother were waiting in the living room.

And that is what you think about?

No. How can a man think about something like that? It would drive him crazy. He slapped his small hand against the side of the grandfather clock. The truth is that I stay home with my wife. I don't know what's gotten into her. She can't get enough.

His face had disappeared. There was bone and flesh: networks of nerves, veins, and arteries laced through the surfaces. He was sitting still, watching the movement of the pendulum. Sometimes it moved so fast that it was almost invisible. Sometimes it stopped altogether.

He stood up. It was time to go home. He put on his coat with the red satin cushion in the pocket.

I see him standing outside the shop, under the awning. I go and visit him in the afternoons and we sit by the grandfather clock, drinking tea and playing chess. He says he has told me all his secrets; but still he tolerates me. I am patient.

SHARON DRACHE · b. 1943

The Scribe

He was sitting by himself, separate from the fashionable visitors loitering in the hotel lobby. Head covered with an embroidered skull cap, he wore an open, taupe overcoat revealing a closely knit sapphire sweater. He was young, this Misha Mikelofsky, only twenty, but he looked even younger, like a boy of sixteen. His blue eyes were intense, busy with his own thoughts, far away from this Montreal foyer, decorated with colourful tapestries, heavy mahogany gilt-trimmed furniture and opulent crystal chandeliers.

Others were waiting too but they were mostly people watchers. Not so with Misha. He sat stiffly, oblivious to all these people, except for Miriam, who had been watching him with intense curiosity. Catching her eye, he smiled and she smiled back with motherly approval. Her two sons also stared at Misha, sitting at the other end of the same champagne-velvet six-seater sofa. Saul, Miriam's husband, was reading upstairs in their seventh-floor suite. He would have been furious with his family: 'People should mind their own business,' he'd say. Miriam thought Saul said things like this because he was a lawyer who spent much of his working life doing just that: minding other people's business.

At Misha's feet sat a worn briefcase, a satchel-type which looked soft as thin cardboard, the two straps shredded and one of the buckles missing. Misha checked his watch every few seconds.

One of Miriam's sons, Michael, played an electronic baseball game while he watched the young man. 'Beep-beep' it sounded with precisioned regularity.

David, Michael's older brother, ogled boldly, the man's eccentricity fascinating to him. But then, David was twelve and Michael was only eight. David had more in his store of memories of similar men he had seen in Toronto on Bathurst Street, about a fifteen minute drive from where his grandparents lived. On those few Sunday visits when his family drove North, they'd see types like Misha.

'Look at the Hasidim!' Saul Bernstein would exclaim, as if he were heralding a momentous occasion. Was this the only time the pious ones left their homes, on one of the three weekends a year the Bernsteins travelled to Toronto? David wondered.

The men wore dark, baggy suits and tiny grey or black fedoras. Sidelocks bobbed at their ears. The mothers and daughters looked equally old-fashioned, arms and legs always covered (even in the thick of summer), their dresses swimming around their concealed figures.

In Ottawa, where the Bernsteins lived, you saw these men only occasionally, but never with their wives or children. First thing Monday morning, they'd get off the bus at the Catherine Street depot. Saul said these Hasidim were from New York: 'Diamond merchants!' he'd tell his sons.

'They're Hasidim?' David once asked.

'Hasidim too need to earn a living!' his father said. 'But usually they negotiate through intermediaries. They don't like to mix,' Saul added, 'At least, most of them don't.'

'You mean some do?'

'Well, the Lubavitcher sect . . .' Saul hesitated.

'The Lubavitcher sect, what?' David asked.

'David, remember the mitzvahmobile, the van with Hebrew writing, parked outside Hillel Academy? The young Lubavitchers invited you aboard to talk about good deeds.'

'Sure, I remember.'

'David, did you think they were just being friendly?'

'Of course, I really liked them.'

'But son, didn't they tell you to come to their monthly meetings at the orthodox shul?'

'Yes, and I wanted to go and you wouldn't let me!' David complained.

'They wanted your mother and me to come along too, didn't they?'

David recoiled, the thrill of the unusual slipping into the inexplicable 'watch out' category.

'David,' his father tried to explain, 'you know we never go to the orthodox synagogue. The liturgy is too rigid. Your mother and I can't sit together. Why, at their meetings, the Lubavitchers would probably erect a wall.'

'I know all about the *mehitzha*,' David spoke out. 'Surely they don't have one at an ordinary meeting?'

His father looked thoughtful for a minute. 'No, David, maybe not . . . but one thing leads to another. They have their way . . . we have ours.'

Then, reconsidering, he said, 'I'll tell you what, David, if they invite us again . . . maybe we'll go.'

'Oh, Papa, I can hardly wait.'

'Soon you will be a man, David. You must learn to wait . . . and sometimes for a long, long time.'

Now, as David watched Misha, he saw him suddenly get up. A couple approached; obviously the people he'd been waiting for. But Miriam seemed to recognize them too. 'Look,' she announced, loud enough for the stranger to hear, 'Grandma and Grandpa's friends from Toronto, Abe and Ida Stein.' Indeed, the Steins also recognized Miriam. They made a great fuss over her and her sons, ignoring the uncomfortable Hasid.

He stood by, awkward as ever, first putting down his briefcase, which he had so hastily picked up, next adjusting his skull cap so that it tipped down on top of his forehead. He shoved his hands into his pockets and even dared to peek covertly at his surroundings, in order not to interrupt the old friends' reunion.

'The boys, how they've grown!' exclaimed Ida Stein. 'The last time we saw David, he was four, and Michael here was barely visible, except in the form of an extended belly, eh Miriam?' Abe Stein teased her while he tousled Michael's hair and Miriam blushed.

'You, Miriam, now you too know how time flies,' Ida remarked. 'But tell me, how are your mother and father? We haven't seen them in over a year,' she rambled. 'You see, Abe and I travel so much now. We're hardly ever in Toronto.' Then, taking a quick breath, 'Now we have stores, not only in Canada, but all over the

world . . . New York, London, Paris, Tel Aviv . . .'
'And next year, if all goes well, we'll open a *Musée Steen* in Rio,'
Abe completed the list.
'That's fantastic, you're an international phenomenon!' Miriam
declared, 'but you've changed your surname?'
'When we incorporated six years ago . . .' Abe hesitated. '*Steen*
goes better with the French *musée*. But Canada is still our base of
operation. Where we began. In fact, most of our contemporary
artisans are Canadians.'
Abe Stein steered his wife toward Misha who looked miserable,
for he hated being referred to as an artisan. He was a scribe! His
work was holy!
'Hello, Misha Mikelofsky of Dunavitch. It's good to see you
again,' Abe Stein greeted him. 'Please, meet our friends, the
Bernsteins.' Misha bowed, lowering his eyes to avoid the women.
'Dunavitch,' he brooded, forcing a smile. Why did Stein have
to mention the village's name? Lately, the Montreal papers were
full of stories of the pious Hasidim descended from the
Dunavitcher Rebbe, a group of zealots who couldn't manage in
their separate enclaves on St Urbain, Jeanne Mance and Fair-
mount, where other Hasidim lived. In the early sixties, these
Dunavitchers moved north of Montreal to establish their own
municipality near the twin towns of Claremont-Ste-Justine. Misha
didn't want to think about Dunavitch now. He offered to show
the two boys the contents of his handbag.
'Yes, by all means, show your wares,' Abe Stein urged. Misha
couldn't hold back his anger. 'Michael, David,' he appealed to the
youngsters, 'inside my bag are Sifrai Torah, tefillin, mezuzzot.
Religious objects are not wares!'
The Steins remained silent. They could see Misha was upset.
'Have you ever seen a Torah up close?' Misha asked.
'Never,' the boys answered in unison. David told Misha the
closest they ever got to the Holy Scroll was during the Torah
procession in the synagogue when they were permitted to kiss
the fringes of their prayer shawls and then with the fringe only,
permitted to touch the beloved Torah.
'How would you like to actually hold a Torah, a real one, not
as big as the ones in shul, but big enough. How would you like
to do that right now?'
'Could we really?' David asked, hardly believing his good luck;

and Michael even pocketed his electronic game.

They moved to the corner of the lobby and sat down on a chocolate-coloured couch constructed around a slab of tan pocked marble. On a coffee table in front of them, purple silk anemones stretched their heads from their pewter pitchers. The boys eagerly peered into the briefcase to discover several packages individually wrapped in embroidered cotton.

'I do needlepoint too,' Misha told them. 'Each box is covered with a cloth on which I stitched a phrase from the Bible.'

Misha pulled out one miniature Sefer Torah, the size of a small prayer book, and placed it in David's hands. After carefully lifting the cover he had Michael hold one of the handles while David supported the scroll in his palms. The script revealed itself to the youngsters as miraculously as it had to 600,000 Israelites at Sinai, as if it had been etched by *The Holy One Blessed Be He*, instead of the hand of Misha Mikelofsky.

The boys marvelled and so did Miriam, while Ida bragged. 'We discovered Misha . . . at the Spanish and Portuguese synagogue book fair, two years ago. Never had we seen such writing! We realized immediately he had talent.' Ida broke off, and Abe took over. 'We're selling his . . . religious objects all over the world,' Abe paused before he said 'religious objects', his attempt to show respect for the Hasid. Then, he suggested, 'Soon we may sell your paintings too?'

'Really, Mr Stein, I'm not an artist. I keep telling you, my work is not for show.'

'The boy's too modest,' Abe continued. 'I tell you, his art is unique. His designs are so intricately executed that his paintings resemble manuscripts. The subject matter is Biblical, the colours pale, while his brush strokes, like a pen, leave only the thinnest trace on the canvas.'

'He's an innovator!' Ida sung.

'Mr Stein, I keep telling you, I'll never sell my paintings. My father lets me pursue painting because I'm his only son, but he warns me that art is heresy.'

'You see, Miriam, how intense Misha is!' Ida said.

'So dedicated,' Miriam agreed. 'Life must be difficult for you, Misha Mikelofsky.'

'Not where I live, Madam. In Dunavitch, I don't worry about selling my work.'

'You sell your scrolls, phylacteries, and mezuzzahs?' Miriam questioned.

'We all do what we must. The community decided to raise outside funds. They needed my help.'

'Selling your paintings would help even more,' Abe added. 'You ought to speak to your father. He could get permission from the Rebbe.'

'Yes, yes, Mr Stein,' Misha laughed nervously. 'He never gives up,' Misha looked to Miriam for support.

'I'll convince you yet, Misha Mikelofsky,' Abe warned before inviting Miriam and her sons to visit the Montreal *Musée Steen*.

'What about it, boys? Would you like to go?' Miriam asked.

'Would we ever!' David spoke for himself and his brother.

They set out together, the Bernsteins, the sofer and the entrepreneurial husband and wife, down Sherbrooke for the *Musée*. 'It's been a long time, Miriam, since you were in our first store. Remember, the one in Toronto, on Eglinton, near Old Park Road? We called it *Stein's Gift Centre*, back in the fifties. You were about David's age when we opened. But we've come a long way since then?'

Unconcerned with Abe Stein's success, the boys were busy questioning Misha: 'How long have you been painting? Why does your father want you to be an artist? What's it like living in Dunavitch? Do you ever shave your beard? Why do married orthodox women wear kerchiefs? What do you think of ordinary Jews like us, really?'

Misha answered, trying his best to satisfy the children. There was a natural closeness between the Hasid and the boys because they sought only a certain measure of fact, accepting on faith what most adults would question.

David asked, 'How does one learn to be a scribe?'

'From an established sofer,' Misha explained. 'I was taught by my Uncle. I watched and practised from the year before my Bar Mitzvah until two years ago. But Uncle said I knew everything in six months. "The boy's a natural," he'd say. "He will succeed me when I'm gone."'

They reached the small museum flanked by a *crêperie* and a *chemisier*. A black grill fence with gold spikes on each iron pole in front of the window and door gave the building a forbidding look.

'Is this a jail?' Michael whispered to Miriam. 'Don't be silly,' she admonished, 'the gallery has many priceless items; the bars are protection against theft.'

'Still looks like a jail to me,' insisted Michael, pulling out his electronic game, even though he had his mitts on. '*Beep-beep*' it sounded, while he stubbornly announced, 'I'm not going in!'

'You're not staying outside. You never know who could be roaming the street.' They crowded together at the door while Abe Stein rang the bell. Michael peeked through the cracks in the coats and that's when he saw her. 'Who is she?' he asked impulsively.

'That's Tzipporah, my little bird,' Stein answered proudly.

A pale thin woman with azure eyes, as intense as Misha's, opened the door. She wore a blue wool dress with long sleeves and a Peter Pan collar, scalloped at the bottom edge. A star of David set in tiny turquoise stones hung from a silver chain round her neck.

'Is she ever pretty!' Michael exclaimed.

Tzipporah's face reddened while Mr Stein proceeded to make introductions. He lingered when he introduced his daughter to Misha, for he had a fondness for the Hasid that went beyond business. But the couple did not need his effort to get them acquainted. They stared at each other in silence, while Miriam and the children began exploring the shop.

There were mahogany and cherry cabinets with bevelled glass doors, gilt-edged bureaus with marble tops. Mr and Mrs Stein pointed out several of their favourite items: a jade lion, a set of nineteenth-century French china, trimmed in 24 karat gold, a dozen Georgian silver tankards, and six bronze daggers with handles set with precious stones.

Tzipporah, stirred to a motherly instinct by Misha's melancholy eyes, lured the boys to the back of the shop where a burgundy curtain hung in deep folds. She pulled a thick yellow pulley and the drape opened, revealing an inner sanctum of Jewish religious objects. Resting on the shelves, which climbed walls of powder blue velvet, were crowns, pointers, breastplates: accoutrements for the Torah. Dozens of filigree spice boxes also adorned the niches.

In one corner of this room, set apart from these objects, were three large tubular cases, the style starkly simple. Michael and David were immediately drawn to this nook.

'What are these things anyway?' Michael asked.

Tzipporah didn't answer but instead suggested the boys look for themselves. 'You can open one if you like, but be careful. The silver is very soft and likely to bend if you apply too much pressure.'

The boys were excited now. Usually in museums you could look at things only through the glass of locked showcases, or if the objects were openly displayed, there would be one of those dreary 'please do not touch' signs.

Stein explained to Miriam that Pablo, a Mexican silversmith, made these Torah holders exclusively for *Musée Steen*. 'Perfectly plain,' Abe said, a trace of Yiddish accent suddenly surfacing. He rarely spoke the language of his youth, but occasionally the tone of the old tongue trickled into his English. Meanwhile David and Michael succeeded in opening one of the silver cylinders. 'Look, one of Misha's Sefer Torahs!' Michael declared, 'And it's almost as big as the Torahs in shul!'

Sensing the boys were ready bait, Abe suggested, 'Pablo fashions the silver without design so we can engrave something personal for each purchaser. For example, *"For David, on the occasion of his Bar Mitzvah"*.'

'Gee, my Bar Mitzvah is next year,' said David, just as Abe Stein knew he would.

Miriam was annoyed. Her detective's mind told her she should have expected Abe's aggressiveness. Not that he means any harm, she rationalized, but still, for old times' sake, and for the sake of the children, she found herself saying, 'I'll ask Saul.' But then she saw the price tag. 'Abe Stein, are you serious? This Torah costs twelve hundred dollars!'

'Miriam, it's an investment. Besides, it's a Torah. Buy one for the boy for his Bar Mitzvah. You won't be sorry!' Abe insisted.

Miriam reached a new pinnacle of disappointment and embarrassment. 'Look, Abe, I can't make an investment like this without consulting Saul.' Then, to prevent a rebellion from her sons, she added, 'I promise, we'll ask Saul as soon as we get back to the hotel, okay?'

Abe agreed, 'Good girl,' he said patronizingly, 'I'll put it away until Saul decides.'

'Abe Stein, you do no such thing, unless you hear from me.'

'If that's what you really want.'

'Yes, that's what I want. Anyway, David's Bar Mitzvah is still a year away. You make me feel like it's tomorrow.'

Michael pulled out his electronic game. He wasn't going to get a Torah. Just David. *'Beep-beep,'* his machine protested.

Misha who had been absorbed in conversation with Tzipporah, had only begun to listen. He was flattered by the heated exchange. After all, it was his Torah they were fighting over. But when he realized how uncomfortable Miriam had become, he interrupted, 'We'd better get busy Mr Stein. It's three o'clock already and I have to catch the four-thirty bus back to Dunavitch.'

'Miriam, before you go,' Abe tried one last time, 'let me put this Torah away. It's the one David likes.'

'Let her go, Mr Stein,' Misha insisted. He took David by the shoulders. 'Your mother is right. The Torah is very costly.' Then he said to the boys, 'I'm really glad you fellows like my work. It means a lot to me.'

Miriam took her sons in tow. 'Abe, we really must leave. Thanks for showing us the gallery.'

'Yes, thanks, Mr and Mrs Stein,' David said as he and Michael trudged unwillingly to the front door.

On the way back to the hotel, Miriam complained about the lengths Abe Stein would go to for a sale. David and Michael couldn't stop talking about Misha. 'Will you ask Dad about Misha's Torah?' David begged, while Michael chimed in, 'If he gets a Torah for his Bar Mitzvah, I get one for mine . . . *"Beep-beep!"'*

It was a year and a half later. The Bar Mitzvah, a pleasant memory, was behind the Bernstein family when they went to Montreal for a weekend break. No sooner had they arrived at their hotel than David reminded his parents of their promise to visit the *Musée Steen.* Michael immediately groused, 'I'm not going back to that jail.' And he pulled out his new electronic game, football . . . *'Buzz-buzz!'*

'You don't want to go because you're not getting anything!' David said, 'Besides you're not interested in religion, remember. Only sports. And for that matter, you're a poor sport. Anyway, you got baseball last year and this year you got football, so what's the big deal if I get a little Torah?'

'A little Torah. . . ?' Michael cried out. 'Did you hear, Dad, a little Torah for twelve hundred dollars?'

'Look, Miriam,' Saul said, 'Michael's right. Twelve hundred dollars is a ridiculous price. You go alone with David to the

gallery. If I'm not with you, Abe will be powerless.'
'Saul, you're coming,' Miriam insisted.
'I am not,' Saul affirmed.
'Saul Bernstein, you're afraid of Abe Stein!'
'Me? Afraid of that millionaire? Are you kidding?' Suddenly, Saul changed his mind, 'Michael, we'll go along with David and your mother to *Le Musée Steen*, but I'm warning everyone: we're not buying, only looking.'

When they arrived at the gallery, it looked closed, the black and gold fence as prohibitive as ever. David rang the doorbell and to Miriam and the boys' surprise, a familiar but somewhat different looking young man opened the door. Capless and beardless, the changed Hasid wore tight blue jeans and a short-sleeved T-shirt which exposed his white, sinewy arms.

'Is it you, Misha Mikelofsky?' Miriam asked. 'I hardly recognized you.' Then Miriam saw Tzipporah approaching from the back of the gallery. Right away Miriam could see the young woman was about six months pregnant. Misha beamed as he introduced his new wife.

'You married her?' Michael questioned, stuffing his football game into his pants pocket. 'I thought Hasidim didn't marry *ordinary* Jews.'

'Michael!' Miriam reprimanded, giving the boy a tug.

'It's all right, Miriam,' Misha protested. 'The boys and I understand each other.' Misha turned to the children. 'We do?' he joked.

'But seriously, boys,' he continued, 'it's very simple. Tzipporah and I fell in love the first time we met, in the museum, eighteen months ago. Remember, you were here?'

Silence.

Undaunted by his young friends' bewilderment and moved to devotion for his beloved, Misha proceeded, 'I proposed to Tzipporah the week after we met and we were married the following month. Abe gave us the gallery. Tzipporah is the manager. I work in the back; my very own atelier. I'm no longer a scribe, but a full-time painter.'

The boys were struck dumb, brutally betrayed by their Hasidic idol. Sensing their confusion, Misha tried to humour them. Imitating Abe Stein, he asked, 'Maybe you'd like to buy a painting for twelve hundred dollars?'

Saul laughed. But not Miriam or the boys.

Misha continued, 'There's no more Judaica in the museum. I needed the space for my paintings. I hope you boys aren't too disappointed.'

In total despair, the boys stared at their shoes while their father suddenly felt tremendously relieved. 'So much for the Sefer Torah, David.'

Feeling awkwardly generous, Saul suggested, 'Maybe we will look at some of your paintings, Misha.'

'Much more in your price range, I assure you. Only seventy-five to one hundred dollars. And I just happen to have a painting here that I think you and your family would be particularly interested in.'

He led them to the back of the store, to a corner cupboard in his studio. As soon as he opened it, the boys saw a single Sefer Torah.

'Do you remember this Torah, boys?' Misha asked. 'It's the one you liked best, David, and it's the last Torah I wrote! If you still want it, it's yours, a present from Tzipporah and me . . . and my in-laws. Abe told me to tell you, Miriam, that he didn't mean to annoy you with the come-on. I quote: "Do you think I get rich taking money from friends?" Take it home, David. It's yours.'

Misha teased, 'Now that I've moved to Sodom, maybe you'll move to Dunavitch, David. Maybe you could even learn to be a scribe.'

'Isn't it enough to own a Torah?' asked Saul, while Miriam suggested, 'You never know, Saul, he might be a sofer, one day.'

David was about to probe his feelings about the future, when Michael pulled out his new football game. 'These batteries are burnt out,' he moaned. 'Dad, will you get some new ones?'

'Sure, son,' Saul said. 'Guess we better be going, Misha, Tzipporah. We'll drop Abe and Ida a note. It was certainly wonderful of you all to remember David.'

'Good luck, kids,' said Miriam, for they were so young, she thought to herself.

J.J. STEINFELD · b. 1946

The Chess Master

The old men seated at nearby tables, playing chess, paused briefly to wave at the bearded man, but Lionel Siedelman did not notice them. He stared through the front window of Kruger's Grocery until he caught the owner's attention. Heinrich Kruger raised a fist and shouted for Lionel to go away. Lionel failed to move. Instead he blew kisses at the grocer through the window and yelled with mock affection, '*Sholom, sholom. . . .*' Lionel wanted to break the window. The last week he had dreamed about the destruction of the grocery—by explosives, by fire, by the wrath of God, but mostly by his bare hands, pulverizing each brick into dust, blowing the dust out of time.

Lionel could see his reflection amid the signs and advertisements in the store window. The shadows of sleeplessness on his face were sharp and incriminating even in the glass. In his mind every can and box and piece of produce was thrown to the floor and crushed under his wild, vengeful dance. Somehow this local grocery had become the source of all his frustration and anxiety and hatred. He swore at the grocer, uttering the most vivid Yiddish curses he knew; he made flamboyant, obscene gestures. Yet every word and gesture was inadequate, hardly more than breezes against a brick fortress. He considered urinating against the front window but had not yet lost all his control.

'Why do you still come here? He's dead,' Heinrich Kruger said as he came through the grocery's front door, repeatedly wiping his hands on his apron.

'Sentimental reasons,' Lionel said, trying to imagine the grocer forty years younger. He would have punched Kruger in the face had the grocer not been so old, had he not resembled so closely his brother Ernst. The eighty-year-old man, trembling with anger, nonetheless appeared rejuvenated by his fury.

'I don't like you around my store.'

'Your brother liked me around. I was good luck to him,' Lionel taunted, stepping closer to Kruger. Lionel thought he saw the dark secrets that were embedded in the old man's wrinkled face, the lines of treachery and disgrace, the traces of an undissolved malignancy.

'He's dead. Go the cemetery. Play chess by the grave.'

'I told your brother I would kill you.'

'So try to kill me, big mouth,' Kruger said, pushing Lionel with all his furious strength but not budging him. If Lionel could have gotten closer to the old man, devoured him with his own body, he would have.

'And turn me into you, perish the thought.'

'You pathetic and pitiful fool,' the old man said with the conviction of a youth defying the world. 'I have no trouble understanding how your brain thinks.'

'*Mazel tov! Mazel tov! Mazel tov!*' Lionel screamed in a voice louder than he knew he had, feeling himself losing control. Ernst Kruger had taught him that control and concentration were essential if one wanted to win at chess.

'Try to kill me now . . . go ahead.' The old man opened his mouth and noisily sucked in air, as if attempting to swallow his adversary.

Shoppers stopped to watch the afternoon confrontation, most from a safe distance. Storekeepers and their customers were summoned outdoors by the arguing voices.

'I loved him. For fourteen years I loved him,' Lionel declared.

'Ernst was my twin brother, don't forget that. We were together during World War II. *Inseparable.*'

'You bastard,' Lionel said, his fingers curling into fists, sealing themselves into an ill-boding permanence.

'Then he was a bastard. Twins are twins, even you must know that.' The old man's face gradually displayed a swollen smile. His eyes indicated enjoyment; the prospect of both calamity and triumph overcame the hard downward slope of his mouth.

'Ernst was not an evil man. He regretted what happened during the War. You enjoyed what happened, you goddamn murderous old bastard.' Lionel moved away from Kruger, closer to the window. The lettering on the signs and advertisements blurred. The old man began pounding on Lionel's back. Lionel thrust his right fist through the window, shattering the glass. The blood that flowed reminded both men of different times.

Riding on the yellow school bus home from Hebrew School made Lionel ill, so he usually walked the three miles from the school to his parents' house. Only the most heavy rains prevented him from walking. Lionel enjoyed walking and thinking, swinging a leather briefcase at his side, imagining himself anywhere but on the streets of Toronto. The briefcase had been a present from Lionel's older brother Zvi.

It was during one of these walks home that Lionel, then twelve years old, first saw the old men playing chess. There were five tables in front of three adjacent stores. As long as the weather was agreeable, even in winter, the men played chess. The young boy associated the sight of the ongoing chess games with an old, orderly, tranquil world.

At first Lionel, always shy with strangers, observed from across the street. Then he would slowly walk past the men. Finally, when the school term was almost over, he stopped and watched, a feverish eagerness running through his body.

'You play chess, boy?' the old man sitting with his back to Kruger's Grocery asked Lionel. At the old man's elbow was a copy of *Deutsche Schachzeitung*; to the side of the chessboard was a bowl packed with oversized apples and moist grapes.

'Not very well,' the nervous boy said, feeling the eyes of all the old men circling him.

'Sit, sit, play with me. This tree stump is no challenge,' the old man said as another man got up from his chair and moved to the next table. 'If he lasts twenty moves it is a miracle. . . . Move first, boy. Do not be bashful. Have fresh fruit,' he said, lifting the bowl toward Lionel, 'it is energy for the brain. For chess, brain energy is required. The great Goethe wrote that chess is the touchstone of the intellect.'

That afternoon Lionel played the old man seven games, stopping only when he realized he would be late for supper.

'Come back soon,' the old man said. 'You have potential.'

'You beat me seven out of seven,' Lionel said sadly.

'You are learning. One day I will submit to your mastery. . . . What is your name?'

'Lionel Lazer Siedelman.'

'Such an elegant name for such a small boy. . . . I am Ernst Kruger. Play me tomorrow again. I am here by my brother's store all the time. I will teach you to play smarter,' the old man said, pointing to his head.

'I can't tomorrow. I have to go to synagogue.'

'Go, go to synagogue, boy. . . .'

'*Schach und matt*. . . . That is how you say checkmate *auf deutsch*,' the old man said as kindly as he could to the young loser.

'I can lose in two languages. Wonderful,' Lionel said.

'But see how good practice and concentration are making you.'

'I'll never beat you.'

'Already you almost win. You are no pushover. I tell you this from the heart. You are a real *schachspieler* now. Patience, you are such a little boy.'

'I'm just about a man,' Lionel said with an attempt to sound older, locking himself into a rigid and serious pose.

The old man's face was tugged by delight and pleasure. He reached a hand across the table but did not touch the boy. Suddenly his hand felt heavy and inflamed.

'Come to my Bar Mitzvah next week, Mr Kruger,' Lionel said eagerly.

The old man shivered, as if something icily foul or pitiless had entered his system. 'I cannot possibly, Lionel.'

'Please,' the boy begged, leaning over the chessboard.

'You will understand why not when you are older.'

'You're my friend, Mr Kruger.'

'Let us play one more game,' the old man said abruptly, casting away the fear that was beginning to dominate him.

They played and Lionel won after a struggle in which neither player spoke or even took his eyes off the chess pieces. The men who were watching the game could not believe the outcome, charging in German that the old man had allowed the boy to win. He accused them of being lifeless old cynics. Soon there was a heated argument, all in German.

Before Lionel left, the old man gave the boy his personal copy of *Modern Chess Openings* as a Bar Mitzvah present. Lionel ran the entire way home, jubilantly, clutching his new book, knowing full well that Mr Kruger had not tried his hardest. Ernst Kruger, the other old men had told the boy, was a chess master.

'My brother's not well,' Lionel told the old man when he asked why Lionel was not concentrating, why so many silly moves today.

'What is wrong with him?'

'My parents won't tell me. Only that it has to do with his nerves. My brother has a bad nervous condition.'

'No one is spared; life is full of problems,' the old man said sympathetically.

'He's in hospital and they won't let me visit. I'm supposed to be too young. My father told me he fought in the Underground in Poland when he was fourteen. I'm fourteen and he treats me like a baby. I'm not too young, am I Mr Kruger?'

'Your parents know what is proper. Your brother will get well, you'll see.'

'I told Zvi about you once,' Lionel said, stopping and pinching his chin in thought. He started and stopped his next sentence several times before he could say, 'Zvi says you're a Nazi.'

'Let us play chess,' the old man said with a sudden, stiff resolution. 'I have an interesting opening strategy to demonstrate to you.'

'Were you a Nazi, Mr Kruger?'

'I tell you, let me show you what is called the Ruy Lopez Opening and a few of the more potent defences against it.'

'Were you a Nazi?'

'That nightmare still lives too odiously in my heart for words.'

Lionel held his white queen in the air, squeezing it. Had the queen been a blade it would have severed his fingers.

'One day I will tell you about that nightmare. When you are more historically inclined.'

'Tell me, Mr Kruger. . . . Tell me,' Lionel said, an interrogator caught in the trance of his own questioning.

'This is a beautiful story, Lionel,' the old man said after he had finished reading the manuscript, kissing the last page in praise.

'My parents think it's foolish. Narrishkeit they call my writing. Science and math, my father says. You can always use science and math.'

'This is a quite serious topic you write about. Your mother talks in such detail about being in the camps?'

'No. She won't talk about the War at all. I read all I can about the War and the concentration camps. The story still needs work. I'm going to rewrite it tonight.'

'So you definitely want to be a writer?'

'Nothing else, Mr Kruger.'

'*Nothing else?* Can you be so sure at sixteen?'

'Yes.'

'Sixteen is not a time for irrevocable decisions. I wanted to be a violinist when I was your age. I was so sure also.'

'Why didn't you become a violinist?'

'Why? Simple: war changed me,' the old man said casually. Then, as if harshly struck by the realization that he might have disclosed something too terrible for words, he quickly added, '*The First World War.*'

'Nothing will change me, Mr Kruger.'

'Do not forget that life is a formidable opponent.'

'I learned to beat you.'

'Yes, on occasion—only on occasion.'

'I'm still young,' Lionel said, smiling, balancing a pawn in his palm, lightly blowing on the chess piece.

The old man shook with a pleasurable laugh, as if a dear friend had poked him teasingly in the sides. 'That is true. So move, my brilliant precocious writer. . . .'

'Why doesn't he like me?' Lionel asked as Ernst Kruger's brother went back into his store.

'Do not worry, Lionel. He sees you differently than I do.'

'As an enemy?'

'Worse. As a reminder of what he was. What he did.'

'What did he do? You're never specific about the past.'

'Let us just play. Chess is more important.'

'Chess *and* writing, Mr Kruger.'

'Yes, chess and writing. You have a new story, I know.'

'How can you be so positive?'

'I know the expression of artistic delight. It ignites your whole body, Lionel. You are very outward with your emotions and expressions.'

'I haven't typed it out yet,' Lionel said as he pulled out a cluster of papers from his old briefcase.

'And you are starting to grow a beard. Quite literary.'

'It'll take me forever and then some,' Lionel said, picking at a few of the immature strands on his cheeks.

'Nothing takes forever, my friend. I can see you one day with the most beautiful full beard,' the old man said, pulling at his own trim white beard. He was going to say that he had not grown a beard until after World War II, but caught himself. 'Read to me. My eyes bother me so much lately. Horrible headaches.'

'"The Chess Master" by L.L. Siedelman,' Lionel began as the old man closed his eyes and concentrated, thinking of when he played the violin and had an abundance of dreams.

'My brother's dead, my brother's dead,' Lionel screamed as he ran toward Ernst Kruger. Lionel was not carrying his briefcase; his eyes reflected terror.

'How is that possible? He was a young man.'

'Zvi killed himself in the garage. *I* found him.'

'I am sorry for you, my poor Lionel.'

'The funeral's tomorrow. I won't go, I won't go. I want to know why Zvi's dead.'

Lionel started to cry, and the old man embraced him. Aside from casual handshakes or a random pat on the back, they had never touched before, as if touching might unearth or destroy the past. Six years of chess playing and afternoon conversations and now they held each other wordlessly, like father and son. The old man let out a wail. The other chess players turned their heads toward Lionel and the old man, and imagined the worst.

The early afternoon was warm, but Ernst Kruger was not at his table. The gap made Lionel think he was on the wrong street, in the wrong world. Lionel sat down and stared at the empty place. He made several moves for the old man, attempted to think the way Ernst Kruger thought. Some of the other men called for Lionel to play with them, but he refused their invitations. He played the game out with his absent friend, Ernst winning with his usual brilliance.

From inside his store Heinrich Kruger tapped at the window and told Lionel to leave. When Lionel did not stir, the grocer came outside, striding with a heavy-footed hostility.

'No more chess playing for you and my brother. He's blind now. Eyeless,' the grocer said in a tone that was at once predatory and overflowing with satisfaction.

Lionel looked up at his friend's brother. The old man could see that Lionel had been crying. Ernst and Heinrich Kruger looked so much alike that Lionel could barely detect any physical dissimilarities.

'What hospital is he in?'

'None of your business.'

One of the old chess players told Lionel where Ernst Kruger was recuperating, then said something to Heinrich Kruger in German.

The grocer's hissing, open-mouthed breathing turned into a fierce discharge of spitting sounds. 'You are bad luck for my brother, a curse,' he finally said, saliva spraying wildly from lips that had lost their durability years ago.

Lionel crossed the street to the northbound bus stop. He wanted to go to the hospital and read a story to his friend.

'You play better than ever, Mr Kruger.'

'You are my eyes, Lionel.'

'It's incredible how quickly you've adjusted. That's really important.'

'I like being blind.'

'*Mr Kruger!*'

'I've seen enough, Lionel. I have seen too much. Think of it, now all distractions from concentration are taken away. I can see the pieces perfectly in my head. The most exquisitely crafted chessmen are within my head. I wish I could have had this extraordinary vision when I was a young man. . . .'

'I'm my brother's age now,' Lionel said with a solemnity that frightened the blind man. '*Twenty*,' Lionel added with a fearfulness that made the word sound grotesque, a denunciation of life and hope.

'You are not your brother. You have a destiny to fulfil,' the blind man said with such determination that his dead eyes momentarily appeared sighted.

'No one wants my stories.'

'In time they will, you wait.'

192 J. J. Steinfeld

'I'm more and more like my brother. You never met Zvi. He was always so sad. Sadder than my mother. You're not at all like your brother.'

'Who can explain these things? Read me a story.'

'I get extremely depressed like Zvi did. I know I have the same nightmares. My parents want me to see a special doctor. Doctors didn't help Zvi.'

'Don't talk yourself into such a dark frame of mind, Lionel. Read me a story or shall I defeat you in ten moves today?'

Lionel smiled and tenderly touched the old man's hands. 'I wrote another story about you,' he said.

'You shouldn't, Lionel.'

'About when you played the violin and soothed all the savage beasts in Germany. . . .'

'I can't believe a story's going to be published. At last an acceptance,' Lionel said, his face radiating excitement like a man bursting forth from a long and profitable solitude.

'Congratulations! See, perseverance pays off. And you are not twenty-one yet. By thirty you will be world-famous. I feel this in my soul.'

'Let the egomaniacs have the fame, I'll settle for a few kind readers.'

'Which publication will be honoured by your story?'

'*Jewish Dialog*.'

'A good start. And which story?'

'The millionth rewrite of "The Chess Master".'

'The first of many publications. You are a natural storyteller. We should have some schnapps for a toast to your success and future.'

'I feel good now, Mr Kruger. . . . I'm going to quit school and write all the time.'

'Finish your degree, Lionel.'

'No, it would be a defeat. . . .'

'Nothing really interests me. Nothing makes much sense. Except for the writing. If I didn't write, I'd end up like my brother. It's as if I was there, in the concentration camps.'

'You have inherited painful feelings from your parents. The past can be transmitted from generation to generation, even through any silence or deafness.'

'Will I pass it on?'

'Through your eyes. Through your stories. Write about your pain and being a Jew. Write, and perhaps the suffering will make sense, Lionel.'

'Zvi's been dead five years and I dreamed last night I walked into the garage and found him again. I was hanging next to him. I wasn't unhappy with my dream.'

'You have witnessed too much already in your life.'

'My brother couldn't take it.'

'You can take it. Listen to a foolish old blind man who has stumbled around this world for as many years as Methuselah.'

'Why won't you talk about the War with me? Let me take you to Germany for a trip.'

'Absolutely no.'

'I could do research for some stories and for you it would be a homecoming. Let's confront the past together.'

'That nightmare. . . . That nightmare is still there for me.'

'But you never killed any Jews, right?'

'That nightmare was bad for everyone. It damaged the souls of so many people, even the unborn. . . .'

'I'm sick and tired of the bullshit and excuses I hear. Goddamn it, I don't want to listen to any more crap from people.'

'Calm down, Lionel. Let us play chess. What is your move? You have not used Bird's Opening in ages. Try Bird's Opening today.' The old blind man reached across the table to touch Lionel's face, but the young man moved away, as if fearing a slap.

'I've figured out how to deal with my past and my future at the same time. I'll kill your Nazi brother.'

'You should not think like that, Lionel.'

'I'll be sent to jail and I'll write there. I'm not writing enough lately.'

'You have written seventy stories.'

'Not enough! I don't belong in this stupid forgetful world anyway. I'll write all the time in jail. If I ever stop writing I'll—'

'Kill me instead, Lionel.'

'I love you.'

'I was a Nazi, too.'

'No!' Lionel screamed as he pushed the chessboard off the

table. All the old men got to their knees and began to pick up the fallen chessmen.

'That nightmare suffocated everyone. I did not fight it. I did not hold back a single salute.'

'You did! You did!'

After a silent, painful moment, Lionel, with his index finger, gently traced a number on the blind man's forearm.

'Your mother's camp number?'

'Yes.'

'I am not worthy, Lionel Lazer Siedelman. . . .'

Lionel began his novel a week after the old man died. For a week he had brooded and drunk excessively. Then he put his fist through the window of Kruger's Grocery. He required twenty-nine stitches to close the wounds, but he began writing that night, fighting the pain. The novel, about a Jewish boy growing up in Toronto and playing chess almost daily with a displaced old German, started out with a grocery in flames.

NAOMI GUTTMAN · b. 1960

Practising

On my way to feed your cats I'm passing a group of tourists,
Americans, when one of them, a man, stops me.
   Pardon, Mademoiselle, parlez-vous l'anglais?
   For some reason I wish I could say '*Non,*' and slide away, wish
I could give a polite shrug, a serene smile of apology, but keep
walking. For some reason, perhaps the earnestness of his delivery
and because I know that you, a fellow American, would help him,
I stop. I even know that if the situation were reversed, you would
try, in your sign language and battered French, and you would
probably succeed.
   Maybe your success would be due to the telepathy that occurs
between men; still, I was the one who grew up on this island, in
this city, not you. I know where the rivers are, though I may forget
their names, and I know that what we call south is south-east,
north north-west. But I can't tell people where to go, I mean, how
to get to where they want to go. I like to give advice, not directions.
   Faced with this flushed and quizzical body of tourists, I do my
duty. I even do more than is necessary, boarding their subway car
and telling them when to get off.
   Between our neighbourhoods the Métro runs in a large U. I've
come to feel a certain attachment to its efficiency, its smooth, fast
ride, the way it connects us. Our underground railroad. Even so,
I don't like coming to your street. It recalls a part of my childhood
not fondly remembered—the site of my failure and my guilt. Here
I learned things about myself that I'd rather not have known. I
used to come here for piano lessons. Now I come only for you.

I get off at Snowdon and, nose in book, stand still on the three flights of escalators it takes to get to the street. The neighbourhood has changed; at least it seems that way as I walk down the hot midday diamond of Queen Mary Road. Of course there was no Métro then, but I think there are more shops, more people on the street than there used to be—or perhaps it's me that's changed. I'm taller, pay my bills, do my own shopping.

I'm glad not to meet the concierge on my way up the four flights to your apartment. I am not the woman you rented the apartment with, the woman who, when they asked, you said was your wife. Of course it wouldn't matter—I'm only feeding your cats.

But they aren't your cats, I remember as I unlock the door, although since we renamed them, they've come to feel like ours. They belong to a friend who's dumped them on you until you can find someone else to give them to.

They're right in front of the door as I walk in—talking to me, reminding me that they haven't been fed for a week even though you only left yesterday. I don't find this endearing, especially because of the cat smell that makes me want to turn around and leave, and the bits of paper and garbage they've managed to get out of the pail in the kitchen and distribute around the apartment.

I curse you for not changing the litter before leaving, then open some windows.

'Fuck you,' I say to Bugs, the fat, soft, furry one who wraps himself around my feet. His mother, Slinky, comes out of the bedroom— she thinks it's safe now—and begins her own form of protest, which is to go directly to the kitchen and meow at the cupboard.

I decide I might as well get it over with and begin with an entrée of crunchies, kibble, which gives me time to open a can. By the time I'm spooning the food onto a plate, Bugs has finished most of the crunchies, while Slinky's just getting her turn at the bowl. I don't want to watch them. I put down the canned food and go into your study.

Mostly it's filled with boxes you're packing for your girlfriend, who's gone back to Japan. I think you let people take advantage of you.

'Wouldn't you do the same thing?' you say. Probably I would, but I won't say it. And then there's your friend with the cats.

'When's he coming back?' I asked before you left.

'I don't know,' you said.

This is your standard response, and it's true—you don't know. But I want you to know. It would make my knowing so much easier. I want you to make the decision. Are the cats going to stay? Are they going to rule our lives, keep us travelling the Métro back and forth through the weeks before you leave? And what about when you're away—who will take care of them then?

These are questions I ask myself as I clean up the mess the cats made. I even wash out the litter box with Javex and leave it on the sill to dry. After collecting the garbage and sweeping up, I notice the sludge at the bottom of your garbage pail. For a moment I consider washing it, but that's going too far. Instead, I sponge the countertops. I open a container and find that the apple cake I brought you last week was never refrigerated. Into the garbage. It's no insult: I didn't make it.

Before leaving, I water the one plant that has survived your girlfriend's departure, and wonder if you would agree to part with its ratty macramé hanger and which window it would do best in at my house.

The piano lessons were given by Miss Ames in her basement apartment, where the halls always smelled of other people's cooking. According to Miss Ames, I had been badly taught by my former teacher. So we spent most of the first year relearning posture, which Miss Ames insisted was the basis of sound piano technique and would also stand me in good stead in later life.

In the beginning I did very well. I even surprised myself by enjoying the scales, the minuets, and marches, those clean pages of notes that translated into the indescribable sensation of music. Miss Ames was pleased and gave me gold stars. My mother was vindicated: she was right to keep me at the piano for an hour while she listened from the kitchen.

In my second year I began to lose patience. The practising had become work, and I didn't want to work. I wanted it to come easily the first time; I wanted to be gifted, to be perfect. Challenged by a new piece, I was keen, eager to have my turn at it after Miss Ames's eloquent preamble and demonstration. I'd work on the first page until I knew it by heart. It was when I got to the sticky part—the patch of thorny black sixteenth notes, the difficult progressions in the left hand, the syncopation that I never seemed able to anticipate—all these hurdles deterred my progress so that instead of forging ahead, 'bar by bar', as Miss Ames reminded me weekly, I stubbornly returned to the beginning of the piece. Perhaps I imagined that the problem would have disappeared or miraculously corrected itself when I got there again.

As time went on, I became contemptuous of Miss Ames and refused to practise at all. I resented the meanness of her tweedy suits and loafers, the smelly halls I had to travel through to get to her subterranean doorway, and the long, cold after-lesson wait for the bus on dark winter afternoons.

There was one thing, however, that did appeal to me about Miss Ames, and that was her hair. If only I could have such hair, hair like Anne of Green Gables, long auburn-red hair. If only she would unknot it from the tightly netted chignon she invariably kept it in. I was sure it came all the way down her back.

'You don't think it's real!' my sophisticated sister snarled when I confessed my envy.

The possibility that she was right nagged at me all week until my next lesson. Arriving earlier than usual, I went to the bathroom. I was relieved to discover that, upon inspection of the medicine cabinet, there was no trace of Miss Clairol, or anything else that would support my sister's cynical remark. But I did find other things, and though I knew it wasn't Miss Ames's fault that I was a bad student, I began to steal.

The morning you left, the phone rang at seven. Of course it's her; I know it before my eyes open. The conversation lasts more than half an hour, and though I'd prefer to be asleep, I can't help hearing the ups and downs of your side. Some of the time you speak in Japanese, probably exchanging the endearments she taught you, the words you couldn't learn in school. Mostly, though, it sounds like English.

You come back to bed with a look on your face, and I feel like I shouldn't be there—I should be home, in my own bed with my own cat. I wish this wasn't the morning you're going away. Even if it's only for five days to visit your family in Washington before heading east to visit her. Far East.

'You okay?' I ask. You've sat down on the mattress, but I can't see your face. I try talking for you, a mistake.

'You know, if you decide to stay, there's nothing wrong with that.' I want to touch you, but I don't.

'Thanks,' you say. I can't tell if you're being sarcastic.

'For what?'
'For being generous.' You're serious.
You let me hold you, but I want to be held, too. We don't talk for a time. Then I say, 'I'm not generous, just realistic.' I wonder what you'd do if she asked you to stay with her. I don't ask. I know what the answer would be: 'I don't know.'

Sometimes it's different. Sometimes you do know, like the other day when we were eating and I said, 'I don't want you to go.' I was trying to tease, trying to keep it pleasant, so I said, 'But I shouldn't think about that.' Brave girl. But you can tell now. You took me on your lap.

'No, you shouldn't. And I'll be coming back,' you said.

That made me feel good for the day. I try to concentrate on the present, on getting to know you, on understanding your jokes, your crossword puzzles, your work. The hats you like to wear around the house. Sometimes I wonder what will happen when we run out of things to say to each other—will it happen? Right now I can picture the way your fingers move to slice an onion, the way your skin feels over mine, under mine, your furry skin, the taste of your kisses, your smells. I can't imagine now that this will ever run out, that we will stop being enchanted by the novelty of mixing our bodies. But what about when it does run out, when we're on firmer ground? Will it stop, this feeling?

They say it doesn't have to. But it takes work, they say. What is that work? That's what I want to know. I can see, from the garbage pail, from the shelf of your broom closet stuffed with paper bags, loose ends of rope and emergency candles, that there are things that will be work—but that work I can understand; I've done it before.

Will it happen that we'll begin to repeat ourselves, that our bodies will become machines that know exactly where and how to give without the touch of thought? It's not that I want it to happen; I'm just afraid. It's the little steps, the ones I don't see coming, that kill me. I want it to come easy, the first time.

'I miss you,' you tell me, calling from your family's home that night.

'I miss you, too.' I know I do. Now I miss you, and I'll miss you even more this summer, when you've gone to be with her. With her for the last time. Maybe. I don't know. But I don't talk about it now; this is our phone call.

'Well, I'll be home soon,' you say, and for some reason this has the soothing effect you mean it to have, and as I put the headset back into the cradle, I realize that it's the first time I've heard you call this city your home.

At first it was old make-up, things I didn't think she'd miss. Dusty compacts of face powder (the kind with mirrors), or crusty sticks of eye make-up—blues, greens, and mauves, in lipstick-like containers. But eventually I took newer things. I couldn't imagine that she ever used them, this cool woman with her strict brow, her no-nonsense wrists. It didn't occur to me that these containers might represent her own small claim to glamour, might signify money hard-earned. Nor did I realize then that when one lives alone, sooner or later everything is missed.

Yet my treachery seemed to go unnoticed by Miss Ames, who broke her silence only occasionally to make some wistful remark about my sister's steady progress. Eventually the novelty of stealing wore off, but she must have known that I was the thief. It was only towards the end of my third year, however, that she pleaded incapable of teaching me how to get both hands moving at the same time, and my mother found me another teacher. I spent yet another first year learning how to sit properly and hold my wrists, making remarkable progress, for a beginner.

So I stole something from someone who had borne me no harm, and what I stole was of no use to me. I was only nine—still too young to wear make-up out of the house—and since, if I had worn it, my sister would have made me account for its origins, my stash lay hidden for many years in the section of a small armoire that was reserved for a growing pile of unused dolls.

I have a dream where she calls you from Japan. She tells you that she's engaged to be married. She asks you to put me on the phone, and you do even though I don't know who you've been talking to. In the dream I see her face clearly, as if in speaking to her on the phone I could also see her, and although I don't recall exactly what is said, it is clear that she is happy, that she is forgiving me because she wants you to be happy.

When I wake up, I do not remember the dream. I only know that I must cross town again to feed those cats. It's when I'm back in your apartment, which is filled with her boxes, that I remember.

On her desk is a black-and-gold box of perfume. I've noticed it there before, sitting in its regal way amidst the piles of papers, books, mementos—things that you haven't yet packed or still can't decide what to do with. It's a brand my mother wears, and I spray some onto my wrist. I remember you telling me about the group of ladies in Manitoba, members of some international agency, who sent her gifts like this—she was their foster scholar. I wonder if she ever wore the perfume, if she would miss it if it weren't packed, and I hesitate. I think of Miss Ames again, of why she didn't say anything. Maybe she had too much to lose then; maybe she needed the money more than the make-up. And why hasn't your girlfriend said anything, she who must suspect, after all the times she probably called you, sure that you'd be home and you weren't ('I was at the library', 'I unplugged the phone'—those were your lies)? Maybe, I think, she has too much to lose. Maybe if you told her the truth, she wouldn't want to see you, wouldn't want you to visit her country, her family. It's perhaps better, after the plans have been made, to save face, to honour commitments. That's how you put it to me when I ask why you must go. 'I promised,' you say, simply, and I think how lucky the child will be who has you for a father.

I put the vial of perfume back into its black-and-gold box and shut it. I take the box from the desk and put it into one of the open cartons of books and clothes marked 'Japan'.

On my way to pick you up at the airport I find myself singing down the highway, trying not to speed. It's sunny and I have the windows down. I've borrowed my sister's car. She knows all about you—now we share our secrets, keep them between ourselves and hide them from our parents. This is part of growing up. 'He'd better come back,' she says to me. He'd better.

Back from your family, you have a suitcase of new summer clothes. You're wearing a straw Stetson that you bought in anticipation of the burning, humid Japanese summer. You will find that it was a good investment because the top of the crown will warn you of the inevitably low doorways. You will eat rice and pickles for breakfast, raw fish for lunch. I will spend some time out of every day thinking about what time it is where you are. I'll wake up, and you'll be setting off to a movie, eating out. Maybe making love.

We drive back, holding hands when we can, getting into bed

as soon as we get back to your apartment. Your body smells sweet—your mother's soap. We could caress each other for hours if we didn't also get hungry. If the cats didn't get hungry.

But already there's something different. You're not as new as you were when you left, five days ago. Maybe I'm not working hard enough, but then I think, maybe we can't keep things new, maybe that's not the job. I tell you this, but you don't say anything. It's not the kind of thing you worry about. The phone rings and you go to answer it.

You're smiling when you come back to me.

'Simon,' you say. 'He's going to take the cats for the summer.'

'Great,' I say. And for a moment I do think it's great. It's deliverance. We can go to the country for a few days like we planned to—spend some time alone before your trip. But then what? What if you don't come back? Maybe you'll only come back if the cats are here waiting for you, if I'm here taking care of them. I know it's foolish, this way of thinking, but it's hard not to. Bugs licks my nose and I scratch him under the chin.

You sit down on the mattress and watch me with those eyes that are almost all pupil. You stroke my head.

'What are you thinking?' you say.

'About the summer.'

'I'll be back,' you say.

There are many things I could say here, but I don't. I think about the dream, about absolution. Maybe I don't want you to come back. What if I'm just getting to that point, the trouble spot, the trill I can't get my fingers to do fast enough? So far it's been easy—we've had to pace ourselves, had to live in the present. If you leave me, it will be your fault it didn't work out, your fault you left. Maybe I'd rather go back to the beginning—the first bars that play over and over in my head, make it ring with first feelings.

I will spend the summer on the other side of the city. The hot, treeless streets east of St Lawrence will sweat dust, grow popsicle sticks in the gutters, and by the time you come back, the neighbours will have begun making their wine, leaving the stained grape cartons buzzing with bees on the sidewalk. I will practise thinking of you, a stranger in another country. I will remember laughing with you. I will be angry that you have gone, and I will remember that you keep your promises. I will practise loving you from a distance, and the hard part will come later.

NOTES ON AUTHORS

ALLAN, TED (b. 1916): Born in Montreal, he served with Dr Norman Bethune in the Spanish Civil War. He now lives in Toronto and Los Angeles. His best-known book is his biography of Bethune, *The Scalpel, the Sword* (with Sydney Gordon, 1952; rev. 1971). In addition to short stories, he has written plays and radio and television dramas, as well as the screenplay for the film *Lies My Father Told Me* (1976).

BOSCO, MONIQUE (b. 1927): Born in Vienna, she came to Canada in 1948, and currently lives in Montreal. She has written poetry, short stories, and novels, including *La femme de Loth* (1970), which received a Governor General's Award, and was translated as *Lot's Wife* (1975).

COHEN, MATT (b. 1942): Born in Kingston, Ontario, he currently lives in Toronto. He has written both novels and collections of short stories, including *Korsoniloff* (1969), *Columbus and the Fat Lady* (1972), *The Expatriate* (1982), *Cafe Le Dog* (1985), and most recently, *Living on Water* (1988).

DRACHE, SHARON (b. 1943): A resident of Ottawa, Drache is the author of *The Mikveh Man and Other Stories* (1984) and a novel, *Ritual Slaughter* (1989).

FAESSLER, SHIRLEY (b. 1921): She currently lives in Toronto, where she was born. In addition to short stories Faessler has published one novel, *Everything in the Window* (1979).

GUTTMAN, NAOMI (b. 1961): Born in Montreal, she lives in Los Angeles. Her stories have appeared in such books as *Celebrating Canadian Women* (edited by Greta Hofmann Nemiroff).

KATTAN, NAIM (b. 1928): Born in Baghdad, Iraq, Kattan moved to Montreal in 1954 and currently lives in Ottawa. He is the author of books of essays, memoirs, and several collections of short stories. *The Neighbour and Other Stories* (1982) is an English translation of some of his most notable short fiction.

KLEIN, A.M. (1909-1982): Born in Ukraine, he came to Montreal with his family in 1910 and began publishing in various journals in the late 1920s. His books include *Hath Not a Jew . . .* (1940), *The Hitleriad* (1944), *The*

Rocking Chair and Other Poems (1948), which won a Governor General's Award, and *The Second Scroll* (1951). His short fiction was collected in *A.M. Klein: Short Stories* (1983; edited by M.W. Steinberg).

KORN, ROCHL (1898-1982): Born in Galicia (now part of Poland), she fled to the USSR in 1939. Returning to Poland after the war, she immigrated to Montreal in 1949. She wrote nine volumes of poetry, including *Dorf* (Country, 1928), *Roiter Mon* (Red Poppies, 1937), and *Varbitene Vor* (Changed Reality, 1977), and two of short stories. Two collections of her poems have been published in English as *Generations* (1984) and *Paper Roses* (1985).

KREISEL, HENRY (b. 1922): Born in Vienna, he came to Canada in 1940 and began teaching English at the University of Alberta in 1947. He has written two novels, *The Rich Man* (1948) and *The Betrayal* (1964), as well as the collection *The Almost Meeting and Other Stories* (1981).

LEVINE, NORMAN (b. 1923): Born in Ottawa, he lived in England from the late 1940s until 1980, when he returned to live in Toronto. His books include *Canada Made Me* (1958), *From a Seaside Town* (1970), *Thin Ice* (1979), and *Champagne Barn* (1984).

LUDWIG, JACK (b. 1922): Born in Winnipeg, he has taught at several universities in the United States. The author of three novels—*Confusions* (1967), *Above Ground* (1960), and *A Woman of Her Age* (an expansion of the story in this volume; 1973), he has also written several books on sports.

RICHLER, MORDECAI (b. 1931): Born in Montreal, where he currently lives after residing in London, England, for many years, he has written such novels as *The Apprenticeship of Duddy Kravitz* (1959), *Cocksure* (1968), which received a Governor General's Award, *St. Urbain's Horseman* (1971), *Joshua Then and Now* (1980), and most recently *Solomon Gursky Was Here* (1989).

ROSENFARB, CHAVA (b. 1923): Born in Lodz, Poland, she was interned at Auschwitz and later at Belsen; she made her way to Brussels in 1945, and to Canada in 1950. She currently lives in Montreal. Rosenfarb has written poetry, plays, and stories, in Yiddish. She received the Israeli Lamed prize for writing, the highest honour for a Yiddish writer.

STEINFELD, J.J. (b. 1946): Born in Munich, he now lives in Charlottetown, Prince Edward Island. He has written several collections of short stories, including *The Apostate's Tattoo* (1983) and *Forms of Captivity and Escape* (1988).

WADDINGTON, MIRIAM (b. 1917): Born in Winnipeg, she moved to Montreal in 1945, and later to Toronto, where she taught at York University until 1983. Among her many books of poetry are *Green World* (1945), *The Glass Trumpet* (1966), *Say Yes* (1969), and *Collected Poems* (1986). Her short stories are collected in *Summer at Lonely Beach* (1982). A selection of her numerous essays and reviews were published in *Apartment Seven: Essays Selected and New* (1989).

WEINZWEIG, HELEN (b. 1915): Born in Poland, she came to Toronto, where she still lives, at the age of nine. She published her first novel, *Passing Ceremony*, in 1973, and her second, *Basic Black with Pearls*, in 1980. Her short fiction was collected in *A View from the Roof* (1989).

WISEMAN, ADELE (b. 1928): Born in Winnipeg and currently a resident of Toronto, she is the author of such novels as *The Sacrifice* (1956), which received a Governor General's Award, *Crackpot* (1974), and several non-fiction books, including *Old Woman at Play* (1978) and *Memoirs of a Book-Molesting Childhood and Other Essays* (1987).